MUMBO GUMBO
MURDER

This Large Print Book carries the
Seal of Approval of N.A.V.H.

MUMBO GUMBO
MURDER

LAURA CHILDS
WITH TERRIE FARLEY MORAN

THORNDIKE PRESS
A part of Gale, a Cengage Company

GALE
A Cengage Company

LIBRARY OF CONGRESS CIP DATA ON FILE.
CATALOGUING IN PUBLICATION FOR THIS BOOK
IS AVAILABLE FROM THE LIBRARY OF CONGRESS

ISBN-13: 978-1-4328-6811-6 (hardcover alk. paper)

Published in 2020 by arrangement with Berkley, an imprint of Penguin Publishing Group, a division of Penguin Random House, LLC

Printed in Mexico
1 2 3 4 5 6 7 24 23 22 21 20

ACKNOWLEDGMENTS

A very special thank-you to my partner in crime, Terrie Farley Moran. I am in awe of your skill with words and completely adore your twisted sense of humor. Major thank-yous also to Sam, Tom, Grace, Tara, Jessica, M.J., Lori, Bob, Jennie, Dan, and all the amazing people at Berkley Prime Crime and Penguin Random House who handle editing, design, publicity, copywriting, social media, bookstore sales, gift sales, production, and shipping.

Heartfelt thanks as well to all the scrapbook lovers, scrapbook shop owners, book clubs, bookshop folks, librarians, reviewers, magazine editors and writers, websites, broadcasters, bloggers, and New Orleans friends who have enjoyed the New Orleans Scrapbooking Mysteries and helped spread the word. You make this possible!

And I am forever filled with gratitude for you, my dear readers, who have embraced

Carmela, Ava, Babcock, Gabby, Tandy, Baby, Boo, Poobah, and the rest of the scrapbook shop gang as friends and family. Thank you so much, and I promise you many more New Orleans Scrapbooking Mysteries!

CHAPTER 1

Monsters were out tonight. As well as two girls who'd definitely come to party.

"Jeepers!" Ava cried. "That skull puppet is a spooky devil."

Malevolent dark eyes peered from the hollow sockets of a bleached white skull. Shrouded in purple velvet, the creature's jagged teeth protruded rudely while its spidery, skeletal fingers reached out to stroke the arms of unsuspecting visitors along the parade route.

"You've never been up close and personal with the Beastmaster Puppets before?" Carmela Bertrand asked her friend. They were standing on a crowded sidewalk in front of Zebarz Cocktail and Cordial House in the French Quarter of New Orleans, watching the kickoff parade for Jazz Fest.

"I've seen puppets at Mardi Gras, sure, but never like this." Ava took a step back as a scabrous wolf head leaned in and tried to nuzzle her ear. "Keep walking, big guy," she muttered.

"Take a look at the skeleton puppet," Carmela said as a brass band blared out raucous foot-stompin' music, a gigantic float glided past, and a dozen Beastmaster Puppets mingled with the crowd to thrill and chill.

"The skeleton does kind of bother me," Ava said.

"Interesting, since you have an entire retinue of skeletons dangling from the rafters of your voodoo shop," Carmela said. She was the proprietor of Memory Mine Scrapbooking Shop over on Governor Nicholls Street; Ava Gruiex owned Juju Voodoo a few blocks away on Conti Street.

"But those skeletons are under *my* control."

"The giant puppets remind me of the bulbous heads on some of the Mardi Gras floats," Carmela said. As a New Orleans native and die-hard parade fanatic, she was loving this, taking it all in practically by osmosis. Fact is, you could toss a string of colored lights onto a goat cart, roll it down Bourbon Street, and Carmela would stand on the curb and cheer. She was that addicted to New Orleans mirth and merriment.

Ava Gruiex, on the other hand, was a different type of party girl. Slightly loose in her ways, she was a free spirit open to trying just about anything. And while Carmela was a jeans and T-shirt gal, Ava favored tight leather pants, skanky tops, and peekaboo lingerie. Of course, they both adored hot music and cold beer.

"The thing that amazes me most is that real people are working their buns off *inside* those puppet costumes," Carmela said.

The Beastmaster Puppets were indeed manned by a myriad of people who were dressed head to toe in black ninja-style clothing with black gauze masking their faces. They were inside the large puppets, functioning as the beating heart of the puppets, and controlled the bobbing and weaving as well as the puppets' arms. On the really jumbo-sized puppets, outlier puppeteers, also dressed in black, manipulated long sticks attached to the puppets' limbs and faces — sticks that when worked carefully made the puppets look both ethereal and peculiarly animated.

"Check this one out," Carmela said as a banshee puppet flitted past, its bug-eyed, witchy face poking forward as a trail of diaphanous garments fluttered behind it.

"Amazing," Ava said.

Carmela was smiling at the puppets, grooving with the mood and the music. In the flickering light from the antique street-lamps, her face fairly glowed with excitement, her nearly flawless complexion enhanced by the high humidity that seemed to hold the Crescent City in a perpetual cocoon-like embrace. Carmela's honey blond hair was a tousled, choppy mop and her eyes an inscrutable ice blue that often mirrored the flat shimmer of the Gulf of Mexico.

Ava shook back the dark, unruly mane that framed her exotic face. "Witches and banshees, those I can handle, no problem," she said. "It's when the puppets become this . . . active, when they take on human dimensions, that I get creeped out."

"I guess that's what makes these giant puppets so popular," Carmela said. She took a quick sip of red wine from her geaux cup and said, "Uh-oh, take a look at what's coming next."

A hush fell over the crowd as the final parade unit appeared. It was a contingent of black-caped, chalk-faced vampires that seemed to crawl stealthily out of the darkness.

"The Vampire Society," someone behind them said in quiet, almost reverent tones.

10

Four masked riders sat astride coal black horses, the horses' coats glistening like an oil slick and reflecting the yellow and red neon signs from nearby bars.

The vampires marched behind the riders in precise formation. Most of the men (and women) were tall, thin, and appeared to glide almost effortlessly.

Ava wrinkled her nose. "With that funky white makeup, they look like a doomsday cult."

Carmela studied the vampires, whose faces were painted a ghostly white. Their eyes were kohl-rimmed orbs, their mouths a glistening blood red that sported glowing white fangs. It was a look that definitely gave her pause.

Not so nice. Not that friendly.

"I guess it's just playacting," Carmela said finally, lifting her shoulders as if to shrug off any sort of malevolent vibe that might hover in the night air. "Perfectly harmless." Then, "Come on, let's follow along behind. We'll head over to Royal Street and check out the food booths."

Ava fluttered a hand. "You just uttered the magic words — food booths. You think they'll have barbecued shrimp, andouille gumbo, and fried crawfish?"

"Gotta go find out."

New Orleans was, of course, a foodie paradise. New restaurants, food halls, cocktail lounges, delis, and bakeries were opening at a dizzying rate. Here's where those uninitiated into the dining delights of the Big Easy routinely lost their minds over gumbo, beignets, po-boys, jambalaya, red beans and rice, plump Gulf oysters, muffulettas, and tickle-your-sweet-tooth bread pudding. To say nothing of creamy, rich crawfish étouffée, which was practically a New Orleans obsession.

Linking arms, Carmela and Ava trailed along behind the Vampire Society.

They turned the corner at Dumaine Street, walked past the Praline Factory and Toups's Italian Bakeshop, and then hung a right onto Royal Street.

"Will ya look at this!" Ava cried. "Royal Street's been turned into a gigantic street fair."

And she was right. All up and down Royal Street, for a good half dozen blocks, were food booths, food trucks, fortune-tellers, musicians, booths selling beads and T-shirts, and street artists. Revelers were cheek to jowl everywhere you looked — a mob of eating, drinking, dancing, good-time folks that formed a bobbling, jostling sea.

"This is what I need right here," Ava said,

diving toward a frozen daiquiri stand. "We need two in . . . What flavors do you have?" she asked the bartender as she scanned the rainbow-hued liquors lined up on the counter.

"Piña colada, amaretto, pineapple, blueberry, mudslide, and strawberry shortcake," the bartender said, rubbing his hands on his red-and-white-striped apron.

"What's a mudslide?" Ava asked.

The bartender shrugged. "Chocolaty rum?"

Ava turned to Carmela. *"Cher?"*

"Amaretto," Carmela said.

"Two amaretto daiquiris, please," Ava said.

The bartender nodded, tipped a bottle into a slurry of ice, and sent the mixture whirring through his daiquiri machine.

Once they'd grabbed their frozen concoctions, Carmela and Ava strolled along the sidewalk past several antique shops. Royal Street was where the absolute primo shops and galleries were located, where even the locals shopped for that perfect crackle-glazed oil painting, French mantel clock, or piece of antique silver to grace their dining table.

"What a perfect night," Carmela said, as they allowed themselves to be swept along with the surging crowd. "Nice and warm . . ." She tilted her head back and smiled at the view over the Mississippi. "With a crescent moon dangling in an indigo blue sky."

"A fitting salute to our Crescent City," Ava said. "Plus, everything you want to eat and drink. It really is a fabulous . . ."

BANG! CRASH!

Like a clap of thunder, the noise rolled down Royal Street, crackling and booming out. Revelers paused, heads turned, a woman let loose a high-pitched scream.

There was a pregnant pause. And then it came again . . .

CRASH! SMASH!

. . . jolting everyone out of their musical-sugary-deep-fat-fried reverie.

"Somebody's shopwindow just got stove in," Ava said. "With this many people boogying, something crazy's bound to happen." She sounded a little shaken, a little philosophical at the same time.

But Carmela was instantly on alert. "That wasn't just any window." She raised up on tiptoes and gazed down the street, not unlike a prairie dog who'd just sensed impending danger. "I think it was the front window at Dulcimer Antiques! Devon Dowling's shop!" She peered down the street again,

14

deeply concerned for her dear friend. "Yes, that's where the crowd's starting to gather. Come on!"

Together, Carmela and Ava weaved and dodged their way along the crowded sidewalk, angling toward Dulcimer Antiques. "S'cuse me, s'cuse me," Carmela said breathlessly as she flew along, stepping on toes and causing several revelers to spill their drinks as she towed Ava behind her.

When they finally got to Dulcimer Antiques, the street in front was a madhouse. A horde of people milled about, screaming and pointing at the large plate glass window that had been shattered. Dangerous shards of glass lay everywhere, and there was an ominous hole right under the letters that said *DULCIMER ANTIQUES. BUY SELL TRADE.*

"Was it terrorists?" one woman shrieked.

Another woman with blood trickling down the side of her face was starting to weep. She'd obviously been hit by a shard of flying glass.

"Something got tossed hard against Devon's shopwindow," Carmela said, making a hurried assessment. She glanced around. "Maybe from the inside?" The gigantic hole in the center of the window was outlined with jagged pieces of glass, as

15

sharp and dangerous as a shark's teeth.

"This is terrible!" Ava cried. "People are hurt!"

"Where's Devon?" Carmela wondered out loud. Worry engulfed her as she shoved her way to the front door. She put a hand on the brass knob, twisted it forcefully, and . . . got nowhere.

"Locked," Carmela said. She knew Devon had to be inside, because she could hear his pug, Mimi, barking frantically.

"Devon!" Ava cried out. Now she was edging toward frightened.

More gawkers gathered as Carmela pushed her way back to the broken window. She peered through broken glass into the dark interior of Devon's shop, trying to fathom what had gone wrong in there. She could see sterling silver teapots, priceless Chinese vases, and antique clocks smashed to bits on the floor. Lamps had been toppled, furniture upended. But it was difficult to make anything out . . . way back in the shadows.

"Devon?" Carmela called out in a strangled voice. Was he in there? Could he hear her? She looked about frantically, saw a man wearing a giant foam baseball mitt that covered half his arm, and snatched it off him.

16

"Hey!" he cried.

Carmela didn't stop to apologize or explain. She pulled the foam mitt onto her own arm and batted aside shards of glass as she lifted a leg and stuck it through the shattered window. She needed to find Devon to see if he was okay. Had he possibly experienced some sort of cardiac incident and collapsed against the window? Was someone in there with him? Had there been a knockdown, drag-out fight? Was Devon perhaps in dire trouble?

Carmela swatted another nasty shard aside and stepped all the way through the window, her shoes immediately crunching hard on broken glass.

"Devon?" Carmela called out, louder this time. "Mimi, sweetheart?" The little pug danced toward her, eyes rolling in fear, still barking frantically.

BANG!

A deafening roar and a shower of bright sparks exploded directly in front of Carmela and sent her reeling. Half-blinded by the smoke and feeling frantic now, she reached out for something — anything — to keep from falling. Luckily, her hands grasped a small walnut desk and she was able to steady herself.

Dear Lord, what was that? Carmela won-

17

dered, even as the words *flash-bang* zipped like jagged lightning through her brain. And was that the slam of the back door she'd just heard? Or were her ears, shocked by the loud explosion, playing tricks on her?

As smoke began to clear, Carmela crunched her way forward into the darkened shop. She moved two steps, then three, and stopped to draw a shaky breath. The place smelled of smoke, dusty furniture, old canvases, and something else . . .

Carmela shook off the foam mitt and reached around blindly. Her heart was beating out of her chest, her breath coming in sharp rasps. Where was Devon? And after that last explosion, had someone outside thought to call the police?

In complete darkness, feeling beyond apprehensive, Carmela finally reached out and touched a lamp. She fumbled for the switch, felt the lamp wobble slightly, and was flooded with relief when she heard a tiny click and the lamp spilled its warm yellow glow.

"Devon?" Carmela called again.

Mimi let out a sharp, terrified yip that pulled Carmela's bewildered eyes downward. And there, sprawled like a rag doll on a priceless Persian carpet, his eyes drooped shut, head in a puddle of crimson blood, was Devon Dowling!

CHAPTER 2

Carmela's hands were shaking so badly she could barely punch 911 on her cell phone. But she finally managed to pull it together and call for help. And even though it felt like hours dragged by, the first responders arrived within minutes.

Carmela scooped up Mimi as two men from Fire and Rescue smashed out the rest of the front window with metal tools, ducked their heads in, and surveyed the scene. Shouting ensued, and the fire guys quickly brought in light stanchions, followed by two EMTs equipped with portable oxygen and medical gear.

As the EMTs performed CPR on Devon and hung a bottle of IV fluid, Detective Bobby Gallant arrived. Gallant was a good-looking, slightly bulked-up detective, who cast a curious eye at Carmela's presence. Yes, they knew each other. Gallant was the right-hand man to Detective Edgar Babcock, Carmela's fiancé. How convenient!

Except it wasn't at all, because if Babcock arrived at the scene, Carmela figured he'd immediately banish her from the premises. The last thing Babcock would want would be for her to get messed up in one of his cases. And, chances were, this would end up being one of his cases.

Carmela touched a hand to Gallant's arm and hastened to explain her presence here. "I heard the crash when his front window broke, and I couldn't find Devon Dowling anywhere!" Her words spewed out in a hot rush. "So I came in to investigate. Hoping that I could help." She gazed at Gallant as she flapped a hand in frustration. "There was a huge explosion, and then I noticed Devon."

"Wait," Gallant said. "There was an explosion *after* you came inside?"

"Yes. Like those flash-bang things you guys use. Oh, and I think I heard the back door slam shut."

Gallant just nodded as Ava stuck her head through the front window, blinked, and then stumbled into the shop on sky-high stilettos. "Oh no," she said when she spotted Devon's body. "Is he . . . ?"

"They're working on him," Carmela said.

"You shouldn't be in here," Gallant said

to the ever-curious Ava.

"She's with me," Carmela said.

But Gallant had bigger fish to fry than dealing with Carmela and Ava. "Getting a pulse?" he asked the EMTs.

One of the EMTs shook his head. "Barely."

"Please try harder," Ava said as she fingered the silver crucifix that hung around her neck.

"They're doing everything they can," Carmela whispered. Still hanging on to Mimi, she pulled Ava away from Devon's body and then slipped an arm around her friend's shoulders.

"Maybe I should say a little prayer?" Ava asked.

"Just stay back," Gallant told them in a no-nonsense tone. He was part of the tight little scrum of Fire and Rescue and EMTs that now surrounded Dowling.

As the EMTs worked on Dowling, another disturbance was suddenly taking place outside: loud shouting, accompanied by howls from the anxious, curious crowd. Then a voice boomed out that Carmela recognized immediately. Detective Edgar Babcock had arrived, and he didn't sound one bit happy.

"Push 'em all back," Babcock shouted.

"Every last gawker. Then get some crime scene tape strung up and post as many officers as possible. Give me a twenty-foot perimeter. No, make that thirty feet."

"Babcock," Ava whispered.

Carmela just nodded. This crime scene — because that's surely what it was at this point — was about to get even more intense.

"And will somebody please unlock this damn door!" Babcock shouted.

"That's my honey," Carmela said under her breath. She watched expectantly as a tall ginger-haired man hovered in front of the broken window. Then she caught her breath as he ducked his head and stepped on through.

Babcock was, to put it mildly, extremely good-looking: tall, broad shouldered, elegant in his carriage and manner of dress, and with intense blue eyes. At this moment, he also looked incredibly on edge. As if his brain was spinning at warp speed, trying to stay one step ahead of . . .

"Carmela!" Babcock blurted out. "What are you doing here?"

"Funny you should ask," Ava murmured.

"We were at the festival and heard a terrible crash," Carmela said, gesturing toward the front window. "We rushed in to investigate."

"Wrong answer. *I'm* the one who rushed in to investigate," Babcock said. But he didn't say it in a mean way, just in a firm tone that confirmed he was definitely in charge.

"Devon and I are friends," Carmela added. She figured that was enough of an explanation for now.

Babcock leaned in to where the EMTs were still administering oxygen and doing chest compressions. "How's he doing?"

"Not good," one of them said.

"Let me through! Let me through!" came another scream from outside.

"What now?" Babcock muttered.

A uniformed officer stuck his head through the broken-out window. "Detective Babcock? We've got a guy outside who says he works here."

"Let me in! Please!" came the frantic voice again. Then a head bobbed in the front window.

"Who're you?" Babcock called out.

"T.J.," the young man said. "Trevor Jackson. I work here!"

"Let him in," Babcock said.

A young man in blue jeans and a tweedy jacket clambered over the glass and into the store. "What happened?" he demanded. "Did we get robbed? Please tell me what's going on!"

"We were hoping you could tell us," Babcock said.

T.J. looked momentarily stunned. Then he caught sight of Devon Dowling lying on the floor surrounded by the pack of first responders, and his eyes went wide as saucers. He opened his mouth but only managed a faint, "I . . . I . . ." T.J.'s dark hair was tousled, his eyes dark pinpricks of worry, and he carried a cardboard tray that held two muffuletta sandwiches and two cups of coffee.

"Do you know him?" Ava asked Carmela.

Carmela shook her head. "No, but Devon mentioned that he'd hired someone to help around the shop."

From that point on, the scene built in intensity. The Crime Scene team arrived as reporters continually tried to break through the barrier to shoot photos and film footage. Peter Jarreau, the NOPD public information officer who worked closely with Babcock, showed up and did his best to handle the always-pushy media, but he looked strained and caught off guard.

"No, no!" Jarreau snapped at the reporters. "We've got nothing to release yet."

"Then when?" the reporters clamored. There were so many camera flashes outside it looked like a Stones concert.

Jarreau pulled open the shop door and shot a look at Babcock, who simply shook his head.

"We'll let you know," Jarreau shouted to the TV and newspaper people. He turned back to Babcock. "The TV guys are hoping to get something for the ten o'clock."

"Probably not going to happen," Babcock said. He was watching the EMTs minister to Dowling. It wasn't going well.

Carmela and Ava remained pressed up against the back wall of the shop, keeping an eye on the law enforcement and medical personnel as they worked on Dowling and mumbled among themselves.

"I wonder what happened?" Ava whispered to Carmela. "Why'd the window shatter?"

"I think there was some kind of fight," Carmela said. It was fairly obvious that someone had viciously attacked Dowling and, in the ensuing struggle, smashed lamps, glassware, a few clocks, and the large plate glass window. The question now was Dowling's medical status. Was he hovering at death's door or was there hope for him?

"Don't let Mimi see Devon looking this way," Ava whispered to Carmela. "If she sees all that blood, she could be scarred for life."

"I'll hang on tight to her," Carmela promised. She leaned down and planted a kiss on Mimi's furry head as she cradled the shivering little dog in her arms. Outside, lights pulsed blood red and police radios blared unintelligible static. Night had settled hard on the French Quarter, and garbled voices from the crowd on the street sounded like a drunken cocktail party.

Carmela and Ava finally got some answers when Babcock stood up, dusted his hands together, and said in a somber tone, "Just leave it in while we transport him."

One of the EMTs frowned. "It's awfully wobbly. Could dislodge at any moment."

Charlie Preston, one of the Crime Scene techs, leaned forward. "Anchor it with a strip of adhesive tape," he said. "We gotta leave it there. It's critical we preserve his body in situ."

Carmela nudged her way into the pack as if she were negotiating a quarterback sneak. "What exactly are you talking about?" she demanded as the metal gurney they'd brought in uttered a dull clank. "How's Devon?"

For a homicide detective who'd seen it all, Babcock looked more than a little rattled. "Now Carmela . . ."

"Leave *what* in?" Carmela asked as she stared down at Dowling's pale face. His head was canted at an odd angle, and his lips were almost blue.

Babcock pursed his lips, still stalling. When he saw the purposeful look on Carmela's face, he knew he had to tell her. "The ice pick," he finally said. "We have to leave the ice pick in for the ME to examine."

"What!" Carmela said, practically shouting now. *"Ice pick?"*

"The one that's jammed in Dowling's left ear," Babcock said.

As one of the EMTs gently turned Devon's head with his gloved hands, Carmela was finally able to see the cause of the physical damage. The worn wooden handle of an ice pick protruded rudely from Devon's left ear.

The floor swayed beneath Carmela's feet, and now, finally, the realization hit her that her friend was dead. "He's dead? That's what killed him?" She gulped hard and drew a sharp breath. "I can't believe . . ." Carmela was stunned by the sheer grotesqueness of the murder even as she remained achingly curious. She'd never heard of such a bizarre way to kill someone. Well, maybe in a B movie. But only ones that involved the Mafia.

"Take him away," Babcock said.

Carmela held up a hand. "Are you sure he's really . . . gone?"

"Sweetheart," Babcock said, "that ice pick didn't just kill him; it made mincemeat out of his prefrontal cortex."

"There's nothing the doctors can do?" Ava asked. She'd wiggled her way in to catch a glimpse of Dowling as well. "There's no hope for a meaningful recovery?"

Babcock grimaced. "Not unless his middle name is Lazarus."

CHAPTER 3

Carmela walked into Memory Mine bright and early on Monday morning, juggling Mimi in one arm and a box of handmade washi paper in the other.

Gabby Mercer-Morris, Carmela's assistant, took one look at Mimi and her face fell. Then she gazed at Carmela and said, "I heard. About Devon Dowling."

Carmela set her box of paper down but hung on to Mimi. She hadn't wanted to leave the little pug at home with her two dogs, Boo and Poobah. They'd been curious about their visitor last night and pretty much on their best behavior. But today, the three of them left alone to their own devices . . . well, you never could tell.

"I suppose the news about Devon is all over the French Quarter," Carmela said.

Gabby nodded. "They're already talking about it at the Café du Monde. Plus, the graphic details were splashed all over TV last night and the front page of this morning's paper."

"So there was actual news footage?"

"It was grainy, but I could kind of pick you out. You and Mimi and Ava."

"Just what I needed," Carmela said.

Gabby stood behind the front counter, one hand worrying the strand of luminous pearls that nestled around her neck. Her other hand nervously smoothed the edge of the cashmere cardigan of her jonquil yellow twin set.

"The look on that little dog's face is breaking my heart," Gabby said.

Carmela had to smile. Gabby was the epitome of sweetness and competence. She'd been with Carmela for so many years that she could be trusted to run the shop single-handedly. But what Carmela admired most about Gabby was her unfailingly sweet nature. She was a champion of hummingbirds, puppies, and toddlers. When kids came into Memory Mine with their moms, Gabby practically lost her mind with joy.

"You should have seen Mimi last night," Carmela said. "You know those awful sci-fi movies where some ginormous alien ship destroys every building in New York City but there's always a tiny kid left crying in the street because its parents were killed?"

Gabby's face crumpled. "Yes?"

"That's what Mimi looked like last night. A poor little orphan."

Gabby reached over and gathered Mimi into her arms, letting the little dog cuddle up against her. "What are you going to do with her?"

"I don't know. But Mimi's the only witness we have."

Gabby put a hand on Mimi's head and rubbed gently. "This sweet little dog is a *witness*? I'm sure she's smart but . . . Carmela, you can't be serious."

"Now you sound like Babcock. I suggested last night that Mimi might be able to identify Dowling's killer, and he poohpoohed the whole idea."

Gabby looked doubtful, but she said, "You think Mimi could really do that? Recognize the killer, I mean?"

"We won't know unless we try. Mimi was right there in Dulcimer Antiques when Devon was murdered." Carmela gave a shudder as she recalled seeing the ice pick protruding from Devon Dowling's ear. It had been a harsh dose of reality.

"Carmela, hold it right there. You do realize you're meddling in one of Babcock's cases again."

"I wouldn't call it meddling." Carmela

paused and squinted, as if carefully weighing her answer. "Well, maybe superficially I am. But it's really all about Mimi. She's involved whether Babcock likes it or not. And right now, I'm the one who's taken custody of Mimi."

"Carmela, I know how your mind works. You have some sort of murder-solving plan, and this poor baby" — Gabby stroked Mimi's head again for good measure — "is going to get mixed up in it."

"Devon was my friend," Carmela said, almost defensively.

"I realize that, but you have to leave a murder investigation to the professionals. And by professionals, I mean Babcock and his team of homicide detectives."

"I haven't actually *done* anything yet."

"But you're thinking about it," Gabby said. "And the thing is, you've already dabbled your little pink toes in a bit of hot water."

Carmela sighed. "I have no idea what you're talking about." But, of course, she really did.

"Perhaps we should address that point," Gabby said. "Does Babcock *know* that your old paramour is opening a gumbo shop in the space right next door to us?"

"Let's get one thing straight. Quigg Brevard is *not* my old paramour. We dated once."

"Twice."

"Who's counting?" Carmela asked.

"I think Quigg might still be counting on you for, shall we say, some serious female companionship." Gabby paused. "If you ask me, Quigg's still a little bit in love with you."

"Quigg is only interested in things he can't have. He's one of those guys who barks at the moon." Carmela gave an offhand shrug. "But there's nothing to worry about. I happen to know that Quigg's already hired a manager for Gumbo Ya Ya."

"That's what he's calling his little gumbo bar?"

"As far as I know, yes. So between Gumbo Ya Ya, his other restaurants — Fishbones, Mumbo Gumbo, and Bon Tiempe — and his St. Tammany Vineyards, he's going to be way too busy to ever show his smiley little face next door."

"He's over there right now," Gabby said. "I saw Quigg walk by, like, five minutes ago."

Carmela inhaled sharply. "He is? You did?"

Gabby's smile was that of a cat who'd licked up all the cream. "It's hard not to notice a good-looking guy like that."

"You really think Quigg is good-looking?"

34

"Yes, but in that swarthy-pirate-bad-boy way."

"I know what you mean," Carmela said, giving a little shiver. Did she ever. Didn't all the women who stumbled into Quigg's aura? He was a handsome, dark-haired spider who'd spun the perfect failsafe web.

The bell above the front door dinged, and two women walked in.

"Are you open?" the younger T-shirt-and-jeans-wearing one asked.

"Absolutely," Carmela said.

"Oh, what a cute dog," the other woman said. She was older and wore a blazer over her T-shirt and jeans.

"What can we help you with?" Gabby asked. She transferred Mimi back to Carmela and walked around the counter.

"Albums," the younger woman said.

"Paper," said her older chum.

"Right this way," Gabby said, beckoning them into the heart of the shop.

Carmela smiled to herself as she gazed around her shop and watched the two women eagerly poring over paper, card-stock, rubber stamps, tempera paints, and all manner of ephemera. With the yellow brick walls and sagging wooden floor, her little craft shop oozed cozy. What better place to display hundreds of scrapbooking papers than on her floor-to-ceiling shelves? Or paper theaters, decoupaged frames, and handstamped pillows. Ditto that for beads, brads, Paperclay, ribbon, tassels, and colored pens. At the far back of her shop was an old wooden table that had been left by previous tenants. This was Craft Central, where all the classes and lessons took place. Off to one side was her small office. A little untidy, yes, but where else was Carmela going to keep her sketches and ideas for her stamping, album-making, and paper classes?

An hour and several more customers later, Carmela was ringing up an order of papier-mâché portfolios and Krylon spray when she heard the first hint of a disturbance next door. Shouting? Yes, it sounded like angry shouting. What on earth was going on over there?

Carmela walked her customer to the door, thanked her, waited for a hot moment, and then stuck her head outside. There. Now she could see and hear a whole lot better.

"I quit!" a screechy voice blurted out.

A tall woman with frizzy red hair suddenly burst onto the sidewalk. She was gesturing like crazy, waving her hands in the air and screaming at the top of her lungs. Not two seconds later, Quigg Brevard rushed out after her.

"You can't do that, Darnelle!" Quigg shouted. He looked upset, as if he'd tried to placate her and failed miserably. And Quigg was not used to failing when it came to women.

"Watch me!" the woman screamed back. As her shrill cries echoed up and down Governor Nicholls Street, Quigg continued to plead with Darnelle, practically begging her to stay.

"Not on your life! I will not put up with this." She spun around, her arms flung outward. "This place is way too dangerous." Then she turned on her heels and rushed down the street.

"Please, Darnelle," Quigg pleaded after the retreating figure. "Don't leave me in the lurch like this." But his words fell on deaf ears. Darnelle not only kept on running, she picked up the pace.

Quigg stood there on the sidewalk, looking puzzled and alone. He shook his head as he muttered to himself and said, "Damn it."

"What was that all about?" Carmela asked.

Quigg spun around as if he'd been zapped with a thousand bolts of electricity. "Carmela, I didn't see you there."

"Looks like you've got a problem," Carmela said. She didn't want to get involved. Well, not *involved* involved. But, truth be told, she was curious about what had just happened. Seems that curiosity gene of hers never could be tamed.

"My manager just quit," Quigg said. He scratched his head, looking puzzled. As if nobody had ever stormed out of one of his restaurants before.

She didn't just quit, Carmela thought. *She ran down the street like she was in a red-hot sprint with Usain Bolt.*

Carmela lifted an eyebrow. "That lady was your gumbo shop manager?"

"*Was* being the operative word," Quigg said. "Darnelle got all freaked-out when she heard about the murder last night."

"Devon Dowling," Carmela said. "Yeah. Ava and I were there. We followed the parade over to Royal Street."

Quigg closed one eye halfway and stared at her. "You saw it happen?"

"Heard it happen. There was this super loud crash of his front window shattering, and then we found Devon lying on the floor. Bleeding all over his Persian rug."

"You guys were friends. I'm sorry."

"Yes, we were. Thank you."

Quigg blew out a long breath. "Tough luck for both of us."

Carmela nodded. "I can see where losing your manager presents a terrible problem." She tried to sound sympathetic even though she was secretly pleased. She hadn't mentioned anything to Babcock about Quigg opening a shop right next door to hers. Now, thank goodness, it was probably a moot point. Quigg would undoubtedly fold the business and focus on his other restaurants like a good little restaurateur.

"I never saw it coming," Quigg said. "Darnelle quitting was like . . . *kerpow.* Out of the blue."

"This probably derails your big opening, huh? Or maybe you've changed your mind completely?" Carmela gazed at the narrow storefront and shook her head. "That space was too small for a gumbo restaurant anyway."

"I completely agree."

Whew, Carmela thought to herself. Saved by a screaming red-haired woman she didn't even know.

Quigg glanced at her, then turned suddenly thoughtful. Which made Carmela's scalp itch. She knew that look. It meant an idea was percolating.

"What?" Carmela asked in a slightly tentative voice.

"To be honest, I've been noodling around

39

a concept for a slightly *different* kind of shop."

"What are you talking about?" Carmela asked. Alarm bells were suddenly clanging inside her head. "You mean like an oyster bar?"

"New Orleans is up to its eyeballs in oyster bars," Quigg said. "No, I don't want to go in that direction, but I can't back out of this three-year lease I signed. The landlord did a complete build-out, and the interior designer is charging me an arm and a leg."

So he intends to stay? To go forward with . . . well, whatever he decides to go forward with? This is so not good.

"Do you know what the absolute hottest retail concept is today?" Quigg asked.

"No, but I have an idea you're going to tell me," Carmela said.

"Have you ever heard of a paint and sip shop?"

Carmela gave a faint nod. "Heard of them, yeah." She was starting to get a queasy feeling. Not exactly a run-for-the-porcelain, toss-your-cookies alert, but something approaching it.

"Paint and sip shops are hotter than ghost peppers right now. What you do is combine wine drinking with some kind of craft."

"Craft," Carmela said slowly. Now Quigg was veering dangerously close to her territory.

"Yeah, you pattern it after a traditional wine bar but include painting on canvas or decorating pottery." Quigg rolled back on his heels and smiled. "If I opened a shop like that, I could call it something like Decant & Design. Or Brush with Wine. What do you think of that?"

"I think you're off your rocker."

"And I think you'd be the perfect person to manage it."

Me! Carmela's horrified shriek echoed all the way down the street, causing a couple of T-shirt-and-bead-wearing tourists to stop dead in their tracks.

CHAPTER 4

"You know what that crazy Quigg Brevard wants to do next door?" Carmela said to Gabby. She was practically frothing at the mouth, and her eyes had gone all googly. Her hair was . . . well, never mind her hair.

"What?" Gabby asked, wide-eyed.

"Quigg's got this insane idea of opening a wine bar where you can also paint your own glasses. Or pots. Or something."

Gabby clapped her hands together. "I love it!"

"And he wants you and me to run it!"

"Oops, maybe I don't love it."

"I know," Carmela said. "Like we could even find the time. We're frantic enough as it is, running around like gerbils on crack."

Gabby tipped her head from side to side and gave a shy smile. "You have to admit, it *is* a cute idea. I know about a gazillion women who'd love to hang out at a place like that."

"So do I," Carmela said. "Fact is, they'd be standing in line. And the place could be decorated like one of those cute little 'she sheds' you see in women's magazines, with poufy pink pillows, velvet curtains, and leopard print chairs. Only with a never-ending supply of wine."

"And maybe a few appetizers."

"The place would be an instant money-maker," Carmela said. "It'd be the first of its kind in New Orleans."

"Honey, it sounds like you might be coming around to the idea."

"No, no, I'm just thinking out loud," Carmela said.

"Okaaay." Clearly, Gabby didn't believe her.

Carmela bit her lip and frowned. "Would a paint and sip shop be that much different from what we're doing now? Would it be a problem?"

"Yes, because then you and Quigg would become business partners. Which . . . oh, let me see . . . might present a huge problem for your soon-to-be *life* partner, Detective Edgar Babcock."

"Yeah, I know. I keep forgetting that I'm engaged."

"How on earth could you forget with that

big rock glittering on your finger like a disco ball?"

"Being engaged, getting married . . . it just doesn't feel like me."

"You're not going to call off the engagement, are you?" Gabby looked horrified. She loved all things romantic and was positive that Carmela and Babcock were absolutely right for each other. Unbeknownst to Carmela, Gabby had even started designing their wedding invitations. Well, she'd only gotten as far as the typography and paper. But still.

"Oh no, I adore Babcock too much," Carmela said. "We're going to get married all right. It's just that I can't picture myself all glitzed up in a white wedding dress and veil. Or white shoes. Yuck."

"You don't have to wear white. Or a veil. Or shoes, for that matter."

"The thing is, even if I wore crimson, I'd still feel like a tarted-up Wedding Barbie," Carmela said.

"Then plan a lovely low-key wedding. Lots of people do. You don't have to get married in St. Louis Cathedral with a gospel choir and a flock of white doves. You could . . . oh, I don't know, get married in a small chapel. Or on a beach. Or in the bayou if you don't mind some bugs and al-

44

ligators. Think of it as the new 'I do.' "

"This is Babcock's first wedding. I think he wants something more traditional."

"Then you might have a problem," Gabby said. "Right along with the problem that seems to be fermenting next door."

"The wine bar," Carmela said.

"What about the name Blush and Brush."

"Jeez, you make it sound like we're seriously considering going in with Quigg on this project."

Gabby grinned. "Well, aren't we?"

By two o'clock they'd had more than two dozen customers come through the doors of Memory Mine. More and more, Carmela was focusing on crafts rather than just scrapbooking. These crafts included handmade wine and jelly jar labels, handstamped wrapping paper, journals, decoupaged tins and cigar boxes, giant paper flowers, invitations, personalized stationery, and so much more.

When there was a break in the action, Gabby crept up to the front counter, where Carmela was going through a stack of invoices, and said, "The crazy thing about the wine bar is — I know we could make it a huge success. There's a million things we could do . . ."

The tiny bell over the front door went *da-ding,* and Detective Edgar Babcock strolled in, looking handsome as ever in a well-cut Brooks Brothers suit. His vivid blue tie perfectly matched his always-searching blue eyes.

As usual when he arrived unexpectedly, Carmela nearly lost her breath at the sight of him. Her hand automatically went to her mouth. When Carmela was really worried, she sometimes fell back on her childhood habit of biting her nails — and she was extremely worried now. How could she possibly tell Babcock about the Paint and Sip, or the Wine and Design, or whatever Quigg ended up calling the place?

"Hello," Carmela stammered.

From her spot in the corner, Mimi gave a tiny yip.

"So I was right," Babcock said. "That dog disappeared from the crime scene at the exact same time you and Ava did. I figured you snatched her up, but poor Officer Toohey just about went crazy looking for her."

"Sorry about that," Carmela said as Gabby headed for the back of the shop, the better to give them some privacy.

Babcock glanced at Mimi. "You still think that dog can eyeball a suspect?"

46

"No, but she might be able to sniff one out."

"So you say."

Carmela moved a step closer to him. "To what do I owe this . . . ?" She let her voice trail off.

"I just stopped by to see how my best girl was doing." Babcock put a hand on Carmela's shoulder and gave a gentle squeeze. "I know you and Dowling were friends for many years."

Were, Carmela thought. *He's already taking about Devon in the past tense.*

"This has to be a terrible shock for you," Babcock said.

"It's awful," Carmela said. "I can still hardly believe it."

Babcock nodded as his cell phone beeped from inside his jacket pocket. "Murder is a ghastly criminal act. And it's even worse when the victim is a close friend. It's hurtful and frightening all at the same time." He raised his phone, said, "Yup?" Then, "Hey, Bobby, whatcha got?"

Carmela figured it was Bobby Gallant and wondered if he was calling about the case. When Babcock moved a few steps away from her and lowered his voice, she knew he was, and she guessed something important had to be up. But what? A clue? Maybe a serious suspect?

"So T.J. didn't turn tail and run. Okay. Yeah, it's interesting." Babcock glanced at his watch. "No, I'm supposed to talk to him in forty minutes or so. You get anything from the lab yet?" He bent forward, listening intently. "Yeah, that is weird. Okay, keep pushing them to try and nail it down. I'll catch you later." Babcock stared at his phone for a second, then turned to look at Carmela.

"What?" she said. Something was going on. She could feel electricity sparking in the air.

Babcock shook his head as if this was all routine.

"Nothing to concern you," he said.

But Carmela wanted answers. *"Everything* about Devon's murder concerns me."

"Carmela. Just . . . no."

"What was that about T.J.? What was Bobby Gallant saying to you?"

"You shouldn't be listening in like that."

Carmela offered him a shrug and a faux-guilty smile. "You were standing, like, two feet away from me."

"Point taken," Babcock said.

"So?" Carmela decided to go for it. "I know Bobby said something about T.J. And by the way, where exactly was this T.J.

person when Devon was murdered? I mean, why wasn't he in the shop? With all the action on Royal Street and potential customers everywhere, you'd think, as an assistant, T.J. would be Johnny-on-the-spot."

"Trevor Jackson claims that, per Dowling's request, he ran out to grab sandwiches and coffee. What we can't seem to ascertain is how *long* he was absent. How long it took him to run down the street to get takeout."

"Maybe he's the one who tossed the flash bomb at me," Carmela said.

"Maybe," Babcock said. "But he didn't have any sort of residue on his hands. And his prints weren't on the ice pick."

"So you're ruling T.J. out?"

"Not necessarily," Babcock said. "For one thing, we know he's not exactly an upstanding citizen. He's a heavy drinker . . ."

"Seriously?"

". . . And a brawler. With a police record."

Carmela felt like she'd been punched in the gut. Had kindhearted Devon Dowling allowed a snake to crawl into his lovely little antique shop? Had his kindness and innocence been his final undoing?

Babcock continued. "It's not a *terrible* record, but Jackson does have two DUIs."

"So you *do* consider T.J. a serious suspect." Could Devon's murder be that easy to solve?

"We're not ruling anyone out at this point," Babcock said. "It's too early."

"Did Devon have any — what do you call them? Defensive injuries?"

"Not that we've determined."

"So someone surprised him," Carmela said. "Except that . . . his front door was locked."

"So maybe he let someone in and locked the door after them," Babcock said. "A customer . . . a friend."

"So Devon might have known his killer," Carmela said, and the notion chilled her.

"It's possible," Babcock said. "Anything's possible."

"And your lab is working on some kind of — what would you call it? Forensic evidence?" Carmela asked.

Carmela saw Babcock's jaw tighten and feared for a moment she'd gone too far, pushed him too hard.

"I mean . . . I couldn't help but overhear . . ."

Babcock seemed to relax then. "There was some sort of forensic evidence found on Devon Dowling — a type of plant matter, possibly native to one of the bayous."

"Do you know what kind of plant?"

Babcock sighed deeply, as if it was all too

50

much for him. Or maybe he just hadn't eaten lunch yet. Carmela knew that when Babcock got super busy, when he was digging into a case, running hard, he forgot to eat and his blood sugar level dropped.

"The plant material . . . I don't know. The crime techs are working on that right now." Babcock gave a faint smile then leaned over and gave Carmela a quick peck on the cheek. Two seconds later he was gone.

"Well?" Gabby was back behind the front counter, clutching a bunch of brown kraft envelopes in her hands. "What did Babcock say about the wine bar? About Quigg?"

"Quigg? I never mentioned Quigg," Carmela said.

Gabby blinked rapidly. "Wha . . . you never? Carmela, you're going to have to spill the beans sooner or later that Quigg is our new next-door neighbor. Even if we don't wind up teaching classes at the Drink and Drizzle — or whatever he decides to call it — and even if you don't actually work with Quigg, he's going to be around. All the time."

Carmela pushed back a chunk of her choppy blond hair. "I know. And I'm working on that aspect of it."

"You better work harder, girlfriend."

"I am. I will." Carmela shrugged. "Can we please change the subject? Don't we have other things to worry about?"

"We've got that greeting card workshop scheduled for tomorrow."

"And I'm looking forward to it," Carmela said. "Though I haven't had time to give it a single, solitary thought."

"Luckily, I have," Gabby said. She picked up a card from the front counter. "I worked on this earlier. See?" She handed the card to Carmela.

"I love this heavy vellum," Carmela said, turning the card over in her hands.

"From that new supplier over in Belle Chasse."

"And your design is terrific," Carmela said. Gabby had used a pearl gray cardstock and rubber stamped a design of three hot-air balloons on the front. But what was really spectacular was that she'd used a multicolored ink pad to get a lovely pastel rainbow effect. Then, using letter stencils, she'd added the words *YOU'RE INVITED*.

"Since I'm forever getting e-invitations from zillions of charities that want Stuart and me to attend their fund-raisers and soirees, I thought we could gently encourage the creation of handmade invitations. You know how swiftly they're fading from our collective use."

Gabby's husband, Stuart Mercer-Morris, owned several car dealerships and was generally known as the Toyota King of New Orleans. This made him extremely popular with the charity and society set.

"That's a genius idea," Carmela said, trying to stifle a yawn.

"Whoops, somebody's having a midday slump," Gabby said.

"I guess I am."

"Time for a coffee run," Gabby said. She glanced at Mimi. "And Miss Mimi, you can come with me and stretch those cute little legs of yours."

Carmela went back to her stack of in voices, secretly hoping that Gabby might return with a couple of beignets as well. Just as she initialed the final invoice, ready to turn the whole pile over to her bookkeeper, there was a bump and a loud knock at the front door.

"What?" Carmela said as the door flew open and whacked hard against the wall.

Peter Jarreau, media liaison for the NOPD, paused in her doorway. He looked hesitant and disheveled, his suit just a tad too large for his skinny frame. His eyes swept the room anxiously while the sweet, sticky aroma of his cologne nearly knocked

Carmela flat.

"Is he here?" Jarreau asked.

"Is who here?" Carmela asked. She knew he was looking for Babcock, but there was something about Jarreau's manner that irritated her.

"Babcock."

"You just missed him."

Jarreau stared at Carmela for a moment, as if trying to comprehend what she'd just said.

Carmela tried again, speaking slowly and enunciating carefully as if to a child.

"Babcock is not here. You'd better try him on his cell."

Jarreau nodded. "Ah. Okay." He seemed to relax then. "I'm sorry you got pulled into that mess last night. Babcock told me you and Dowling had been friends."

Carmela blinked hard, trying to keep the tears from flowing. "It's never easy to lose a friend."

"Well, sorry to disturb." Jarreau tipped an imaginary hat and was gone.

"Whew," Gabby said when she came back some ten minutes later, leading Mimi and carrying two large coffees in paper cups. She wrinkled her nose. "What is that . . . ungodly smell?"

"Peter Jarreau stopped by. He was looking

for Babcock."

"Oh, the Cologne Ranger. Of course."

"How'd you know we call him that?"

Gabby gave a mischievous grin. "Ava told me."

At five o'clock, Gabby clicked the lock on the front door.

"If you're staying late, be sure to keep the door locked," Gabby said. "You never can tell what's going to happen. Some crazy person could be targeting French Quarter shop owners."

"I'll be careful," Carmela said. "I'm going to put Mimi in my car out back and then run back in and double-check everything."

"Okay, I'm just going to pack up and grab the outgoing mail."

Carmela scooped up Mimi along with a couple of *Somerset Studio* magazines and put them in her car.

"You sit tight," she told Mimi. "I'll be back in a flash."

But when Carmela went back inside, Gabby was standing at the front door, gazing at a handsome man with two delicious streaks of gray in his well-coiffed dark hair. The man was peering through the glass at her.

"I'm sorry, we're closed," Gabby said

through the closed door.

The man nodded and smiled, then pressed a business card up against the glass. It was a thick, cream-colored card with raised black type that read RICHARD DRAKE, PRESIDENT. Underneath were the words VAMPIRE SOCIETY.

"I'll handle this," Carmela said. She looked at his card and said, "You're kidding, right?" And to herself, *This is way too wacky for words.*

The man shook his head. "I need to talk to you about Devon Dowling."

Carmela unlatched the door and pulled it halfway open, just far enough so they could converse without yelling at each other. But she kept her foot pressed against the door in case she wanted to close it in a hurry.

"What's up?" she asked, curious about this strange but very good-looking visitor. "Mr. Drake, is it?"

"I understand you were the one who discovered Devon Dowling's body last night," Drake said. His hazel eyes bored into her, but they were kind eyes. His cheekbones were pronounced, and his lips carried a sensual curve.

"That's right." Carmela decided this was a man she should be wary of.

"Your discovering Mr. Dowling was not

56

an accident," Drake continued. "I understand that you and he were good friends."

When Carmela remained silent (and puzzled), Drake tried again.

"I was wondering if your friendship was casual or if you were a confidante of Mr. Dowling's, a trusted friend. Someone he might share his thoughts with?"

"Why, exactly, are you asking me these questions?" Carmela was aware of Gabby hovering in the background.

Drake seemed to waft closer to her, as if pushed along on a slow evening breeze.

"Because my cohorts and I believe that Mr. Dowling possessed something extremely important. More important than anyone could ever imagine."

"What exactly are you talking about?" Carmela asked. She wondered if he was inquiring about some precious antique. Had an extremely pricey piece also been stolen from Devon's shop?

"It's something we all want very badly," Drake continued.

Carmela stared at him as if trying to decipher his words — and his bizarre performance. "I'm sorry, but you're talking in circles. You're going to have to do a lot better than that. Just spit it out, okay?"

"Yes, of course." Drake licked his lips and

leaned in close. "There's a strong rumor that Mr. Dowling had somehow come to possess a small piece of Lincoln's coat."

"Lincoln," Carmela said. What exactly was this fine-looking man rambling on about? Then her brain finally caught up with the conversation. "Whoa, buddy." She made a referee's time-out signal with her hands. "Do you mean *Abraham* Lincoln? Devon has a piece of his *coat*?"

From the back of the shop, Gabby uttered a little shriek.

"From the coat Lincoln wore the night he was assassinated at Ford's Theatre," Drake said.

Carmela put a hand to her throat as a startling thought rumbled through her brain: *Dear Lord, if this story is true, it definitely raises the stakes!*

CHAPTER 5

In the tiny kitchen of her French Quarter apartment, Carmela busily chopped onions and avocado slices. Popping a piece of avocado in her mouth, she glanced through the doorway into the dining room. And smiled with satisfaction at the soft glow of candlelight that came from the elegant white tapers she'd placed on her refinished walnut dining table.

The rest of her combination dining-living room was just as inviting and cozy. Over the last couple of years, Carmela had given her place the Belle Époque treatment with antique chairs, fringed lamps, and prints in elegant gold frames that hung on her brick walls. She also had a leather chaise lounge, a small fireplace, and a collection of vintage children's books. A blue and peach Aubusson carpet served as a favorite napping spot for dogs.

Carmela's gaze swept past to the wine rack.

Yes.

Carmela put down her knife, hurried over to the wine rack, and scanned her collection of bottles. Because she was searing bay scallops and mushrooms in white wine sauce, and both she and Ava preferred drinking a red wine, she decided a rosé would be the perfect complement and compromise. Back in the kitchen, she plunged her bottle of Matthiasson rosé into an ice bucket just as there was a loud knock on the door. Ava. And right on time.

Poobah immediately bolted for the front door. He was an energetic, shaggy-haired mongrel that Carmela's ex-husband (Shamus, aka the Weasel) had found wandering the streets and adopted. And Carmela had inherited. Carmela's chunky little Shar-Pei, Boo, followed languidly after Poobah. Mimi, who was asleep on the Persian carpet, raised one eyelid, not sure what the fuss was about.

"Boy, am I pooped," Ava declared as she waltzed in. She dropped her shoulders as if she were a beast of burden tasked with carrying a hundred-pound sack of coal. "If my schlep across that courtyard was any longer, I'd be too worn out for dinner."

"It's a killer," Carmela agreed. Juju Voodoo, Ava's quaint little voodoo shop, was a hop, skip, and a jump across their shared courtyard with its palmetto trees and pattering fountain. Ava's studio apartment, which was festooned in leopard prints and painted Pepto pink, occupied the floor directly above her shop.

Ava brightened. "But a free meal is always worth the effort, so thanks for the invite and here I am."

Woof.

Poobah nudged Ava's knee, signaling, *Treat time, Auntie Ava.*

"I wouldn't forget you, sweetie," Ava said. She pulled a handful of dog treats out of her studded leather purse and bent to feed the two dogs. As she did so, her corset top gapped dangerously. "Oops, Auntie Ava almost had a wardrobe malfunction." She bunched her top an inch higher, still offering a fine display of cleavage. "And Mimi, there you are, you little dickens. Get over here. I've got a treat for you, too."

"Wine?" Carmela asked.

"That should definitely take the edge off. What a day, honestly!" Ava readjusted her purple corset and plopped down onto Carmela's leather chaise lounge. She watched Carmela work the corkscrew. "Seems like every wacko beat a path to my shop today. But not a single one of them was a good-looking billionaire who was interested in my incense, talismans, or magic charms." She fluffed her mass of dark hair. "Or my own personal charms."

Carmela handed her a glass that held two fingers of wine. "Try this."

Ava stopped her rant long enough to chugalug her wine. "Mmn. Bold taste for a rosé. Mama likes it. I'll have some more, please."

Carmela promptly filled Ava's glass.

"Yes'm, everyone showed up to ask the same stupid questions without buying a thing. 'Do you have candles that will raise the dead? Or at least figure out where dead Uncle Hughie buried his gold coins? Is there an incantation that can make a woman look thirty years younger right before she's forced to meet her ex-husband's new trophy wife?' Seriously, *cher,* what the hell's wrong with people? Is it too much trash TV? Social media? Or is something in the ozone?"

"Come sit down for dinner and we'll figure it out," Carmela said. She carried out two avocado, tomato, and Vidalia onion salads and placed them on the table along with a basket of warm French bread and a pot of honey butter.

Ava pushed herself off the chaise and sat

down in a cane-backed chair. "Now this is what I call pure deliciosity. I can't tell you how happy I am that my BFF is also a gourmet cook." She held up her wineglass. "Cheers, baby." Then, "How was your day? Any fallout from last night?"

"Babcock stopped by Memory Mine this afternoon," Carmela said.

"To see how you were faring after last night or to warn you to back off his investigation?"

"A little of both, actually."

"It's not your fault you discovered poor Devon's body last night. I mean, it's terrible. I feel awful about it. But, honestly, when Babcock showed up, he acted as if we were trying to annoy him personally. When that wasn't the case at all."

"He knows that," Carmela said. "At least I think he does."

"The real litmus test is if the wedding is still on." Ava chewed thoughtfully. "Is it?"

"He's been pushing me to set a date," Carmela said.

"Then you *should* set the date. What's the holdup? You're not getting cold feet, are you?"

"Nooo."

"So what's the problem?" Ava asked. "A

man like that . . . ai, yi, yi. Such a great catch."

"Hold that thought," Carmela said, "while I grab our entrées."

"Ye gadz, what do we have here?" Ava asked when Carmela set a plate in front of her. "Scallops? Be still my heart." She dipped her fork in and sampled the wine sauce. "Your seasonings!" she raved. "They're so fresh and perfect. Me, I've still got a can of paprika in my kitchen cupboard that's so old Hungary was still a Communist country when it was packaged."

"I'm happy you're enjoying dinner," Carmela said.

"Oh yeah. So. You were saying. About the wedding and everything."

"Well, there's been a sort of monkey wrench thrown in where I didn't expect it."

"How so?" Ava asked.

"Guess who rented the empty space right next door to my shop."

"I don't know. A donut shop? Tattoo parlor? I might want to get a rose or a dove or something on my hip. Or maybe my tush."

"Sorry, but you're out of luck. The new tenant intends to open one of those paint and sip shops."

Ava gestured with her fork. "I've heard

64

about those. Where chicks get together to quaff wine while doing something creative like painting plates or small canvases."

"Well, they asked me to help with the crafty aspect," Carmela said.

"That sounds real nifty. You make a few extra bucks while you drive business to Memory Mine. Who's the shop owner? Anybody we know?"

"It's Quigg."

Ava's fork clattered to the table. "Quigg *Brevard*? That Quigg? Holy griddle cakes, Carmela, what did Babcock have to say about him being next door?"

"I haven't told him yet."

"Babcock's going to burst a blood vessel when he finds out you're going to be working with Quigg! He's gonna have a full-blown thrombosis!"

"But I don't know if I am going to work with him. Right now it's just an . . . idea. It's out there spinning around in the ether."

"But you said Quigg signed a lease?"

"Yes."

"Then it's not just spinning, that sounds pretty darn solid, sweetie."

Carmela shrugged. "I guess."

"When are you going to break the news to Babcock?"

"Tomorrow?"

"Better fix him a gourmet dinner first. And get him liquored up, too."

Carmela took a sip of wine. "Yeah, well, there's more I have to tell you. You remember that Vampire Society group we saw marching in the parade last night?"

"How could I forget?"

"The president of the society, Richard Drake, stopped by my shop today."

"Vampires are into scrapbooking now?"

"No, but it was the weirdest thing. Customers were in and out all day, and when Drake arrived it was like, *pouf!* There he was. Like he just floated in and appeared somehow. I was a little creeped out."

"What'd this guy Drake want?"

"Here's where it gets weird. He wanted to know if I was one of Devon's confidantes."

"A confidante about what?" Ava asked as she took a sip of wine. "Etchings? Antique cameos?"

Carmela took a deep breath. "Drake asked me if I knew that Devon might have owned a small piece of Lincoln's coat."

Ava started choking on her wine. "Agh, agh . . . wait, you mean *Abraham* Lincoln's coat?"

"That's right."

"Why would Devon possess something as weird as that?"

"You know antique dealers. They poke around in odd places and find all sorts of different things like old books, rare paintings, and valuable stamps. It gives them bragging rights. Plus, they're a little bit fickle . . . sometimes dealers sell an item as soon as they find it. Try to turn a quick profit."

"Did you tell Babcock about this Lincoln's coat thing?"

"Not yet. But I know he'd pretty much pooh-pooh it," Carmela said.

"Well, I'm intrigued," Ava said. "And what's this Drake guy like? I've never met an actual vampire before. You think he can handle a Caesar salad, what with the garlic and all?"

"Drake's not a real vampire, but I want to tell you, the man is drop-dead gorgeous. He's very intense with these sensual lips and two distinguished streaks in his hair. And his hazel eyes . . ." Carmela stopped abruptly. "The only problem is, I think Drake was playing me. For all I know, *he's* the one who killed Devon when Devon wouldn't give him or sell him the piece of coat. *If* that piece of coat even exists."

"So you think Mr. Vampire was spoofing you today because you discovered Devon's body and you've got a super tight connection to Babcock."

"That's a possibility, yes," Carmela said.

"Carmela, you're the French Quarter's very own Nancy Drew. If there's a riddle to be solved, you're the girl to dig in and untangle it. And if there's something shady about Drake, I bet you can sniff it out."

"Why would I want to?"

Ava leaned toward her, a serious look on her face. "Because any information you learn could help lead to Devon's killer."

"Gulp," Carmela said.

"I know, I know. Babcock warned you to stay away from his case. But face it, honey, it's kind of our case, too."

They finished their dinner then, talking quietly about Devon Dowling. Reminiscing about the fun they'd all had together, the committees they'd served on for the Children's Art Association.

Carmela stood up and began clearing the plates. "You want another glass of wine? Something for dessert?"

"I'm stuffed, *cher.* I ate and drank so much I'm sick to my stomach." When Ava saw the look of concern on Carmela's face, she added, "But in a good way."

"Sure."

Ava picked up the wineglasses and snuffed out the candles. "But I've got some news for you," she said as she followed Carmela into the kitchen.

"What's that?"

"I've decided to take control of my love life."

"Um . . . what?"

"I made an appointment with a genuine matchmaker."

"What's it called?" Carmela asked. "Dudes R Us?"

"No, it's with Penelope something at Turtledove Matchmaking. You should read her ratings on Yelp. Talk about satisfied customers. Some scored actual marriage proposals!"

"Were these customers male or female?" Carmela asked.

"Both! What I have to do now is go for an interview – that way they pick my brain to find out all my likes, dislikes, preferences, and deal breakers. That sort of thing."

Carmela lifted an eyebrow. "When is this interview supposed to take place?"

"Wednesday night. And, *cher,* will you pretty please come with me? This isn't the kind of thing a girl can do alone. Heaven forbid I leave out something important."

"What is this all about, really? Did you just take one of those *Cosmo* quizzes?"

"Mostly it's because I have so much

trouble connecting with men," Ava said in complete seriousness.

Carmela laughed until she almost choked. Finally, when she could control herself and had wiped away the tears that were streaming down her face, she said, "Ava, you connect with men just fine. You've basically broken the land speed record for making men fall in love with you. It's the *caliber* of men you connect with." Carmela hesitated for a second, because she wanted to say this next part with as much kindness as possible. "Face it, honey, you've dated every dingbat, peckerwood, dolt, dunce, and dullard that New Orleans has to offer."

"You're saying I've just about run through everyone?"

"Well, no. I wouldn't go that far," Carmela said. "But you do tend to date more men in a single year than other women do in a lifetime."

"What was it you just said? Dolt, dunce, and dullard? That sounds suspiciously like a law firm."

"Ava, you just need to raise your sights a little more, that's all. You deserve a good guy, a nice guy," Carmela said.

"But that's exactly *why* I need a matchmaker. So she can turn up an entirely new crop of men. Some really good guys." Ava gave a little wiggle. "After all, I'm not getting any younger. I have to buckle down and get serious about a relationship. Why, I haven't even had a starter marriage yet!"

Carmela sighed. "When you walk down the street, men practically throw themselves at your feet."

"I need a gentleman, not some goombah with a foot fetish." Ava suddenly looked stricken. "You know that eastern European bag boy at the Picky Quicky Grocery? The one with the crazy eye?"

"Yeah?" Carmela said.

"I put a little shine on him, and he didn't respond."

"He may not be the best subject."

"C'mon, Carmela, using a matchmaker is basically outsourcing my dating life and using an expert who can push me in the right direction. You found Babcock, now I need to find a guy who's not a self-centered dingbat."

Carmela put her arms around Ava and gave her a hug.

"It's true, I do have Babcock now," Carmela said. "But please don't forget that I bumbled my first marriage with the lying, cheating Shamus Meechum."

"That's exactly what I'm trying to avoid — marrying a spoiled, selfish jackhole like

Shamus. Or his doppelgänger." Ava sighed. "So will you come with me?"

Carmela nodded. "Of course I will." *If only to make sure this matchmaker is really on the up-and-up.*

CHAPTER 6

"I think I had a nightmare about Lincoln's coat fragment," Gabby said. It was nine o'clock Tuesday morning, and Carmela had just arrived at Memory Mine. Correction, she was there physically, but she still needed to jump-start her brain with a cup of industrial-strength chicory coffee.

"You're worried about *that*?" Carmela asked.

"Not me, per se, but my subconscious. Ever since that guy Drake came here and cornered you, I've been seriously creeped out. I mean, it can't be true, can it?"

"I don't know, stranger things have been known to happen," Carmela said. "I mean, look at all the relics that are purported to exist around the world. There are all sorts of cathedrals in Europe that claim to have pieces of the true cross or the bones of St. Peter or the original crown of thorns."

"How about the Shroud of Turin?" Gabby said.

"There you go." Carmela lifted a hand. "More proof positive in the case for relics. And relic hunters."

"I think there's even supposed to be some saint's bones preserved at that church in the Garden District," Gabby said.

"And didn't someone truck a vial of saint's blood through here a couple of years ago?"

"So there's a precedent," Gabby said.

"There is in New Orleans anyway. Where just about anything hinting at the supernatural is warmly embraced." Carmela was dead serious. New Orleans claimed to have had more haunted houses, hotels, and cemeteries than anywhere else on earth. A few voodoo priestesses, too.

Gabby fingered a roll of purple velvet ribbon. "You didn't bring Mimi along today."

"She's back home ruling the roost. Nipping at Boo's and Poobah's heels."

"Good for her," Gabby said. "I'm glad she's fitting in with the pack." Then, "I've been thinking more about our greeting card workshop this afternoon. Really looking forward to it."

"Me too."

"In between customers this morning I

should probably gather up our stash of cardstock."

"That would be great," Carmela said. "Plus, you can haul out that big box of paper snippets and remnants that we've been saving since time immemorial."

"You mean since we first opened," Gabby said. "But you're right, the best cards always happen when you add little bits and pieces of paper and fabric and build up several layers of color and texture."

"And add twine, colored ribbons, and raffia."

"A lot of card shops *used* to sell handmade cards like that, but you don't see them so much anymore," Gabby said.

"Probably too cost prohibitive."

"Have you, um, thought any more about Quigg's wine bar?" Gabby asked.

"Thought about it, yes. But I'm still weighing my options."

"It might be fun," Gabby ventured.

"I wish the wine bar thing hadn't come right on the heels of Devon Dowling's murder." Carmela picked up a basket filled with brads and beads and started sifting through it. "It feels like there's too much going on."

"Is there anything new concerning Devon? About suspects or when the police might apprehend his killer?"

Carmela shook her head. "Prying information out of Babcock is like trying to scrape a hunk of fossilized chewing gum off the bottom of your shoe. It's probably not going to happen." She tossed a couple of packets of gold brads onto the counter. "On the other hand . . ."

"What?" Gabby asked.

"Maybe I could make it happen."

"Carmela." Gabby's voice carried a warning tone.

"Not in a big way or anything. But I was thinking maybe I'd pop into Devon's shop and have a quick confab with that guy T.J., Devon's assistant. I might learn something."

"Is the shop even open?" Gabby asked.

Carmela smiled. "I guess I'll just have to mosey over there and find out."

Devon Dowling's shop wasn't open. In fact, it was locked up tighter than a drum, and the front window was completely boarded over with plywood. But that didn't stop Carmela. She banged hard on the front door until T.J.'s face finally appeared in the door's small rectangular window, looking nervous and frightened.

"Mr. Jackson. Trevor," Carmela said, knocking again. "May I come in?" When he still didn't respond, she said, "We kind of met the other night even though we were never properly introduced."

"You," T.J. said, recognizing Carmela as he creaked open the front door. "You're Devon's friend."

"I'm Carmela," she said. "Carmela Bertrand."

"Yes, Mr. Dowling mentioned you many times. Please come in."

"Thank you, Mr. Jackson."

"T.J. Call me T.J."

"All right."

Carmela walked in and glanced around the shop. The pieces that had been smashed had been cleaned up and a few new things put in their place. And even though a small table had been placed over the bloodstain, the carpet was still discolored. Awful.

"Are you planning to reopen for business?" Carmela asked.

T.J. shook his head. "I don't know what the future holds. Everything's up in the air right now."

"I'm so sorry this happened," Carmela said. "It strikes me that you and Devon were quite close. Please accept my sincere sympathies."

"Thank you, that means a lot to me right now." T.J. wore khaki slacks and a rumpled

77

denim shirt. His dark hair was disheveled, and he hadn't shaved. His face looked narrow and haunted with hollows under his eyes. It was a stark contrast to the polished, good-looking young man of the other night.

"I don't mean to insult you," Carmela said, "but you do look absolutely devastated."

"Because I am. I thought the world of Mr. Dowling, and now he's gone." T.J.'s voice was rough with emotion. "On top of that, the police grilled me for two full hours yesterday."

Carmela was shocked. "Wait a minute, the police think *you* murdered Devon?"

"I'm apparently suspect numero uno. Unbelievable, huh?" T.J. shook his head. "The police kept saying things like, *We're just trying to assimilate all the facts,* but I could tell that under all their nicey-nice talk they had their beady eyes focused directly on me. They didn't want to believe me when I told them I worshipped the ground Mr. Dowling walked on. Mr. Dowling was a gentleman and a true professional. Nobody, but nobody, could discern a legitimate Erté from a knockoff like he could. Or tell a handloomed silk Bokhara carpet from a machine-made wool rug from Pakistan."

"Devon knew his antiques, that's for

sure," Carmela said.

"He was one of the best. Maybe *the* best."

"So. The police who questioned you . . ."

"It was the same two who showed up Sunday night," T.J. said. "That Babcock guy and his henchman Gallant."

"I see." But Carmela really didn't. Why were the police looking so hard at T.J.? Did they have a legitimate reason? Had they discovered a hidden motive? Or were they wasting their time while the real killer chuckled at their antics and watched from the sidelines?

A knock on the front door startled them both.

"Now what?" T.J. muttered as he started for the door.

But it turned out to be Roy Sultan, the landlord. He was a portly, silver-haired man with a benevolent-looking basset hound face who owned a half dozen buildings in and around the French Quarter.

Once Sultan had introduced himself to T.J. and Carmela, he was quick to admit that he, too, was absolutely devastated by Devon Dowling's murder.

"Devon was the best commercial tenant I had," Sultan said. "He's been in this same location for almost fifteen years. Never a problem, never a peep. My other tenants,

they're forever demanding this or that —
upgraded wiring so they can run Wi-Fi. Or
they want new paint, carpeting, and AC. I
can't imagine who I'll ever find to replace
Devon Dowling."

Sultan was still shaking his head, bemoan-
ing the loss of his tenant as he shuffled out
the front door.

"What's going to happen to the shop?"
Carmela asked once Sultan had left.

"I don't know," T.J. said. "Keep it going,
close it for good, whatever's in the cards."

"Does Devon have family?"

"His brother is flying down from Chicago
for the funeral."

"When's that supposed to be?"

"Tomorrow. At St. Roch Chapel."

"So soon," Carmela murmured. It felt like
it'd been all of five minutes since she'd
discovered Devon's dead body.

"Apparently, his brother is some kind of
high-test business executive. Doesn't want
to drag things out."

"Clearly, his brother has no concept of
how New Orleans works," Carmela said.
New Orleans wasn't called the Big Easy for
nothing. Time was a concept that was
routinely dismissed and generally kicked to
the curb. New Orleans took its own sweet,
rapturous time to sort things out. The city

moved as lackadaisically and as leisurely as the Big Muddy that flowed through it.

"I'm guessing Mr. Dowling's brother will make a fast decision about the shop," T.J. said. "About whether it will stay open. Or if someone else stands to inherit."

Carmela thought about this for a few moments. If there were designated heirs, would that have been a reason to kill Devon? After all, Devon dealt in high-end antiques. Baccarat glasses and decanters, sterling silver teapots, Tiffany lamps, oil paintings from the eighteenth and nineteenth centuries.

"Did Devon leave a will?" Carmela asked.

"I assume so."

"Where do you think that would be?"

"In the safe?" T.J. said.

Carmela decided to take a gamble. "Do you by any chance know the combination?"

"No, but I know where Mr. Dowling kept it. He wrote down the numbers and told me once that he kept them under his desk blotter."

"Did Devon keep a lot of things in his safe?"

T.J. gave her a wary glance. "Valuables, sure. Stuff like estate jewelry, some old mine cut diamonds." His brows pinched together. "But why? Why are you asking?"

Carmela drew a deep breath. "Because I

81

heard a rumor . . ."

T.J. held up a hand. "Stop right there. I know exactly what you're going to say."

"A piece from a coat. A snippet."

"Lincoln's coat," T.J. said.

"Well? Did Devon really have it?" Carmela asked.

"He told me he did. But I don't really know for sure." T.J. hesitated. "Do you think we should . . . take a look?"

Carmela's heart blipped with excitement. "What harm could it do?"

The combination was right where Devon said it would be. From there it was only a matter of spinning the dial and letting the tumblers fall into place.

"Exciting," T.J. said, from his kneeling position in front of the squat safe in Dowling's office.

Carmela was practically holding her breath. She was hoping there might be some critical piece of paper stuck in the safe that would offer a clue to help ferret out Devon's killer.

No such luck.

"There's nothing in there," T.J. cried when he pulled open the door of the safe. "No will, no diamonds, no nothing!"

"No piece of Lincoln's coat?" Carmela asked, leaning forward, eager to see. But the safe was completely empty, just like T.J. said it was.

"We've been robbed!" T.J. cried. "Cleaned out!" Then his anger fell away and his face crumpled in exasperation. "Aw, crap. It means I have to talk to the cops all over again."

This time Babcock arrived with only one man accompanying him. A uniformed officer named Harlan Boyce.

"What are you doing here?" Babcock asked when he saw Carmela. He was taken aback and looked slightly annoyed.

"I came to pay my respects to T.J.," Carmela said.

"I'm sure," Babcock said, with little conviction. Then, "What's this about a safe being ransacked?"

"More like cleaned out," T.J. said. "When we opened up the safe, it was completely empty." He sounded nervous bordering on hysterical. "I mean, what else could possibly go wrong?"

"Do you think whoever killed Devon also cleaned out the safe?" Carmela asked Babcock. "Maybe that's why Devon was killed. Because he wouldn't open the safe to an armed robber."

"But he obviously did," Babcock said. "Or

someone did. The possibility also exists that Mr. Dowling emptied the safe at an earlier time."

But T.J. was adamant. "My guess is that Devon was killed defending its contents."

Babcock focused on T.J. "Do you know what those contents might have been?"

"Some loose diamonds, gold coins, miscellaneous jewelry, um . . . supposedly a shred of fabric that . . ."

"Yes, I've heard the rumor," Babcock said. He threw a quick glance at Carmela, then put a hand up and scratched his head. "The thing is, there have been a rash of art thefts in New Orleans, specifically in the Garden District."

"Do you think that was the case here?" Carmela asked.

"Has anyone else been murdered?" T.J. asked.

"It could have been an art theft," Babcock said slowly. "And no, none of the other theft victims were injured in any way. In fact, most of the art thefts occurred while the homes were unoccupied."

"Do you have any suspects for these so-called art thefts?" Carmela asked.

"There's a guy by the name of Sonny Boy Holmes, aka Stanley Holmberg, who's been known to crack a safe or two," Babcock said.

"After serving four years in Dixon Correctional, we thought he'd pretty much pooped out. But you never know, maybe Sonny Boy hung out his shingle again."

"The shred of fabric that T.J. mentioned before," Carmela said. "If it really was an actual piece from Lincoln's coat, that might explain this robbery."

"Would it really?" Babcock asked. He sounded testy. "Does something like that actually exist?"

"T.J. thinks it did," Carmela said.

"Mr. Dowling told me it did," T.J. said.

"But who would have known about it?" Babcock said. "Better yet, who would have cared?"

Someone did, Carmela thought to herself.

While Officer Boyce took a statement from T.J., Babcock pulled Carmela outside onto the sidewalk.

"What's going on?" he asked. The expression on his face was a mix of concern and impatience.

"Like we just told you, T.J. opened the safe and it was completely empty."

"Nice try, but that's not what I'm talking about."

"It's not?" Carmela said.

A horse-drawn wagon clip-clopped by,

85

chattering tourists streamed past them, and a street musician banged out a bluesy version of "Round Midnight" on his saxophone. The French Quarter was alive and kickin', but Babcock remained focused only on Carmela. "I was just over at the Licensing Bureau in City Hall. Imagine my surprise when I overheard your name being put on a permit for some kind of wine bar."

"*My* name?" Carmela was suddenly the picture of innocence.

"Do you know another Carmela Bertrand?"

Carmela's eyes were drawn to a shiny black Maybach that pulled to the curb. She entertained a fantasy of running over, flinging herself into the front seat, and driving away. Then she turned her attention back to Babcock and said, "Well . . . no."

Babcock continued. "And . . . this is the really choice part. It seems the permit being issued is for a partnership in a wine bar, between you and Quigg Brevard, your old boyfriend."

"He's not my old boyfriend and I'm not really a partner." *Yet. Until I make up my mind.*

Babcock cocked an eye at her. "You've got some 'splaining to do, my dear."

"Would you believe it if I said I've been

86

semi-railroaded?" Carmela asked. She tried to sound contrite.

Babcock actually laughed out loud at this. "Nice try, Carmela. I'll give you an A for effort. I hear what you're selling, but I'm seriously not buying it."

"I received an offer from Quigg on a crazy idea he had concerning a wine bar, a kind of paint and sip. But I promise I haven't said yes to anything yet."

"Hmm." Babcock was stroking his chin, looking like a thoughtful scholar.

"Lawyers would have to be consulted, papers drawn up. We're not even *close* to having any kind of agreement."

Babcock took her hand and held it gently in his. "Not like our agreement, right?" He turned her hand so that her three-carat engagement ring sparkled outrageously in the sunlight.

"Of course not, Edgar," Carmela said.

"I want to believe you, sweetheart." Babcock gripped her hand tighter as the saxophone music continued, haunting and sweet.

"Then do."

"Set a date then. Buy a dress. Get some bow ties for the dogs. Let's stop fooling around and do this."

"I promise," Carmela said. "I'll do all that

and more." But even as Carmela made her heartfelt declaration, she was still trying to work out the circumstances surrounding her friend's murder. The ice pick, the missing jewelry, a piece from Lincoln's coat. If only . . . if only she could come up with the tiniest of clues, maybe then she could help set things right. And find a tiny bit of justice for poor Devon.

CHAPTER 7

"How'd it go at Devon Dowling's shop?" Gabby asked the minute Carmela set foot in the bustling scrapbook shop. "Was anyone there? Did you learn anything new?"

"Devon's safe was robbed," Carmela said in a half whisper so as not to disturb the customers who were shopping.

"What!" Gabby screeched. So much for maintaining a calm and quiet atmosphere.

"I kind of convinced Devon's assistant, T.J., to open the safe. And when he did, the safe was as empty as a fridge in a college dorm room."

Gabby's eyes widened. "So a robbery, too? You're thinking the perpetrator was the same person as Devon's killer?"

Carmela shrugged. "Maybe."

"So you have to report this, right?"

"Already did," Carmela said.

Gabby gave a knowing nod. "Ah. That's why you look so discombobulated. As if you just stumbled off a Tilt-A-Whirl. You guys called the police . . ."

"And Babcock obligingly came over," Carmela finished.

"And gave you a slap on the wrist."

"Something like that, yeah. Plus, he made no bones about the fact that he doesn't want me involved."

"Good," Gabby said. "Truth be told, neither do I."

"But I am involved."

"So you say. But, Carmela, you've got to be a little more chill about this. About everything." Gabby reached under the counter and grabbed her Coach bag. "Okay, 'nuff said. I'm going to run out and grab us some lunch. What do you feel like having? A salad from Pirate's Alley Deli or should we throw caution to the wind and pig out on powdered-sugar beignets?"

"I have to stuff myself into a wedding gown one of these days."

"Right. A salad it is." But Gabby still didn't make a move to leave. Instead, she stood there, a knowing smile on her face.

"Well, maybe it wouldn't *kill* me to have one last oyster po-boy."

"Attagirl. I thought there might be some fried food in your future."

■ ■ ■ ■

While Gabby was gone, Carmela walked casually through her shop, offering help to customers and answering questions.

One woman wanted rubber stamps with floral motifs, so Carmela found some lovely iris and rose stamps for her as well as pink and purple ink pads.

Another customer, a regular named Angela, wanted to make free-form pendants out of polymer clay.

"How do I get them nice and thin so they're comfortable to wear?" Angela asked.

"I'd recommend putting your polymer clay through a pasta machine," Carmela said. "That way it comes out super thin. Makes it easier to cut your clay or sculpt it into the shape you want."

"And then I bake it?"

"Yes, but you should first texture the surface with coarse sandpaper," Carmela said. "And don't forget to poke holes to allow for jump rings or pieces of cord."

"Then I bake it and paint it," Angela said.

Carmela gave an encouraging nod. "It's as simple as that."

Carmela was busy ringing up two people at the front counter when Gabby returned with lunch. She immediately slipped a brown paper bag to Carmela and smiled at the customers.

"Here, let me package this up for you," Gabby said. "Give you some free samples, too." She reached for a couple of cellophane packets. "Got some new stickers here . . ."

Carmela ducked into her office to eat lunch, noodle around some ideas, and work on a few sketches.

She was balling up her paper sack and frowning at a grease splotch on her sketch pad when Quigg popped his head into her office.

"Hey, sweetheart, we're all set," Quigg said. He wore a chambray shirt tucked into faded blue jeans. His dark hair was slicked back, and his eyes sparkled in a very come-hither way. Basically, he looked like trouble.

"Please don't call me sweetheart," Carmela said, swiveling in her purple leather desk chair to face him. "And what are you jabbering about? What exactly are we all set about?"

"I put an order in with my sign painter. Decided to make an executive decision and call the place Blush and Brush."

Carmela stood up so fast her chair just about flipped over. "No!" she cried out. Somehow she had to make Quigg under-

92

stand that he couldn't just run roughshod over her and make partnership assumptions. That he had to recognize the error of his ways.

"Yes." Quigg smiled back. "Surprised? Excited?"

"You do know that Babcock found out about this wine bar?" she said.

Quigg pursed his lips and made a rude raspberries sound. "So what?"

"Babcock despises the idea of you and me doing any sort of collaboration."

"At the risk of repeating myself, so what?"

"Quigg, you can't just go around railroading people. Maybe I don't want to be your partner in this wine bar thing."

Quigg looked hurt. Or maybe he was just pretend offended?

"You really don't want to be my partner?" He looked like he'd just had his jelly beans stolen by the playground bully.

"Well, I do and I don't," Carmela said. "I mean, the idea is tempting . . ."

"I'm glad that's settled. Jeez, I hope you're not this conflicted when it comes to getting married." He squinted at her. "You are still getting married, aren't you? To what's-his-name?"

"Of course I am. That's why I've been trying to impress upon you the fact that

Babcock doesn't want this partnership to happen. He's not, um, comfortable with us working together."

"But it's a done deal," Quigg said.

"No, it's not," Carmela said.

Quigg winked at her as he held up an index finger. "Think about your first project. Whether you want the customers to paint plates or wineglasses."

"Quigg!"

But he was already out the door, a confident smile spread across his handsome face.

Gabby was standing at the back table, sorting through cardstock, when Carmela came out of her office.

"How'd it go with Quigg?" she asked.

"He won't take no for an answer," Carmela said.

"I don't think Quigg's *ever* taken no for an answer."

"He's pulling me one way and Babcock is pulling me the other."

"It's lonely right there in the middle, huh?" But Gabby smiled as she said it.

"I just have to decide," Carmela said.

"Maybe that's one decision you can put on the back burner. Because I just saw Baby and Tandy walk past the front window."

And two seconds later, the two women

rushed into Memory Mine like they owned the place.

"Carmela!" Tandy Bliss shrieked at the top of her lungs. She was the super expressive one, a skinny forty-something in a body-con red knit dress that perfectly matched her fluff of hennaed red hair. But what Tandy lacked in body mass index she made up for in enthusiasm. "It's been what, you guys?" she practically shouted. "Two whole weeks since we've been here?"

"Feels longer," Carmela said, playing along with her. In reality, Tandy and Baby had stopped in last week, shopping for stencils. But who's counting?

Baby Fontaine was slightly more demure. A doyenne of the Garden District, Baby was a fifty-something social butterfly with pixie blond hair and an impish sense of humor. Today she wore a pair of ripped denim jeans along with her navy Chanel jacket.

"I love your outfit!" Gabby exclaimed to Baby.

"You don't think it's a little too outré?" Baby laughed.

Carmela leaned in and gave Baby a warm hug. "Your outfit's perfect. It's you."

Five minutes later, they were joined by three more women who were all atwitter about creating their own greeting cards.

"How do we start? How do we start?" a woman named Peggy jittered.

Carmela held up a folded blank card. "With a folded piece of cardstock that's pretty much a standard card size."

"And we want that size why?" Peggy asked.

"To fit in a standard card envelope," Carmela said. Then, "Gabby, will you pass out a few blank cards?"

"With pleasure," Gabby said as she worked her way around the table.

"We're starting with cream-colored cardstock," Carmela said. "But that doesn't mean your cards have to be boring or traditional. I want you to think way outside the box. Use paper, fibers, copper wire — whatever you want — to decorate your cards. Color them, edge them in gold, or use rubber stamps if you like. At Memory Mine, it's perfectly okay to bend, spindle, and mutilate your cards. In fact, it's encouraged."

"Mutilate?" one of the women said.

"That means you can rip, deckle, or shred the edges," Gabby instructed. "To make your card more tactile and interesting."

"Ah," the woman said, a light bulb suddenly going off over her head. "I think I'm going to enjoy this card-making class."

"The most important thing about card making," Carmela said, "is to build up a number of layers."

"Give us an example," Peggy said.

Carmela took a yellow stamp pad and smeared it across the front of her card. Then she did the same thing with a green stamp pad — only she used this color slightly more judiciously. She glued on a piece of checkered paper, grabbed a rubber stamp, and stamped the image of a wineglass. With a red colored pencil, she colored in the wine. Then she took a squishy marker and wrote *YOU'RE INVITED TO A WINE TASTING.*

"Wow," Tandy marveled. "You did that in like eight seconds flat."

"You guys will get the hang of it, too," Carmela said.

"How about a birthday card for one of my grandkids?" Baby asked.

"Got a rubber stamp of a toy train right here," Gabby said, always on the ball.

"How about a save the date card for a wedding?" one of the women asked.

"I'd add a few squares of gold paper or vellum, stamp on a set of rings, and maybe add a gold string and tassel," Carmela said.

"Wow," Baby said. "I can't wait to dig in."

Everyone got to work then, coloring their cards, pasting on bits of colored paper, gluing on the occasional brad or button. Every card was unique and every card was (amazingly!) creative.

"For all you paper savants," Carmela said, "I'm also offering a Paper University class next week."

"What is that, please?" Tandy asked.

"That's where we go even more crazy with paper," Carmela explained. "Handmade paper, mulberry paper, Japanese rice paper, ephemera, that kind of thing. But you don't necessarily have to make cards. You can create paper jewelry, fun labels, miniature theaters, tags, foldout albums — whatever you feel like."

"Count me in," Tandy said.

"Me too!" came a chorus of voices.

Carmela was restocking one of the paper bins when Baby sidled up next to her.

"I read about poor Devon Dowling in the newspaper," Baby said in a low voice.

Carmela's face fell. "It was awful. I was there."

"So I understand. And besides Devon being murdered, his shop was also burglarized?"

"How do you know about that?"

"Del overheard a rumor at the courthouse." Del was Baby's husband, a hightest attorney.

"Um, the police *surmise* that's what happened," Carmela said. She didn't want to let the cat out of the bag quite yet.

Baby frowned. "Funny. One of my neighbors was burglarized last week."

"Who's that?" Carmela asked, instantly on alert.

"Jeffrey Cummins," Baby said. "And his wife, Melinda. It was terrible. While they were attending a charity dinner someone slipped in and stole their Kandinsky right off the wall!"

"Wow," Carmela said. She wondered if Sonny Boy Holmes might be back in business after all.

At four o'clock, Babcock called.

"I hope I wasn't too tough on you earlier today. Apologies. It's just that I've got a lot on my mind."

"I know you do and I understand, I truly do," Carmela said. "I know how hard you work, how much pressure is put on you to solve cases."

"Well . . ."

"Why don't you come over for dinner tonight? I could fix that cornbread-stuffed chicken you like so much."

"That's not entirely a bad idea. We really do need to talk."

"Six o'clock?"

"How about seven?" Babcock said.

"Perfect. I'll see you then."

Once Carmela and Gabby cleaned up the back table and straightened out the paper bins, Carmela ducked back into her office to put together a menu.

She'd kick things off with ice cold martinis, then serve an arugula salad with bacon, snap peas, and pickled beets. Then she'd segue into her cornbread-stuffed chicken and add a side of fried green tomatoes.

It wasn't the most heart-healthy menu, but it was the perfect menu to win Babcock's heart. Once he was fed and his appetite sated, she could carefully and logically present the paint and sip idea to him. And prove to him, once and for all, that he had absolutely nothing to worry about.

Carmela smiled to herself as she doodled a row of X's and O's on her paper. Babcock would come around. Because, when all was said and done, he really was a reasonable guy.

CHAPTER 8

Oops. Turned out, Babcock was *not* a reasonable guy. And he *didn't* come around to her way of thinking.

"I don't understand," Babcock said, jerking his hand and spilling part of his martini down the front of his Brooks Brothers shirt. When he felt dampness seep through, he growled, "Damn. See what you made me do."

Carmela put down the bowl of arugula salad she'd brought out from the kitchen and handed him a crisp linen napkin. Babcock yanked it out of her hand and began to furiously blot the mixture of gin and vermouth.

"Now I smell like a gin mill."

"Listen, please. I'm trying to explain things to you," Carmela said.

"Tell me again why it's suddenly such a marvelous idea to go into business with your old boyfriend." Babcock looked at Carmela from beneath furrowed brows.

"I haven't decided. The business thing is still up in the air. And, once again, for the record, Quigg is *not* my old boyfriend."

"A wine bar," Babcock grumbled as Carmela grabbed the martini shaker and refilled his drink. "Doesn't every café, restaurant, bistro, and bar in New Orleans *already* serve wine?"

"This would be something totally different," Carmela said. "Geared more for women with an accent on crafts."

Boy, was Babcock ever crabby tonight! Even though Carmela was secretly pleased that Babcock was jealous of Quigg, the last thing she wanted was for his jealousy to cross the line and for him to become super possessive. Because just suppose she *did* decide to join Quigg in his paint and sip business — was Babcock going to get hysterical and carry on like this forever? She'd been on her own for too long to put up with this kind of silliness.

Carmela drew a deep breath. "Like I said, I haven't formally agreed to anything yet. But if I want to enter into a business agreement . . ."

"Then you'll probably do whatever you damn well please. Yeah, I get it."

"No, Edgar, you don't get it. *You* are the

man I dearly love, the man I am going to marry. But that doesn't rule out my having business arrangements with other people. I want to be your wife, I'm dying to be your wife. But if I decide it's a smart, proactive thing to do, I'll be Quigg's business partner." She put a hand on his arm. "Do you get that?"

"I may get it but I don't like it."

Carmela had really hoped this evening could be a sweet, romantic interlude, but so far it wasn't looking good. Maybe some food would help to calm tempers down? She counted to ten, smiled sweetly, and said, "Why don't you sit down and I'll serve dinner."

With a grumpy face, Babcock placed his glass on the dining table, pulled out a chair, and sat down. Boo and Poobah lay down quietly at his feet under the table, while Mimi remained on the sofa.

Carmela grabbed her antique silver salad servers and mounded her arugula salad onto Babcock's plate. "Here you go. I topped it with that tangy balsamic and mustard dressing you like so much. Go ahead. Have a taste."

"Buttering me up with mustard and vinegar, that's a novel approach even for you." Babcock nibbled at his salad. Then, as if he, too, had decided not to ruin their evening, said, "Mmn, you do know how to zip up a salad."

"Thank you." The tight knot of tension that had formed in the back of Carmela's neck loosened slightly. The battle may not have been won, but at least there would be a degree of détente during dinner.

By the time Carmela brought out their main course of stuffed chicken, the temperature in the room had thawed considerably. Babcock had relaxed (a second martini helped) and seemed to actually be enjoying himself.

"Cornbread-stuffed chicken with a side of fried green tomatoes," Carmela said. "Bon appétit." She sat down, picked up her fork, then set it down again. "I forgot. You brought along a bottle of wine. Do you want me to . . . ?"

"Naw, let it go. I'm enjoying dinner too much. Besides, I've got work to do later. So I'd better keep a sober head. Two martinis is my limit tonight."

"More like one and a half."

"Touché."

They continued their small talk for a while, keeping it light and breezy, but Carmela was itching to bring up Devon Dowling's murder. Was there any new information? Were there any suspects? Had anything come of the investigation into the robbery of Devon's safe today? Carmela knew her questions might shift Babcock back into a cranky mood, but she had to know. Was dying to know.

"Have your Crime Scene techs tracked down the plant matter that was found on Devon's body?" Carmela asked. She figured that was a safe opening salvo.

Babcock blinked, then cranked his head hard to the right. "Whoosh. That question certainly came shooting out of left field. Almost nicked me."

"Well, I'm curious," Carmela said.

"No kidding."

Babcock pursed his lips and cocked his head, as if deciding whether or not to satisfy her curiosity. Finally, he relented.

"They identified the smidgen of the dark green leaf as probably a piece of water hyacinth."

Carmela shook her head. She wasn't all that familiar. One green plant looked like another to her. And out in the bayous, most everything was green.

"The water hyacinth's an invasive plant that snuck up here from the Amazon basin a hundred or so years ago. Been running amok in our waterways ever since. Anyway, our tech guys tried to isolate the source but weren't all that successful. They think this particular piece is likely from Bayou Terrebonne, Bayou Petit Caillou, or even the Barataria bayou."

"Barataria is where Shamus has a camp house." Shamus was not only Carmela's ex, he was the indolent scion to Crescent City Bank. "You don't suspect Shamus, do you?"

"Not this time."

"Thanks a lot." Carmela was surprised that she still felt protective toward her annoying ex.

"Hey, you went ahead and married the dufus. You knew he had a lousy reputation," Babcock said.

"Actually, I didn't know," Carmela said. She hadn't realized that Shamus was a certified hound dog until he crawled home one morning at 4:00 A.M. reeking of Jim Beam and Shalimar perfume. Heavy on the Shalimar.

Once they finished dinner, Carmela cleared away their dishes, then brought out a plate of molasses cookies.

"Here you go, Mr. Crabbypants. Care for a sweet?"

Carmela waited until Babcock took a bite of her cookie, then said, "Now that you've identified the water hyacinth, did it point you in the direction of any pertinent suspects?"

"Not the plant matter, per se. But I quizzed T.J. again today, trying to jog his memory about anyone who might have been angry or upset with Dowling. And, obviously, where they might live."

"Did he come up with anyone at all?"

"I kept asking him to tell me anything and everything that might be related — you know, do a kind of data dump. But the poor guy's mind was pretty much a blank slate. The only name he came up with was a client who was unhappy with an art appraisal that Dowling did. A fellow named Colonel Barnett Otis."

"Devon gave him a bad appraisal?" Carmela asked.

"Not exactly. It turns out Otis owned a very pricey painting. The only problem was — it was stolen."

"What?" Carmela leaned back in her chair. This felt like something that might be important. "How did Devon figure that out?"

"Don't be so impressed, Dowling just checked with the FBI's art registry file. It's pretty standard for high-end dealers to check with the Feds when someone brings in an expensive piece for sale. Or, in this

107

case, an art collector hoping for a rather large appraisal."

"So you think this Colonel Otis might have killed Devon because Devon discovered that the painting was stolen?"

"I don't know."

"It sounds flimsy to me."

"However tentative, it's a lead that needs to be followed up," Babcock said.

Carmela still wasn't buying it. "And then Colonel Otis came back and burglarized Devon's safe? I mean, what on earth would he have been looking for?"

"You've just landed in the same place I am," Babcock said. "Who knows what's going on or what the sequence of events was?"

"You sure don't have much to go on," Carmela said. She couldn't imagine how Babcock and Gallant were going to track down Devon's killer, make a case, and present enough evidence to the prosecution. It all felt like . . . smoke and mirrors.

"I'm afraid there's more," Babcock said with a kind of grim determination.

"There is? Tell me."

"I don't . . ."

"Please?"

Babcock looked unhappy. "Now that we're laying our cards on the table, I might as well tell you. During the autopsy, the ME found trace evidence of cocaine."

Carmela clapped both hands on top of her head and shouted, "What? On Devon's body?" She couldn't believe what she was hearing.

Babcock stared at her now, his eyes searching her face. "You knew Devon well. Was he a user?"

"No! Of course not! I mean, I don't think so." Carmela blew out a long glut of air and then felt dizzy. "Oh jeez, this is terrible."

"It complicates matters, yes."

"No," Carmela said. "What you just told me . . . it's gut-wrenching." This was the last thing Carmela had expected. Now she feared that Devon Dowling's sterling reputation might be tarnished with hints of drug use. "It couldn't have been his cocaine. It had to be . . ."

"From someone else? Perhaps. But who?" Babcock asked.

"I guess you've got to look harder at T.J. And obviously this Colonel Otis."

"We will, we are."

"And maybe . . . well, I didn't tell you about this. But a man named Richard Drake stopped by Memory Mine yesterday afternoon."

Babcock shook his head. "I don't know who that is."

"Drake is president of the Vampire Society," Carmela said.

Babcock narrowed his eyes. "What?"

"The Vampire . . ."

"Yes, I heard that part. I meant go on . . . continue," Babcock said. "Even though this sounds like some kind of bad joke."

"This Drake guy quizzed me on how well I knew Devon. And if I knew anything about the piece of Lincoln's coat that Devon supposedly owned."

"This guy Drake could be trouble."

"Could he be a suspect?" Carmela asked. "Do you think he might be dangerous?" Her words were getting tangled. What she really meant to say was, *Do you think Drake killed Devon?*

"I certainly need to have a chat with this Richard Drake," Babcock said. "And by the way, please don't allow him back in your shop if he happens to show up again."

Carmela knew that was pretty much impossible, given the laissez-faire attitude of shop owners in the French Quarter, but she nodded anyway to appease Babcock.

"Okay," she said. Then, "There's something I need to ask you about. An idea that's been rumbling around inside my head for the last two days."

"What's that?"

"Stand up, please."

Babcock stood up as Carmela came around the table to face him. Boo and Poobah stood up, too, watching them with guarded eyes.

"If the ice pick was stuck in Devon's left ear, then his assailant had to be right-handed, is that correct?" Carmela asked.

"Only if they were facing each other," Babcock said.

"So if the killer snuck up behind Devon, he was probably left-handed."

"Right. Correct."

"Do you know . . . was the ice pick driven straight in, or did it go in at a downward angle?"

"This is very grisly, Carmela. And something you should leave to the medical examiner and trained investigators."

"Like you."

"Like me."

"I realize that, but I'm curious. I can't get the ice pick image out of my head."

"Sweetheart, this is not something you should . . ."

At that exact moment, Babcock's phone began to vibrate. When he pulled it out of his pocket and glanced at the screen, his demeanor changed instantly. He was suddenly all business. "Babcock," he barked.

He listened for a few moments and then said, "When?"

Carmela mouthed, *"What?"* but he ignored her.

Talking in a low voice, Babcock did his usual move and stepped to the far end of the room.

Honestly, Carmela thought, *he acts as if I'd listen in.* And then she stood perfectly still, straining to catch a word or two. Unfortunately, the only word she could pick out was "Bobby." So he was either talking to Bobby Gallant or asking about his colleague's whereabouts. Either way, it didn't bode well for the romantic evening Carmela had been hoping for.

Babcock clicked off his phone and grabbed his suit jacket from the couch, dislodging a sleeping Mimi in the process.

"You're leaving?" Carmela was disappointed at the abrupt end to their dinner. Babcock had loosened up considerably and had been starting to spill secrets.

"There's been a . . . Something needs my attention," he said.

"*I* need your attention, too."

Babcock placed his hands on her shoulders. "Carmela, be reasonable. Duty calls. I have to go to work."

Carmela crossed her arms. "We had a

lovely dinner together and even exchanged ideas concerning Devon's murder. Now, suddenly, you have to fly out of here like Batman?" She gave a little shrug. "Hmm, I thought maybe I came first."

Babcock leaned in and gave her a swift peck on the top of her head. "You always come first. I promise." And then he really did fly out the door.

Carmela looked at Mimi who was looking back at her with expressive brown eyes. "Mimi," she said, "he sure has a funny way of showing it."

CHAPTER 9

"Imagine my surprise," said a low, sexy voice, "when I discovered my ex-wife was involved in yet another murder investigation."

"Shamus!" Carmela cried. Her phone had rung five minutes after Babcock had slipped out the door. And, like an idiot, Carmela figured it must be Babcock calling to apologize for being such a jerk. No such luck. Though Shamus Allan Meechum was certainly the ideal stand-in when it came to all-time jerks.

"You never disappoint me, Carmela."

"And you constantly disappoint me, Shamus," Carmela cooed into the phone. They'd been married for less than a year when Shamus had started creepy-crawling home at all hours of the morning, his shirts untucked, his . . . well, you get the picture.

"That's my Carmela, always heaping dishonor upon my head," Shamus said, though he sounded completely unfazed by her words.

"Nothing you haven't earned," Carmela said.

"So here's the thing, darlin'. I'm right here in your neighborhood, like two blocks away, and I thought I'd pop in quick to see the dogs."

"You're at a bar," Carmela said. She could hear crowd sounds and the tinkle of ice cubes through the phone. "You know Boo doesn't like the smell of alcohol on your breath."

"So I'll gargle. Come on, whadya say? I've still got joint custody, in case you've forgotten."

"Yes, I know." Shamus had been a lousy husband, but he was a loving and attentive pet parent. Go figure.

"Is my dropping by a problem? Or do you have company? Maybe that traffic cop you've been dating?"

"He's a homicide detective, and we're engaged to be married."

"So you say."

"I have a ring, Shamus." Carmela smiled to herself as she fluttered her fingers and watched her diamond shimmer and dance as it caught the light.

"Have you set a date?" Shamus asked in a

snide tone.

Carmela stopped smiling. "I'm working on that. Okay, come over. I'll tell the dogs you're on your way."

Much to Carmela's dismay, Boo and Poobah went batshit when Shamus walked through the front door. They barked, spun around like crazed circus acrobats, jumped up and knocked him over, and then practically licked him to death.

"That's some lovin'," Carmela observed dryly from her post in the kitchen.

"They know their daddy misses them," Shamus said, climbing to his feet, hands still grabbing for both dogs as he tussled with them. "And that he really, really loves them."

"Uh-huh." Carmela was sipping a glass of Sauvignon Blanc that was as dry as her response.

"Got one of those for me?" Shamus asked. His tongue was hanging out as much as the dogs.

"I suppose." Carmela poured a glass of wine for Shamus and handed it to him. She watched as he took a healthy gulp. Still lean and boyish-looking, Shamus was handsome in a casual rich-boy way. Tonight he wore an expensive black leather jacket over gray slacks and had not a single hair out of place. He was the scion to the Meechum family's banking fortune and was as tightfisted as Scrooge McDuck. Hammering out a divorce settlement with him had been a nightmare. Like walking across hot coals.

"Whoa!" Shamus cried when he came up for a breather from his wine and finally noticed Mimi. "Where did that little cutie come from?"

"That's Mimi, Devon Dowling's dog."

"Oh yeah?" Shamus made a wry grimace. "Poor thing." He reached out a hand for Mimi to sniff. "You gonna keep her?"

"I don't know." Carmela paused. "Mimi's staying with me for now because she's kind of a witness."

Shamus set down his wine and picked up Mimi. Much to Carmela's surprise, the small dog cuddled right up to him. "You're telling me this little girl can ID Dowling's killer?"

"She was right there when it happened. And she's awfully smart."

"I suppose if dogs can sniff out drugs and all sorts of contraband, why not a killer?" Still holding Mimi, Shamus grabbed his wineglass, walked into the living room, and plopped himself down on the leather chaise lounge as if he owned the place. "So. Your upcoming nuptials. Am I invited?"

Carmela gazed at him with hooded eyes. "Would you really want to come?"

"Yes," Shamus said. "Well . . . no. Probably not. It might be bad luck or something." He set Mimi down and frowned. "Or maybe that's only if the groom sees the bride in her wedding dress under a full moon on an odd-numbered day."

"Or something," Carmela said as a knock sounded at her front door.

Carmela hurried to answer it, thinking, *Please, please, please don't let this be Babcock!*

It wasn't.

"Am I interrupting?" Ava asked.

"No. In fact, I'm glad you dropped by." Carmela rolled her eyes. "Shamus is here."

"Oh?" Ava threw her a questioning glance.

"He came to see the dogs, not me."

"In that case," Ava said, stepping inside, "I'll come in and give him a few body punches."

"Ho ho, are you playing Sherlock Holmes, too?" Shamus boomed when he caught sight of Ava.

"No, I'm the amazingly cute, incredibly brilliant sidekick," Ava said.

"Watley," Shamus said.

"Watson," Carmela corrected.

"Ah. So Devon Dowling was murdered . . . why?" Shamus asked. "He always seemed like a pleasant enough guy. Really knew his stuff, probably didn't have any enemies."

"It turns out there was also a robbery at his shop," Carmela said.

"What!" Shamus cried.

"When?" Ava asked.

"We just discovered it this afternoon," Carmela said. "I dropped by to talk to T.J. — that's Devon's assistant," she said to Shamus. "And we decided to open the back room safe and — boom. It was empty!"

"Did you call the police?" Ava asked.

Carmela made a face. "T.J. did."

"I can't imagine that Devon had all that much of value," Shamus said.

"It turns out, there might have been one thing in particular," Carmela said.

"The coat," Ava murmured.

"A fur coat?" Shamus asked.

"Hang on to your suspension of disbelief," Carmela told Shamus, "because Devon Dowling reputedly owned a piece of Abraham Lincoln's coat."

"The one Lincoln was assassinated in," Ava added helpfully.

Shamus scrunched up his face. "You gals are pulling my leg."

119

"It's the honest truth," Carmela said.

"Who'd want to own something like that?" Shamus asked. "I mean, would it be worth anything?"

"To the right collector, absolutely," Carmela said.

Shamus stood up so fast his knees sounded like someone was cracking a pair of walnuts. "Every time I come over here there's something weird or spooky going on." Boo, Poobah, and even Mimi were suddenly forgotten.

"Tell the truth," Ava said, giving him a smile that contained very little warmth. "You love it, don't you? You wish you could join our little cabal." Ava liked to needle Shamus as penance for bugging out on Carmela.

"No, I don't," Shamus said, heading for the door. "You girls are plum crazy. You're always poking your noses where they don't belong. Getting involved in a séance or a creepy murder or some spooky-ass business like a dead president's coat."

"Always nice to see you," Carmela called after his departing form. "Don't let the door hit you in the . . ."

WHAP!

"Backside," Ava snickered, as the door closed behind Shamus. She stared at Carmela with mischief in her eyes. "Well, that was an amusing little interlude."

"I'm glad someone sees the humor in it," Carmela said.

"What I really came over for was to ask if you wanted to wander down the block and have a drinky-poo at Pedro Wang's."

"Why not?" Carmela said. "I've been chastised by my future husband, scorned by my ex-husband. Maybe I'll get lucky and be insulted by a perfect stranger."

Pedro Wang's was jammed for a Tuesday night. Then again, bars in New Orleans were always jammed. It was a freewheeling, hard-drinkin' city.

Carmela and Ava elbowed their way through the crowd, headed for the bar. To their right were tables and booths, and through a door was an open-air courtyard where two guys twanged away on guitars, singing about hard times and workin' on the river.

"Those are college kids from Tulane," Ava said. "They got rich daddies and never worked on the river a day in their lives."

"I suppose it's the spirit that counts," Carmela said. "And it helps that they're in tune."

They found two seats at the bar and

settled in. Ava ordered a jalapeño margarita while Carmela opted for shoo-fly punch, which was basically bourbon and ginger beer with orange slices.

"This is nice," Ava said. She slipped her jean jacket off and wiggled her bare shoulders. "Lots of nice men here. A girl could have herself quite a fun time."

"Speak for yourself," Carmela said.

"I always do, *cher*. Oh, hello!" Ava leaned back as a silver-haired man in a string tie leaned in and smiled at her.

"Buy you a drink?" the man asked.

"Maybe later," Ava said, batting her lashes.

"You know what? Maybe this wasn't such a good idea," Carmela said. "I make a lousy wingman. And what about all your fancy talk about meeting a real gentleman instead of hooking up with some random dude?"

"I gotta have a little fun," Ava said. "Besides, you can't up and leave me so soon. At least stay and finish your drink."

CLINK! SMASH!

A glass shattered behind them, somebody yelped sharply, and ice cubes spun wildly across the barroom floor.

"Nope," Carmela said. "I gotta go." She'd had enough of smashed and bashed glass to last her a lifetime.

"Watch it there, buddy!" an angry voice

shouted.

Someone staggered up to the bar, half spilling their drink and mumbling, "Sorry. Sorry."

When Carmela saw who it was, she did a double take. "T.J.?" she said. "Is that you?"

T.J. — Trevor Jackson — stared back at her with rheumy, glazed eyes.

"You," T.J. said as if he half recognized her.

"Carmela," she said. "Remember me from this afternoon?"

"Ayup." T.J. gave an answer that was halfway between a yes and a burp.

Carmela pointed to Ava. "And Ava?"

T.J. sipped his drink, rocked back on his heels so far it looked like he was about to fall over, then finally managed to straighten himself up. "Gee, it's nice to see a familiar face," he slurred. *Face* came out *faysh.* "Can I . . ." He reached in his shirt pocket, fished out a soggy twenty-dollar bill, and studied it. "Can I buy you ladies a drink?"

"No, thanks," Carmela said.

"We're all set," Ava said. "In fact, we were just about to join some friends out on the patio." She flashed Carmela a let's-get-out-of-here look.

But Carmela, kindhearted Carmela, had concern on her face. "Are you okay?" she

123

asked T.J., because he clearly wasn't in great shape.

T.J. just nodded and waved a hand at her, as if to wish her well.

"You've had a rough couple of days. Maybe you ought to go home and take it easy," Carmela said. "Remember, Devon's funeral is tomorrow."

"You're gonna come?" T.J. asked.

"We'll be there," Carmela said. She planned to bring Ava and Mimi.

T.J. favored her with a lopsided grin. "You are *show shweet,*" he told her. "But I'm fine. Really, I am." He dropped his head forward and stared resolutely into his glass.

Carmela didn't think T.J. was fine at all. In fact, she wondered if he was drinking hard because he was shattered over Devon's murder, or drinking himself into oblivion because he had a guilty conscience. She didn't know what his problem was, but either way, this strange, drunken performance tonight was something Babcock definitely needed to know about.

CHAPTER 10

Ava opened the passenger door of Carmela's Mercedes, stuck one foot in, caught her heel, and nearly fell on her face. Clunk!

"You okay?" Carmela asked as she loaded Mimi into the back seat.

"It's these shoes," Ava said, righting herself and pushing back masses of curly dark hair. "They make it supremely difficult to get into a car. Or go up steps. Or walk. If they weren't so devilishly sexy, I'd donate them to the Bridge House Thrift Store." Ava slid into her seat gingerly and lifted one delicate foot so she could admire her patent leather stilettos. "See how long and lean my legs look in these four-inch heels? Don't you think they're especially perfect with my black satin shorts?"

Carmela lifted an eyebrow at Ava's wardrobe choice for a funeral. It was a little out-there. Then again, Ava was a little out-there. Of course, *everything* was loosey-goosey in the Big Easy, where ladies' underpants were routinely tossed from Mardi Gras floats. So . . . to each his own.

"Just shut your door so Mimi doesn't jump up and try to make a break for it," Carmela said.

Ava pulled the door closed and glanced over her shoulder where Mimi was ensconced on a furry sheepskin rug. "You're sure it's a good idea to bring Devon's dog along to his funeral?"

Carmela cranked on the ignition, double-clutched into second, and felt a surge of adrenaline as the engine roared and she peeled away from the curb. "I think it's a genius idea. You know how Babcock always ghosts into the funerals of his murder victims? Why do you suppose he does that?"

"I think you once told me that he wants to see if anyone suspicious turns up — i.e., the killer."

"Bingo," Carmela said as she turned down Royal Street. "And Mimi here is a star witness to Devon's murder. So she's our best chance of identifying the killer, if he decides to show his face at the funeral this morning."

"Okay," Ava said as she glanced out the car window. "Oh, this is so sad. We're driving right by Dulcimer Antiques. The place still has plywood over the windows and . . ."

"What!" Carmela suddenly yelped. She swerved around a bright yellow horse-drawn carriage and stomped hard on her brakes. Ava rocked forward, her head almost smacking the windshield. Mimi tumbled sideways on her soft bed.

"Whoa!" Ava cried. "What's wrong? We hit somebody?"

Carmela pointed. "Look at that sign!"

Directly above the boarded-up window of Dulcimer Antiques, two workmen were hoisting an enormous red and white sign to hang on the building's façade.

COMING SOON! LUXURY CONDOS!

A phone number filled the lower left-hand corner of the sign; a web address was on the lower right.

A horn blasted directly behind them, making Ava shriek, so Carmela hastily pulled to the curb.

"When I talked to Roy Sultan, the landlord, he praised Devon Dowling to high heaven. Said he was a model tenant. Now Devon's not even properly buried and Sultan can't wait to convert the building to condos? How is that possible?" Carmela asked.

"I'm impressed they even have a web address," Ava said. "You don't get one of those things overnight. But *cher,* this didn't just happen. This had to be a long-term plan."

"Well, it's a terrible plan. I mean . . . come on!"

"It's, like, disrespectful," Ava said.

"It's more than that," Carmela said. Her mind was turning somersaults, going in a new direction that was dark and ominous. What if Sultan had *wanted* to move Devon out? What if Devon had been gently prodded to leave the building but had a long-term lease that protected him?

But there's not much protection from an ice pick, Carmela thought. *Imagine that it's full-on dark, there's a noisy crowd outside, and the landlord has a passkey . . . Good-bye, Devon.*

Carmela slid her car forward until she was parked directly in front of Lotus Floral. "Let's pop in and talk to Betty. If anybody can give us the lowdown, it's Betty Doucet."

"Should we bring Mimi?"

"She's okay. We're only going to be in there for two minutes."

Betty was standing behind the counter, trimming dead leaves off a phalaenopsis when Carmel and Ava came in. When she saw who it was, she took off her glasses and smiled.

"Carmela, Ava. Good morning, ladies,"

Betty said.

"Hey, Betty," Carmela said as Ava grabbed a rose from a tall silver pot filled with red roses and stuck it behind her ear.

"Carmela, when am I going to design the flowers for your wedding? Tell me, have you and your handsome detective set a date?" Betty asked.

"We're working on it," Carmela said. "But I promise, as soon as I know, you'll know."

"It's important to plan ahead," Betty said. "I get brides in here all the time who are scrambling to order bouquets, boutonnieres, flowers for the altar, centerpieces for their reception. They don't realize that special orders take weeks. Sometimes months."

"Speaking of things that take time. How weird is it that the building across the street from you is suddenly going condo?" Carmela asked.

Betty looked suddenly unhappy. "I know. And right on the heels of Devon's murder." She set down her clippers. "He was such a sweetheart. But I suppose now that he's gone, the owner decided to jump on the condo fast track." She shook her head. "Unfortunately, that's been the fate of a lot of fine old buildings in the French Quarter."

"It's a dang shame," Ava said.

Betty nodded at the building across the street. "It seems like those condos went on the market just minutes ago. Pre-sale, I think they call it. Where you can look at the building as well as renderings of the units themselves. I understand the building owner was hoping to do that for a couple of years. Problem was, he had a holdout with a long-term lease."

"Devon Dowling," Carmela said.

Betty nodded. "I guess that's right."

"Now Devon is dead and can no longer hold out or lodge a complaint. How convenient for Sultan," Carmela said.

"We're on the way to Devon's funeral right now," Ava said. "Over at St. Roch."

"Oh my. Then you'd better let me put together a nice bouquet for you," Betty said. She grabbed a half dozen stems of lilies, added a grouping of white roses and baby's breath, and accented the bouquet with a few leafy greens.

When Carmela tried to pay for it, Betty shook her head no. "The red rose is gratis, too," she told Ava. "Just say a little prayer for Devon."

"You've got that sneaky-peaky look on your face," Ava said as they climbed back into Carmela's car. "Like something's stuck in

130

your craw."

Carmela glanced at Ava as she pulled out into traffic. "Do you think Roy Sultan could have murdered Devon just to get rid of him?"

"I never met Roy Sultan, but I do know this. Space in the French Quarter is almost as valuable as Fabergé eggs. And every time a newly renovated building comes on the market it's got more and more high-end amenities. Penthouses, balconies, gardens, underground parking, yoga studio, juice bar, you name it. Yeah, I think Sultan could have had dollar signs in his eyes. I also think this could be a red-hot lead for Babcock."

"Maybe it is. But let's not tell him yet. First, I want Mimi to take a good long sniff of Roy Sultan. Then we'll see."

"But before that, you have to find him," Ava said.

"There is that," Carmela agreed.

Five minutes later, Carmela drove through the gates of St. Roch Cemetery past hundreds of aboveground crypts and vaults that were all tightly crowded together.

Ava let loose a good long shudder. "I don't know why so many people choose St. Roch Cemetery as a funeral and burial site. The chapel is beyond creepy what with all those crutches, prosthetic arms, and wooden legs

131

hanging on the walls in the healing room. Not to mention glass eyes, dentures, and body braces."

"But those are like talismans," Carmela said. "St. Roch helped heal plague victims eight hundred years ago, and people still come here to be healed. What you think of as creepy are signs of hope to all those people."

"Still . . ." Ava said.

They drove into a small parking area and pulled into a space next to a banged-up red Mustang with an oxidized paint job.

"Junker alert," Ava said. "I wonder what loser's driving that piece of crap." Then she gave a surprised but knowing nod as T.J. emerged from the old car. His shoulders were hunched, his eyes looked bloodshot, and he hadn't bothered to shave. He seemed morose and painfully hungover.

Carmela stepped out of her car and regarded him. "You look exactly like what my momma used to call 'the morning after the night before.' How are you feeling, T.J.?"

T.J. grimaced. "Like I need three aspirin and some hair of the dog. And, please, keep your voice down."

"Speaking of hair of the dog," Ava whispered.

Carmela reached into her back seat,

grabbed Mimi, and gently deposited the little dog in a large fabric tote bag.

"You're bringing Mimi to the funeral?" T.J. asked.

"Why not?" Carmela said. "She's family, after all. And St. Roch is the patron saint of dogs and miraculous cures."

"Which is what I need right now," T.J. said, limping away.

Carmela and Ava crunched along the narrow gravel path and entered the small chapel.

"I wonder how many people are going to show up?" Ava murmured as she dabbed two fingers in a bowl of holy water and crossed herself. Inside, the chapel was dimly lit and quiet as a tomb. In the front of the church, a few pews were already filled with mourners. An urn and two flickering candles sat on the marble altar. Above it was a statue of St. Roch himself, flanked by four painted wooden panels depicting his various good deeds.

"I wonder if anybody is hanging out in the prayer room next door?" Carmela asked. She turned sideways to duck through the narrow doorway and suddenly found herself face-to-face with Roy Sultan. "Mr. Sultan," she said, sounding surprised. "How interesting to see you here."

"Excuse me?" Sultan said.

Carmela held Mimi up in front of her so the little dog could get a good sniff.

Sultan went glassy-eyed. "You brought a dog? To a funeral?"

"Devon's dog. Want to pet her?"

"Not really."

"Want to explain why your building has suddenly gone condo?"

Sultan's bushy brows knit together. "That's really none of your business."

"It is if Devon was the one standing in the way of your red-hot real estate plan."

Sultan shook his head. "That condo plan was in the works for a long time. Devon was coming around to seeing the wisdom of it all. He also stood to gain a generous buy-out."

Carmela pushed Mimi a little closer to Sultan, but the pug clearly had no interest in her former landlord. If Sultan was guilty, Mimi wasn't going to be the one to point a finger. Or paw.

Feeling as if her Mimi ploy might not be working all that well, Carmela made her way back into the chapel and joined Ava.

"Anything?" Ava asked.

"Mimi didn't react to Sultan at all."

"Maybe he bought her off by feeding her a pound of hamburger while he was busy jamming an ice pick in Devon's ear."

"What a horrible thought," Carmela said.

Ava nudged her. "Hot guy alert. Who's the sex on a stick that's walking toward us?"

"Oh man, that's Richard Drake."

"Intro please," Ava whispered.

But Drake's dark eyes were focused solely on Carmela.

"Miss Bertrand," Drake purred. "Lovely to see you again even under these dreadful circumstances."

"Good day, Mr. Drake," Carmela said.

"Have you by chance learned anything more about the item Devon Dowling supposedly had in his possession?" Drake spoke in an old-fashioned, almost formal manner.

"Not really," Carmela said. She wondered if Drake had heard about Devon's safe being robbed. Maybe not. And maybe she wouldn't be the one to tell him. Better to see how this whole thing played out. She shifted Mimi in her arms so the dog was facing Drake, but Mimi didn't react and neither did Drake. Ava, however, was on full alert.

"Ahem." Ava cleared her throat delicately.

Carmela made hasty introductions.

"So you're the president of the Vampire Society," Ava said with a seductive smile. "Dare I ask if you sleep in a coffin?"

135

Drake seemed mildly amused. "I'm afraid I do not, Miss Gruiex. My interests regarding *vampyr* legend and lore are strictly historical and metaphysical."

"Would that be . . ." Ava began.

But Drake bowed gracefully at both of them and turned away.

"Do you see?" Ava fumed. "Do you see why I need a matchmaker? I'm losing my mojo. That man could care less about my pretty neck and décolleté."

"You don't want him, he's a player," Carmela said.

But Ava was still miffed. "I smiled at him, I used *facial muscles.*"

"What worries me more is that we're losing suspects right and left. I was so sure Mimi would spot Devon's killer."

"I'm sorry it's not working out, *cher.*"

"I think I'll put Mimi in the car where she'll be more comfortable. The weather's still cool, but I'll crack the windows anyway and pour her some Fiji water."

Once another two dozen or so people had crowded into the chapel, the service began. Carmela and Ava sat in the back row, with Carmela craning her neck to see if Babcock would show up. Nope. She didn't see him. She did, however, see her friend Jekyl

Hardy. He was hard to miss in his black European tailored suit and dark hair pulled back in a neat ponytail.

The minister gave an opening welcome, led them in a few prayers, and then introduced David Dowling, Devon's brother.

Dressed in a three-piece business suit, David stepped to the lectern, gripped it with both hands, and faced the crowd of mourners. With a clear, nonemotional voice, he thanked everyone for coming. Then he launched into a sort of bio on Devon.

"He sounds like he's giving a marketing pitch," Ava whispered.

"Or a PowerPoint presentation," Carmela said.

As David Dowling continued to outline his brother's life and accomplishments, Peter Jarreau slid into the seat next to Carmela.

"Did I miss anything?" Jarreau whispered to her.

Carmela shook her head. "Not really." The not-so-subtle scent of Paco Rabanne wafted around him like a miniature weather system.

"Got stuck in traffic," Jarreau said. "A semi jackknifed out by Avondale." He nodded toward David Dowling. "Who's that?"

"David Dowling, Devon's brother." Carmela happened to notice that T.J., sitting in the front pew, seemed more interested in his cell phone than the service.

"Ah," Jarreau said, settling back.

David Dowling droned on with his testimonial, getting chirpier as he went along. Finally, after what felt like an eternity, he wrapped it up. The minister, looking greatly relieved as he stood up, asked everyone to turn to page thirty-six in their hymnals and join together in song.

After one false start, everyone managed to pull it together and sing a slightly off-key rendition of "Amazing Grace."

"Blessings to you all and thank you so much," the minister intoned afterward. "And now, Mr. David Dowling has asked me to kindly invite all of you to join him for brunch at Brennan's Restaurant."

"Hot dang," Ava said.

Now that the service was finally over, Carmela fairly flew out of her seat to see if Babcock had shown up. She found him outside, standing in a shaft of sunlight, watching the mourners exit the chapel.

"You came," she said.

Babcock offered her a crooked smile. "Did you think I wouldn't?"

"After last night . . ."

He waved a hand. "We're okay, right?"

"I guess." Carmela hesitated, then said,

"After you left, Ava and I went out for a drink." She decided to leave Shamus's impromptu visit out of the equation. Babcock didn't need to know about that.

"Hmm, you really were upset with me."

"No. It was still early, and Ava and I just felt like hanging out," Carmela said. "But the thing is, we ran into T.J."

Babcock lifted an eyebrow. "Ran into him where?"

"At Pedro Wang's."

"And . . ." He was suddenly focused on what Carmela was saying.

"T.J. was loaded to the gills. Really smashed. You were right about him. He's a heavy drinker and kind of an angry, irritable guy. I think, without much goading, he wouldn't hesitate to mix it up with a few punches."

"Yeah," Babcock said, though his expression betrayed nothing.

"T.J. also doesn't seem to be taking Devon's death particularly hard. I think he was tippy-tapping his way through social media the whole time the service was going on. Do you think that he could have . . . ?" She let her voice trail off as Peter Jarreau stepped out of the chapel and joined them.

"It's early days, Carmela," Babcock said. "We'll keep riding T.J. See if he reveals anything . . . or cracks wide open." He turned his gaze on Jarreau. "Where's the car?"

"Parked outside the gate," Jarreau said. "Want me to go get it?"

"Naw, I'll walk out with you," Babcock said. He smiled at Carmela. "Later, okay?"

"Okay," Carmela said.

"Until we solve this murder," Jarreau said, shaking his head, "I'm finding it awfully difficult to spin our investigation to the public. We need to keep everyone informed and updated — especially the media — but we don't want to upset all our Jazz Fest visitors, either."

"Figure it out," Babcock snapped. "That's your job."

CHAPTER 11

Carmela rumbled down the alley behind Memory Mine and pulled up next to the loading dock. Grabbing Mimi, she said to Ava, "I'll just be a sec." Then she ran in the back door and deposited the pup in front of Gabby.

"Ooh, hello, princess," Gabby exclaimed when she saw Mimi. "Look what I bought you." She spoke in the high-pitched, sing-songy voice people generally reserved for adorable babies and equally adorable pets. "It's your very own bed. Now you won't have to curl up on that junky old chair cushion anymore."

Mimi flopped down on her brand-new red and green plaid bed, let loose a deep sigh, and immediately closed her eyes.

"How was the funeral service?" Gabby asked. "Did you manage all right? You and Devon were such good friends, it must have been heartbreaking."

141

"The service was fairly well done, considering . . . well, you know the atmosphere at St. Roch's," Carmela said.

"All those crutches," Gabby murmured as she absently fingered the string of pearls around her neck.

"I had hoped Mimi would sniff out Devon's killer, but no such luck. If the killer was lurking among the mourners, Mimi didn't see him. She didn't react at all."

"That's too bad," Gabby said. "I know you were counting on her doggy instincts to make something happen."

"I'm still hoping I can sleuth out a few shreds of information at the funeral luncheon. Can you hold down the fort a little longer?"

"No problem. Where's the luncheon being held?"

"Brennan's."

"Oh, yum. Lucky you if they serve their fabulous crawfish and mushroom omelet."

"I'm praying for egg yolk carpaccio," Carmela said over her shoulder as she flew out the door.

When she climbed back in her car, Ava was fidgeting with her black satin jacket. "I was just flirting with the cute UPS driver who was parked next to us," she said, looking happy and a trifle smug.

"You were flirting with a strange man? In an alley? Hmm. Maybe you do need a matchmaker after all. Professional help, if you can call it that."

But Ava was impervious. "Do you think my jacket looks better when it's open? Or should I close up the bottom two buttons so it stays tight around my waist?"

"These are the things you worry about?" Carmela asked. "Not world peace or global warming?"

Ava sat up straighter. "Well, I do want people to get a good look at my red satin bustier."

"By people, you mean men."

"Obviously."

Carmela cranked the ignition. "Are you sure you want to show that much cleavage at a funeral luncheon?"

Ava gave a slow wink. "Honey, the funeral's over and done with. A girl can't run around in black mourning clothes forever."

"You don't think there's like a three- or four-hour time frame that calls for some sort of decency and decorum?" Carmela laughed as she drove down the alley.

"Not if those hours include a party at Brennan's with some fine-looking men. You were right about that vampire guy, *cher.* He's luscious."

"Down, girl."

Carmela drove along Decatur Street and slid into a parking spot a few doors down from the pink brick façade (the color was technically called Tomato Cream Sauce) and wrought-iron balconies of Brennan's Restaurant.

The maître d', whose handlebar mustache and pork chop sideburns complemented his tuxedo, greeted them effusively, glanced in his reservations book, and said, "Ah yes, the Dowling reception. Please follow me to the Audubon Room."

As he led the way, Ava popped open another button on her jacket and whispered, "I was hoping the event would be in the Courtyard. It's such a pretty day to be outside."

The maître d' opened the double doors to a large, elegant room with apricot-colored walls, sunlight streaming through the high, wide windows, a large group of people milling about, and the most enticing aromas.

But before they could go facedown in the food, Carmela and Ava had to make their way through an abbreviated receiving line.

Carmela put on a solemn face as she introduced herself to David Dowling.

"Carmela Bertrand," she said, offering a hand. "I was a good friend of your brother.

And this is Ava."

Ava, who was busy putting on hot pink lip gloss, just smiled and said, "Howja do."

David Dowling lifted an eyebrow but remained cordial.

"And this is Reverend Wright, who conducted the service," David Dowling said, indicating the man on his right.

The minister smiled at Carmela, took one look at Ava, and coughed loudly. Turning bright red, he took a hasty step back.

No problem, Ava just waltzed right past him and waded into the crowd.

Carmela, on the other hand, made a beeline for her friend Jekyl Hardy.

"Darling, you made it," Jekyl said, taking both of Carmela's hands in his as they exchanged elaborate air-kisses. "I was beginning to wonder."

Lean and wiry, his dark hair pulled into a small, sleek ponytail, Jekyl Hardy was dressed impeccably in his traditional black, which made him look somewhat ethereal and predatory, not unlike the infamous vampire Lestat who frequented New Orleans via Anne Rice's novels. Jekyl was the head float designer for the Pluvius and Nepthys krewes but made his living as an art and antique consultant. As he'd once confided to Carmela, "The float building's for sport, the art and antique consulting is for actual money."

"What did you think of the service?" Carmela asked him.

Jekyl's shoulders lifted a notch. "Adequate. I myself would prefer something a bit more Gothic and grand."

"Of course you would." Carmela glanced around the room. "I was hoping I'd run into Colonel Barnett Otis at the funeral, but no such luck."

"He's right over there," Jekyl said.

"Where?" Then, "Oh, you mean the guy with the bushy white mustache that makes him look suspiciously like a walrus? That's him?" Carmela smiled as she patted Jekyl on the shoulder. "Excellent. I'll be right back."

Colonel Otis had just picked up a plate and was about to go through the buffet line when Carmela waylaid him.

"Excuse me," Carmela said. "Could we talk for a moment?"

Colonel Otis turned and looked at her. "Hmm?" he said. He looked supremely disappointed that the beef bourguignonne would have to wait.

Carmela didn't believe in beating around the bush.

"I understand that Devon Dowling was

the one who discovered that a painting you acquired was stolen?"

Colonel Otis puffed out his cheeks and peered at her. "Who are you, please?" Carmela thought he looked like a British officer in an old World War II movie. All he needed was a uniform and a bunch of medals on his chest.

"Oh, sorry. I suppose I'm getting ahead of myself. I'm Carmela Bertrand, I was a good friend of Devon Dowling's."

"Ah," he said politely, as if that explained everything. "And you were asking about . . . ?"

"Your painting," Carmela said. "Devon was the one who discovered that your painting had been stolen?"

Colonel Otis stepped out of line and nodded at Carmela. "Yes, it was a new acquisition, and I wanted Mr. Dowling to appraise it for insurance purposes. When I found out it was stolen, I was absolutely devastated. Obviously, once the police complete their investigation, the painting will have to go back to the museum it was stolen from."

"How awful for you."

"And for my art collection," Colonel Otis said.

"Where will the painting be returned to?"

"A museum in Denver."

"But you must have some recourse with the painting's seller, am I right?" Carmela knew she was being pushy and didn't care. In her mind, this counted as a legitimate investigation.

"The seller was a private dealer who had actually contacted me. He seemed to have all the appropriate credentials and provenance," Colonel Otis said.

"This was someone you knew? That you'd worked with before?"

"Not really. And I clearly won't ever again. This particular dealer contacted me out of the blue, and I suppose that probably should have been a warning sign in and of itself." Colonel Otis gave a rueful smile.

"Do you know how this disreputable dealer got your name?"

Colonel Otis favored her with a tolerant smile. "Probably because I'm listed as a gold patron donor with the New Orleans Museum of Art."

"I have two words for you," Ava said to Carmela a few minutes later. "Buffet line. As in let's hustle our tushies over there right now. Before the food gets cold. Or is depleted by hungry, voracious guests."

"Okay," Carmela said as they walked over and grabbed plates. "Let's do it."

They helped themselves to panfried veal grillades, crab-stuffed crepes, eggs Sardou, home fries, red beans and rice, and baked apples in pecan sauce.

"So what did you find out from talking to Colonel Mustard over there?" Ava asked.

"Colonel Otis. And to answer your question, not a whole lot. He basically told me he'd been snookered in an art deal."

"Did you believe him?"

Ava's question gave Carmela pause. "Probably. I mean, the police got involved. On the other hand, Colonel Otis is kind of a big-time collector . . ."

"And you think he may have collected something from Devon Dowling?"

"It could have happened that way." Carmela helped herself to a small cup of seafood gumbo. "Colonel Otis impresses me as a bit of a fat cat. And fat cats often have a tendency to get what they want. Never mind how they go about it."

"The snippet of coat?" Ava asked.

"Maybe."

They carried their plates over to Jekyl's table and sat down to eat. One of the servers had brought over a bottle of Chablis, and now Jekyl carefully poured out drinks for them.

"To Devon," Carmela said as she raised

her glass. "May he rest in peace." The three of them gently clinked glasses in a toast to their fallen friend.

Once they'd tucked into their entrées, Jekyl said, "I have news."

"Now what?" Carmela asked.

"No, it's good news," Jekyl said. "The Corinth krewe asked me to do some preliminary sketches for their Mardi Gras floats."

"I thought Julian Bragg was designing their floats," Carmela said.

Jekyl looked pleased, more than pleased. "He was. But now it appears as if he's completely skipped town. Maybe he ran off to join the circus, maybe he skipped out on his bar bill at Commander's Palace. Whatever the reason, I couldn't be more pleased."

"Congratulations, then," Carmela said. "I'm happy for you."

"This is nice," Ava said as she nibbled her eggs Sardou and took another sip of wine. "All of us lunching together. It's so terribly civilized."

The word *civilized* had barely escaped Ava's mouth when a loud noise ripped across the room, startling everyone. Either a steam locomotive had exploded or a T. rex had stumbled in. Then a fist hammered down on a table, jouncing silverware and tipping over wineglasses.

"Now what?" Carmela cried. But as she spun in her chair and gazed across the room, she saw Richard Drake standing over T.J., who was still seated at his table. Not only had Drake assumed a threatening posture, he was screaming at the top of his lungs.

"You did it!" Drake cried. "I know it was you!"

"Get out of my face, you overage poseur!" T.J. yelled back. "Why don't you go back to whatever *Twilight* movie you crawled out of!"

"You won't get away with it!" Drake screamed.

T.J. jumped to his feet. "Back off, jerkwad, before I call the cops!"

"Ooh," Ava said. "This is getting serious."

Hands balled into fists, Drake and T.J. circled each other like a couple of wary prizefighters. Guests craned their heads, and chairs squeaked as everyone shifted to get a better view. Would there be a fight? A hush fell over the room as everyone waited expectantly.

"I just found out that Devon's safe was robbed," Drake said. Now he dropped his voice to a low, menacing snarl. "And I know it was *you* who did it!"

"You're crazy!" T.J. spat out.

"You stole the piece of Lincoln's coat,"

Drake continued.

"The cat's out of the bag now," Ava said as an excited murmur ran through the crowd.

"No way!" T.J. shouted back.

"That relic was promised to the Vampire Society, and we want it *now.*"

"You want it?" T.J. bounced on the balls of his feet. "Okay, asshole, I'll give it to you." He swung wildly at Drake, not a championship punch but enough to clip him upside the head. A loud *thwok* rang out, like a ripe watermelon being thumped.

Drake staggered sideways, looked like he was about to collapse, but managed to recover at the last moment. He came back at T.J. like a ball of fury and landed a right uppercut square on his jaw.

Ava said, "Vampire guy is not only good-looking, he isn't afraid of a fight."

T.J. wobbled for a split second and fell backward, sprawling inelegantly in the lap of a very startled woman who wore a large black hat with netting that was either a messy bow or a scraggly crow.

"S'cuse me," T.J. said to the woman as his eyes goggled. Then he pushed himself up and staggered forward. When his eyes managed to refocus on Drake, he snarled, "You seriously wanna mix it up? Good." He looked like a bandy rooster ready to explode. "Now I'm *really* gonna let you have it!"

"Can't you do something?" Carmela whispered to Jekyl.

"I'll try," Jekyl whispered back. He leaped to his feet and charged across the room, threading his way through tables of stunned guests, heading for the two fighters. "Gentlemen, gentlemen," he said, trying to sound appeasing. Trying to sound reasonable. "This is hardly the time or place . . ."

Drake heard Jekyl's plea and gave a slight nod. He unclenched his hands and looked as if he was willing to back off.

T.J., on the other hand, decided to up the ante. Bellowing like a raging bull, he reached out, grabbed an upholstered chair, and hoisted it over his head. He staggered for an instant, then swung the chair in a wide arc directly at Richard Drake.

At the very last second, Drake saw the chair hurtling toward him and managed to twist his body. The chair struck him on the shoulder with such force that he dropped like a sack of flour.

Then the chair, carried by centrifugal force, turned completely upside down, made a loud *BOING* as it bounced once, and proceeded to hit Jekyl squarely in the chest.

"Oof," Ava said as four startled waiters suddenly rushed toward the three men. "Bummer for Jekyl."

Two minutes later it was all over. T.J. stomped out, Drake apologized to a nearby table, and Jekyl was still trying to catch his breath.

"Do you want us to take you to the ER?" Carmela asked Jekyl.

Jekyl shook his head. "I'm good," he gasped. He fluttered a nervous hand in front of his mouth. "Just need to . . . catch my . . . breath."

"I think there's one of those doc-in-the-box places over on Rampart," Ava said. "Maybe you could suck some O's."

But Jekyl shook his head. "I just want to . . . go home," he rasped.

Carmela was still feeling stunned. "That was awful," she said. "If Drake and T.J. can act this crazed, one of them could have easily smashed up Devon's shop. And maybe even murdered poor Devon."

Ava nodded. "You just said a mouthful, *cher*."

CHAPTER 12

With a heavy heart (and an impending case of heartburn) Carmela dropped Ava at Juju Voodoo, then drove back to Memory Mine.

Why did Drake and T.J. have to fight? she wondered. Why did they have to ruin a perfectly good funeral luncheon? And could Richard Drake be right about T.J. stealing the coat fragment from Devon's safe? If so, had T.J. also murdered Devon? Or had Drake been the thief as well as the aggressor? It all felt murky and confusing with nary a single answer to shed any light on a nasty, baffling situation.

Carmela's mood didn't improve when she walked into Memory Mine.

"There you are," Gabby said. "Quigg's been looking for you."

"For me?" With all that had happened today, Carmela had practically forgotten about Quigg and his wine bar. Had relegated him to the back burner.

"Yes, you. Quigg's been getting things all set up next door." Gabby smiled. "It's really starting to take shape and, my goodness, he *is* an attractive man, isn't he? I can see why you . . ."

But Carmela was already out the front door.

Her heart in her throat, she pushed her way into Blush and Brush. And stopped dead in her tracks when she saw the flurry of activity. "Oh no!" The little wine bar really was starting to take shape.

Quigg saw Carmela standing there with a look of utter panic on her face and, with a burst of enthusiasm, said, "Isn't it great?"

"No!" Carmela shot back.

Quigg flashed his trademark grin and pretended not to hear. Then, like a genial host introducing his guests, he said, "Carmela, you remember Dewey and Ardice, don't you? Part of my inner circle at St. Tammany Vineyards?"

"Hey there," Dewey said as he shifted white marble tables around the shop, as if trying to find the perfect spot for each one. He was mid-fifties, tan from working outdoors, and wore white overalls, the kind housepainters often wore.

Ardice, who was busy unpacking wine bottles from their crates, gave a little wave and said, "Hi, Carmela." Ardice was mid-thirties, African American, and the business manager at St. Tammany Vineyards. She also did the buying for their gift shop.

"Hi," Carmela said back in a small voice. *This is definitely beginning to look like a legitimate wine bar. I'd better straighten things out right now before Babcock sees this place and has a coronary.*

"What . . . what are you doing?" Carmela asked Quigg.

"Are you kidding me? What does it look like we're doing? We're prepping for our big grand opening. Have you made up your mind yet, Carmela? Are our customers going to paint plates or wineglasses?"

"Grand opening? But I haven't even decided if I should be your partner yet. You can't rush me on this! I told you before, I've run into some, um, serious resistance."

Quigg gave her a look of supreme innocence. "Certainly not from me."

Carmela frowned. "You know who."

"That's for you two lovebirds to work out. Meanwhile, Dewey and Ardice are doing a bang-up job of getting us set up."

Dewey's ball cap, decked out with the New Orleans Saints' fleur-de-lis, slid to one side as he shifted a crate of wine bottles from the floor to the countertop. "You

157

should come visit the vineyard more often. You're greatly missed. Ain't that right, Ardice?"

Ardice held up a wine bottle. "We always love company at the vineyard. But this . . ." She swept her hand to indicate the shop. "This is going to be spectacular. We're so happy you bought into Quigg's concept." She flashed a smile at Quigg. "He's quite the marketing genius."

"Uh-huh," Carmela said.

Quigg made a show of consulting his oversized gold Rolex. "The interior decorator and her crew should be here in twenty minutes or so," he told Carmela. "To handle the wall finishes and the rest of the décor. Meanwhile, we're moving in as much wine as we can."

Ardice held up a bottle of Bayou Sparkler. "Remember this one, Carmela? Our finest bubbly. And for white wine drinkers we brought along our Sauvignon Silver, a terrific blend of Sauvignon Blanc and Blanc du Bois."

"Tell her about our newest wine," Quigg urged.

"Jazz Fest Red," Ardice said, her long gold earrings swishing against her neck. "A smoky Grenache with hints of cherry and apple. Perfect for an artsy setting like the

158

French Quarter."

"Plus we'll be serving our Mardi Gras Medley and our Cajun Cabernet," Quigg said.

Carmela felt overwhelmed as she backed out of the shop. "And you say you've got a decorator coming in?"

Quigg glanced at his watch again. "Any minute now. Don't worry, I'll let you know when you can come back and get a peek at the finishing touches."

"What's wrong?" Gabby asked when Carmela returned to the scrapbook shop. She looked dazed and walked with the stiff-legged gait of a zombie.

"Everything," Carmela said. "If I say white, Quigg says black. If I say no, he says yes. He . . . he doesn't *listen*."

"Carmela." Concern flooded Gabby's face as she hurried around the counter and embraced her in a gentle hug. "Don't worry about it. Everything's going to be fine."

"You really think so?"

That stopped Gabby dead and caused her to reboot her words. "Well . . . you know me. I'm generally the optimistic one."

"You are. And I love that about you. But this wine thing . . . it's got me in a huge kerfuffle."

"Imagine that," Gabby said, smiling. "I'm sure . . . no, I'm positive, that your dear sweet Detective Babcock will end up being completely supportive. After all, it's just a little painting and crafting now and then."

"Uh-huh."

"Now. Tell me something good. Like how was the luncheon at Brennan's? Did they serve eggs Sardou and their famous cornmeal-battered shrimp?"

"It was more like assault and battered," Carmela said.

"What on earth are you talking about?"

"There was a fight."

"Mercy!" Gabby cried, taking a step backward.

So Carmela laid it all out for Gabby. Gave her the rundown about quizzing Colonel Otis, Ava's outrageous flirting, and Richard Drake and T.J. getting into a knock-down, drag-out fight. Finally, she told Gabby about poor Jekyl getting hit in the cross fire.

"Was Jekyl hurt?" Gabby asked.

"More like a bruised ego."

"That will heal. But poor Jekyl . . . and poor you. How about a cup of tea to help you calm down? We've got hibiscus and chamomile that we ordered from that lovely tea shop in Charleston."

"Chamomile tea would be great," Carmela

said. "And thank you."

"No problem."

Carmela was standing at the front counter, sipping her tea and sketching a design for a miniature theater, when Babcock walked in.

"Hey, you," he said, smiling at her.

"Hey, yourself," Carmela said. "This is unexpected." Then, "Come on back to my office."

Babcock followed her back and slipped into one of the director's chairs that faced Carmela's desk. "I heard about the fisticuffs at the funeral luncheon," he said. "Not good."

"You're telling me?"

"I can't let you go anywhere, can I?" Babcock stretched out his long legs, bumped her chair with his toe.

Carmela raised her hands as if in surrender. "Not my doing. T.J. and Drake just started going at it like a couple of rabid polecats."

"Are you sure you weren't an instigator?"

Carmela shook her head. "No way. Not this time. I was merely an innocent bystander."

"That's the way I like my sweetheart — innocent until proven guilty and *not* embroiled in the thick of things." He pointed to her sketch pad. "What are you working on?"

Carmela picked up her sketch pad and showed him. "Just an idea for an Italian theater. It's going to be kind of a triptych. You know, three-sided, three-dimensional."

"Cute."

Then, because Babcock seemed to be in a relatively good mood and Carmela couldn't resist, she said, "How's the investigation coming along?"

"Which one?" Babcock gazed at her benignly.

"You know which one," Carmela said.

"Carmela . . ." Now his voice carried a warning. "You know we're doing the best we can."

"There's something you should know about. Something I didn't get a chance to tell you this morning," Carmela said.

"Tell me about what?"

"Devon's building has gone condo."

"So?"

"Don't you find it suspicious that, like, two minutes after Devon is found dead in his shop, his landlord suddenly decides to take the building condo?"

Babcock leaned forward. "This condo business is for sure? How do you know about it?"

162

"Roy Sultan, the building's owner, put up an enormous sign."

"So you think . . . ."

"I think maybe Sultan wanted Devon Dowling out of that building, *tried* to get him out, but Devon was holding up progress. Maybe he'd signed a long-term lease that couldn't be broken."

"Roy Sultan," Babcock said in a thoughtful tone. "He's kind of a big wheel in real estate."

"I don't care if he is. He should be investigated. If Devon was costing him millions in lost revenue, then Sultan had a serious motive." She paused. "A motive for murder."

"He's an older guy," Babcock said slowly.

"He still could have hired someone. People do it all the time. There's no shortage of jerks who'll do any kind of dirty work for money." Carmela stared at Babcock. "You want this case solved, don't you?"

"Absolutely. It's brutal to have an unsolved murder hanging over our heads. Especially during Jazz Fest. Not conducive to tourism."

"Or for those of us who live here," Carmela said.

Babcock got to his feet. "Okay. Point taken."

"So you'll look into this?"

Babcock bent forward and kissed her on the tip of her nose. "I will."

Carmela heaved a sigh of relief as she walked him to the door. Babcock had not only taken her seriously, there'd been no mention of the wine bar. Maybe Gabby was right. Everything would all work out.

"You look happy again," Gabby said, once Babcock had left. "And relieved."

"You have no idea," Carmela said. "And you were right about . . ."

The front door whapped open, and Babcock charged back into the shop like a wounded bull. His eyes blazed, his tie was askew, his face was a veritable thundercloud.

"Carmela! I thought we talked about this! I thought we'd finally come to some *agreement.*" Babcock's voice got louder with each word he spat out.

"Talked about what?" Although it was probably a lost cause, Carmela tried to project innocence.

"I walk out the door and, right there, staring me in the face, is a huge sign being raised on a pulley. *BLUSH AND BRUSH.*" Babcock paused for dramatic effect. "And what else do I see? Blatantly printed at eye level?"

"Um." Carmela's heart was pounding so

164

hard it felt like an anvil being hammered. She hadn't seen Babcock this angry in . . . forever.

"I see two names at the bottom of the sign! 'Quigg Brevard . . . Carmela Bertrand. Proprietors.' "

"I can explain," Carmela said. Although she had no idea what she was going to say to him. It was difficult to make excuses when you'd been caught red-handed.

Babcock didn't give her half a chance anyway. "Make this go away and make it go away now," he said. He let loose an angry huff, spun on his heels, and disappeared out the door.

The silence in his wake was deafening. Good thing there weren't any customers in the shop. Gabby, a hand clutching her throat, stared at her.

"Carmela? What are you going to do?" Gabby looked like she was about to burst into tears.

"I don't know," Carmela said. "But dragging Quigg into a swamp and leaving him for a hungry alligator definitely comes to mind."

"Carmela — and I ask this with complete love and respect — if you knew this wine bar was going to cause such an enormous rift in your relationship, why did you ever

165

agree to work with Quigg?"

"I don't know. It just kind of happened."

Carmela wasn't sure how she'd been dragged into a semi-partnership with Quigg. Maybe she still had a soft spot for him, maybe she liked the thrill of tackling a new challenge, maybe she just hadn't kept her eye on the ball. Whatever the reason, she was drowning in problems now.

"I didn't mean to make everyone so unhappy," Carmela said. "I know I screwed up and caused Babcock a lot of pain."

"With the right words, with a heartfelt apology, I'm sure it's nothing that can't be fixed right now," Gabby said. "Think of it as a . . . a victimless crime."

If it were only that simple, Carmela thought.

CHAPTER 13

Carmela was making pillow-shaped gift boxes out of red paisley cardstock when she got a call from Helen McBride, the editor in chief of *Glutton for Punishment*. It was a wildly popular New Orleans webzine filled with restaurant reviews, interviews with local chefs, recipes, wine recommendations, and top-ten lists that included fun things such as Most Romantic Restaurant, Sexiest New Orleans Chefs, and Best New Rosé Wines.

"Congratulations!" Helen cried. "I hear you're going into partnership with the Dreamboat of the Delta."

"Excuse me?" Carmela said. Helen was prone to theatrics, but what was this about?

"With Quigg Brevard," she trilled. "You two are opening a fancy new wine bar together, no?"

"No. We're . . . wait a minute. Does everybody know about this? Because I haven't *formally* agreed to do anything with Quigg." *In fact, I'll never get to talk to him again if Babcock has his way. But that's another story.*

"Why do I not believe you?" Helen asked. "I mean, a wine bar. How fun is that? I can't wait to write a glowing review, give the two of you some well-deserved — and free, I might add — publicity."

"But I wouldn't actually be running the wine bar," Carmela explained. "I'd be the one honchoing the painting and crafts." *If I do it at all. And if Babcock ever speaks to me again.*

"Don't sweat the small stuff, sweet cheeks," Helen advised. "Just have fun with it."

"Sometimes that's not as easy as it sounds."

"Remember, you can always tell the pioneers by the arrows in their back," Helen laughed. Then she turned serious. "It's definitely no picnic being an entrepreneur these days. Hey, I know how tough it can be . . . finagling loans, writing start-up marketing plans. You get rolling, start feeling a burst of confidence, and boom! You're back at square one. Why, just this morning I had a couple of guys quit on me." Helen snorted. "Millennials. Constantly job hopping and searching for a so-called *new experience.*" She paused, practically out of breath. "But that's not why I called. To complain, I mean."

"You wanted to ask about Blush and Brush?" Carmela said.

"Not exactly. I wanted to see if you'd do me a huge favor by judging our Roux the Night Gumbo Cook-Off this Friday."

"Me?" Carmela was taken aback. "What qualifications would I possibly have?"

"You eat food, don't you?" Helen asked.

Carmela chuckled. "Sometimes too much."

"There you go," Helen said. "Besides, the gumbo cook-off takes place right in your neighborhood at the Marquis Hotel. We've got almost two dozen restaurants entered in the competition. Plus, Abita Beer and NOLA Brewing are doing sponsorships. Should be loads of fun."

"What would I have to do?"

"Gargle a bottle of Pepto-Bismol so you don't singe your gullet, do a whole lot of gumbo tasting, and then render your fine opinion."

"That doesn't sound too bad. But are you sure you want me?"

"What can I say?" Helen said. "You're in the neighborhood and, for some reason, people seem to like you. *I* like you."

"Okay, but . . . I won't be the only person judging, will I?"

"Naw, I roped a couple of other deadbeats into this as well. Come on," Helen urged. "It's one of the premier Jazz Fest events. Pretend to be civic-minded, would you?"

"Okay, then. I guess . . . yes," Carmela said.

"Attagirl."

Carmela hung up the phone and turned to Gabby. "Helen at *Glutton for Punishment* just asked me to help judge a gumbo cook-off Friday night."

"That sounds like fun. Are you going to do it?"

"I told her yes. Helen's also under the impression that I'm going into business with Quigg."

"Well, aren't you?"

"Not really," Carmela said just as the front door flew open and Quigg popped his head in.

He gave Carmela a sexy wink and rolled a hand in a *follow me* gesture. "C'mon, cupcake. We're ready to go."

"Go where?" Carmela asked. Confusion was written all over her face. Was she missing something? Or was Quigg deliberately keeping her unbalanced so he could continue to railroad her?

"Come on over and see the place. The decorating's pretty much done."

"It is?" Carmela said. "Already?" If she was going to change Babcock's mind, she'd have to work fast.

Quigg wiggled his eyebrows. "I also took the liberty of inviting a bunch of people, some of my restaurant regulars, to our new place so we could have a quiet opening tomorrow night. Think of it as a kind of test run."

"You're opening the wine bar just like that?"

"*We're* opening it. Because it's all done, babe. Everything's in place."

"What about the paint, the pottery, the whatever?" Carmela felt like she was in a fun house with shrieking clowns popping out of hidden spaces, floors shifting like crazy, and everything moving way too fast.

"It's all been taken care of," Quigg said. "Paint and canvases are ordered and will be delivered later today, the plates are already here. All you have to do is show up tomorrow night at seven o'clock and lead your class. My people will be there to handle the wine."

"Wow," Gabby said. "When you move, you move fast."

"Don't be so impressed by him," Carmela said to Gabby.

Gabby grinned. "But I am. Kind of."

"See?" Quigg said. "Gabby likes me, why don't you?" Then, "Come on. I want you to see what we did with the walls."

The walls were fantastic, of course. As was everything else. Quigg had hired Letitia Jeffries, who he always referred to as Decorator to the Stars, to do the place up right. Letitia, much to her credit, had invoked a semi-cool New Orleans palette of pinks, corals, and tropical greens, which gave the little wine bar the flavor of a classic Creole cottage. Green and cream palm leaf–printed fabric was stretched across the back wall. The side walls were the original yellow brick hung with framed wine labels. Sisal carpets covered the floors, and the white marble tables were now surrounded by chairs made of bent willow with pink-bordering-on-apricot seat cushions. Frosted green and white wineglasses were stacked on the wine bar, along with dozens of bottles of wine. A list of wines available by the glass was scrawled artfully in black marker on the smoked mirror that hung over the bar.

"It's gorgeous," Carmela cried. She couldn't help herself; the place looked utterly adorable. "But when did all this happen?"

"It's been happening right along," Quigg said. "You just haven't been paying attention." He was pleased that Carmela liked the décor. Now if he could just get her to seriously commit. "Tomorrow night's going to be exciting, yes?"

Carmela turned to face him. Quigg bounced on the balls of his feet, looking practically ecstatic. She hated to disappoint him.

"Tomorrow night's only going to be a rehearsal, you understand," Carmela said.

"Absolutely," Quigg said. "A quick way to test the waters and work out all the bugs."

Great. He's talking about water and bugs while I'm worried about my entire future with Babcock.

"And if it works out . . ." Carmela said.

"It will work out."

"*If* it works out, you understand I'll only be available one night a week. I have other, um, concerns. Commitments."

"I get it, I really do," Quigg said. He reached over and grabbed the top plate from a stack of plates sitting on the counter. "Unfired bisque," he said, handing it to her. "Maybe for your very first project tomorrow night you'd like to paint one as a sample?"

"How was Blush and Brush?" Gabby asked when Carmela returned to Memory Mine. She was packing up, leaving a little early today. Stuart had asked her to attend a Toyota zone manager's reception and dinner with him. "Quigg's got it all glammed up?"

"The place is cute as a bug," Carmela said. "All pinks and corals and greens. You could move in a truckload of flowers and turn it into a jewel box of a florist shop. Or you could spread jewels on the counter and make it a boutique."

"So you're saying it's adorable. That women will love it."

"It's so adorable *I* can barely resist it," Carmela sighed.

"And I take it you'll be leading a painting class tomorrow night?"

Carmela held up the bisque plate Quigg had given her. "The blue plate special, yes."

"This is going to work out," Gabby said. "I can feel it in my bones. You just need to do the dance of the seven veils for Babcock and you'll have him eating out of your hand in no time flat." She picked up her tote bag. "Want me to roll the phones to the answering service? Or are you going to stay for a while?"

"I still have to work on that frame project for Glissande's, so don't worry about the phones."

"Okay," Gabby said. "But I'm going to lock the door behind me. Don't go opening up to any strangers."

You got that right, Carmela thought as she wandered back to the craft table. She was halfway through a decoupage project for Glissande's Courtyard Restaurant, which was located right across the street from her. Toby Brewer, the manager, had asked her to rework a framed mirror that had been hanging in their entryway. It had a two-inch-wide frame made of brushed copper. And, over the years, it had faded and flaked. Now Toby wanted Carmela to update it with a country French look.

Carmela had pondered that notion for a while, then come up with the idea of taking images and typography from old French cookbooks. So she'd scoured used bookstores for French cookbooks, then gone through them for just the right images. She'd snipped out bits of recipes, as well as images of mustard pots, crockery, soup pots, bunches of onions, leeks, chickens (*poulets!*), and all manner of crustaceans. After artfully arranging a few images on the frame, she thought they looked perfect. But maybe the theme was a little too earthy for Toby's refined tastes?

A quick call to the restaurant and she was hurrying across the street, carrying her half-finished frame.

Toby Brewer met her at the hostess stand.

"Come on back to my office," Toby said. "We're open but right now it's mostly just folks in our cocktail lounge. Early happy hour, don't you know."

Carmela carried the frame back to Toby's office and placed it on his desk.

"I like it," she said. "But you're the one who has final say."

Toby crinkled his brow as he studied the frame. He touched an index finger to his upper lip (a good sign?) and finally said, "I like it."

Carmela let out the breath she'd been holding.

"No," Toby said. "Actually, I *love* it."

"Whew. I thought I was on the right track, but you never know."

"It's genius. I mean, *it's* country French, *we're* country French."

"So I'll go ahead and finish it then," Carmela said. "And brush on a lacquer topcoat to preserve the images. I'm guessing you need this frame sooner than later?"

"How about yesterday?" Toby said, and they both laughed. Then Toby got serious. "I was so sorry to hear about your friend." He meant Devon Dowling. News of Devon's untimely death really had swept through the French Quarter like wildfire. "Are the police any closer to catching his killer?"

"I don't think so," Carmela said, thinking about her own stalled investigation.

Toby shook his head. "We bought two paintings from Devon, you know. The wine bottle still life that hangs in the bar and the lovely, moody riverscape that hangs in the dining room. That was a terrible, gruesome thing that happened to Devon. Whoever killed him should be caught, hog-tied, and made to pay for their sins."

Carmela couldn't have agreed more.

CHAPTER 14

Turtledove Matchmaking had their offices directly above Hoby's Bar and Grill, a raucous dive bar with hot pink neon signs that announced *GIRLZ! GIRLZ! GIRLZ!* Although the last part of the sign had a couple lights knocked out, so it read *G LZ!*

"I ask you, does this inspire any confidence at all?" Carmela said as she and Ava trucked up the narrow wooden steps. They could still hear the *plinkety-plink* from the piano and the crack of pool balls being racked below as they walked down the hallway.

"*Cher,* I'm desperate. I need professional help."

"You've always got me. Maybe I could . . ."

"You mean well, but last time you set me up on a date it was with an actuarial accountant. Borrrring."

"It's your nickel," Carmela said as Ava

pushed open a pink door emblazoned with *TURTLEDOVE MATCHMAKING* spelled out in gold glitter.

Miss Penelope, the owner of Turtledove Matchmaking, was waiting for them in her small one-room office. The walls were decorated with hearts and cupids, a pink beaded curtain hung in the window, and two black leather director's chairs were covered with white fur throws. The decorating did not inspire confidence.

"You must be Ava," Miss Penelope said, reaching out to shake Ava's hand.

Ava nodded. "And I brought along my friend Carmela. I hope you don't mind."

"Not at all," Miss Penelope said, taking a seat behind her desk and indicating for Carmela and Ava to sit in the fuzzy director's chairs.

"Great place you've got here," Carmela said, looking around. "Casually elegant but without that formal decorator look."

"Thank you," Miss Penelope said. "It's home."

Miss Penelope herself was a slightly over-the-hill bleached blonde with a tendency to squint. She wore a black leather skirt and a hot pink sweater that buttoned up the front with about a zillion teeny-tiny white pearl buttons. Every time she moved in her chair, to tug down her skirt or shift her weight, another button seemed to pop open. Carmela wondered if Miss Penelope might not moonlight downstairs. Maybe she was one of the GIRLZ.

Once Ava had filled out her questionnaire, Miss Penelope got down to brass tacks. She picked up a ballpoint pen and held it poised, ready to make notes on a long piece of lined paper decorated with a row of dancing purple hearts across the top.

"I need to get an idea of how your mind works," Miss Penelope said. "It will help me decide which one of my fabulous clients would make a good partner for you."

Ava leaned forward expectantly. "Okay."

"So tell me, honey, what are the top three attributes you're looking for in a man?"

Ava grinned. "That's easy. Good looks never fail to jump-start my heart. And neither does money."

When she saw disapproval on Miss Penelope's face, Ava waved a hand in front of herself as if to scrub away her answers. "No, just kidding. Really. I, um, I really love a guy with a great sense of humor."

"Humor," Miss Penelope said as she jotted it down.

"But not juvenile humor," Ava said. "No

pie-in-the-face, seltzer-down-your-pants humor."

"No pranks or stupid pet tricks," Carmela put in. "Those would definitely be a no-no."

"Okay, humor is one attribute you like in a man. What else?" Miss Penelope asked.

Ava screwed up her face as if in deep thought. "Um . . . ah . . . how many did I come up with so far?"

"One."

"Okay," Ava said, "how about 'Likes cats'?"

"Cats," Miss Penelope said and wrote that down, too.

"But not like a hoarder or anything," Ava said. "Like those crazy people you see on TV that have infestations in their sofas and stuff."

Carmela, who'd been relatively quiet until now, spoke up. "How about kindness, a good work ethic, and fiscal responsibility?"

"Yeah, yeah," Ava said. "Those are all good traits in a guy." She tapped a bloodred fingernail on the desk and stared at Miss Penelope. "Be sure to write those down."

"She's writing them," Carmela said.

"Whew, this dating stuff is a hell of a lot harder than it looks," Ava said. "I thought maybe there'd be a bunch of photos stuck on the wall and I could just kind of mosey along and point to the guys that turned me on."

Miss Penelope made a noise in the back of her throat.

"No?" Ava said.

"But most of all you're looking for romance, right?" Miss Penelope said.

"Sure. And a man with a soft, sexy voice," Ava said. "But nobody who's into texting. My guy better be able to dial the phone rather than text, text, text all the time."

Miss Penelope looked confused. "That's a first. Most women love the attention."

"She doesn't like to text, but she's okay on Snapchat," Carmela said.

"Oh," Ava said, as if the thought had just occurred to her. "And I don't want a man who grumbles about how long it takes me to get ready. Guys always want you to be all juicy and delicious at the drop of a hat. They don't realize that all that Spackle, makeup, paint, and powder takes time to apply." She curled both hands to indicate her face. "I mean, I wasn't *born* this gorgeous." She glanced at Miss Penelope. "Don't write that down. It'll be our little secret."

Miss Penelope nodded and tapped her pen, ready to get down to the important points.

"Sweetheart, how many previous relationships have you had?"

Ava scrunched up her face again, thinking hard. "I'd say about . . . a hundred?"

Miss Penelope sat back in her chair, eyes popping, along with two more buttons. "No, that isn't possible," she said in a breathy, almost disturbed tone of voice. Miss Penelope herself probably hadn't had that many actual clients.

Carmela nodded vigorously. "Yes, it is."

"Why don't we, um, approach your particular case from a different angle," Miss Penelope said. "How many *serious* relationships have you had?"

"Oh, then it would only be around forty or fifty," Ava said.

"Honey, I don't mean a one-shot coffee date never to be seen again. Or a bump and tickle in a bar. I'm talking about relationships that blossomed into something with actual . . . potential."

"When I meet a yummy man, I always think the future is ripe with potential. But then . . . it's not," Ava said.

Miss Penelope dropped her pen, letting it hit the desk with a hard *CLUNK*. "Tell you what, dear, I'm going to compile all your information and search my roster of current clients. Then I'll get back to you with a list of prospective matches."

"That'd be great," Ava said. She stood up. "Thank you so much. This is going to be fun."

"I hope so," Miss Penelope said in a faint voice.

"Why did that sound like a threat?" Carmela asked as they headed back down the steps.

But Ava remained upbeat. "I think this matchmaking thing is going to work out great. I have complete confidence that Miss Penelope will find a man who'll give me everything I want."

"Right now, I want a glass of wine," Carmela said.

"Ooh, twist my arm, *cher*."

"C'mon, we'll head over to St. Peter Street. There's supposed to be a good zydeco street party going on tonight."

They strolled along Chartres Street as moonlight dappled the cobblestones and bounced off wrought-iron grillwork on timeworn brick storefronts. Baskets of fanciful pink bougainvillea hung down from balconies and gas lamps glowed in the dark as Ava and Carmela walked past oyster bars, raucous cocktail lounges, a T-shirt shop, and an art gallery. At first the music that drifted

184

toward them sounded faint, like an old-fashioned radio signal fading in and out. But as they finally rounded the corner and hit St. Peter Street, they were suddenly enveloped in an earsplitting, riotous cocoon of good old-fashioned zydeco music.

Sittin' here in La La
Waitin' for my Ya Ya
Uh huh, uh huh

"Love this!" Ava shrieked.

On a brightly lit stage, dead center in the middle of the street, the Zydeco Boyz were playing their hearts out to hundreds of revelers. Dressed in purple and green T-shirts and faded jeans, the two fiddlers, accordion player, drummer, and guy with a rubboard on his chest played their tunes in a superfast tempo. People clapped, danced, and sang along. Dozens of street vendors trolled their way through the crowd hawking everything from Jazz Fest T-shirts to salted peanuts and colored beads.

"It's wine o'clock," Carmela said as they waded through the crowd to a nearby wine bar. "Merlot?"

"Why not?"

Carmela got them two glasses of merlot in plastic geaux cups. She handed a cup to

185

Ava, took a sip, and said, "This is what I love most about New Orleans. Look at this crowd, young and old, tourists and homies. Everybody happy and singing together like old friends."

"It's a super mellow vibe," Ava agreed.

They listened to the music for a while, then eased their way down the block as a court jester on stilts walked by tossing out strands of colorful Mardi Gras beads. A handful landed on Ava's shoulder.

"Thank you so much, tall, dark, and . . . tall," Ava called out.

She draped a few strands of beads over Carmela's head, then dropped the rest around her own neck.

"Maybe we should grab something to eat?" Carmela said.

They strolled to the end of the block where a half dozen food trucks were parked, perfuming the night air with the most delicious aromas. There were muffuletta and roast beef sandwiches, fried green tomatoes, bell peppers stuffed with shrimp and rice, andouille sausage, and onion rings.

"Definitely the fried green tomatoes," Ava said.

"With remoulade sauce for dipping," Carmela agreed.

"Uh-oh, there's my downfall over there, a

potato po-boy. French bread stuffed with French fries, gravy, and mayo."

"You'll for sure boost your caloric intake if you eat that," Carmela said. She was always amazed at the variety of po-boys out there. Beef, shrimp, crawfish, crab, oyster, sausage, catfish, pork, tofu, and (her tastes didn't run that way, but a few people's did) even sweetbread po-boys.

Halfway through their jumbo basket of fried green tomatoes, the Zydeco Boyz wound up "Zydeco Boogaloo" with a flourish, reveling in the applause from the appreciative crowd.

"It's not over, is it?" Ava asked.

"The band's just taking a break," Carmela said. "Not to worry, they'll be back soon."

Ava bounced up and down on the balls of her feet. "But we need music!"

Carmela held up a hand. "Listen."

Ava looked around. "Where from?"

"You hear that, right?"

Ava listened carefully. "Yeah. The faint strain of a jazz saxophone." She bobbed her head. "I love a sax."

"The joy of sax," Carmela said. "What's not to like?"

"Let's go find . . . whoa!" Ava said. She was suddenly brought up short as two creepy-looking Beastmaster Puppets brushed past her. She whirled toward Carmela. "Did you see those guys? I'm not hallucinating, am I?"

"Not on one glass of wine."

"That was a couple of honkin' big Beastmaster Puppets that just whipped past us," Ava said.

"I would say so."

"Let's follow them. I bet they're on their way to some kind of private party."

Carmela, who tended to err on the side of caution (except when she was hot and heavy into an investigation), said, "You think?" But they both started to edge their way down the block in the direction the two giant puppets had gone.

"I think they kind of ghosted their way into that old brick building that used to be a mask shop," Ava said.

They were a half block down Dauphine Street now, walking past a small grocery store, jewelry shop, and coin shop that were all closed up tight for the night.

"Kind of dark down here," Carmela said. "Not so many people."

"The action's over on St. Peter Street," Ava said. Then she squinted at the brick building with its purple door and small brass lamp flickering next to it and said, "Or maybe not."

"What is this place?" Carmela asked.

"I don't know, but it looks mysterious. And I'm pretty sure it's where those two puppet guys disappeared into."

They walked up to the purple door, hesitated for a moment, then Carmela got up her courage and knocked.

Like the proverbial drawbridge in Dracula's castle, the door creaked open slowly to reveal a man in a shiny black cape with a chalk white face.

"Jeepers," Ava said, taking a step backward.

CHAPTER 15

The keeper of the door may have been kitted out like a Transylvanian count, but his accent was pure Southern good old boy.

"Hep ya?" he asked. His voice sounded slightly muddled because he had to talk around his fake incisors.

"We're here for the party," Ava said. With the door open, music and the buzz of conversation seeped out, along with the clink of ice cubes in glasses. "Definitely party time in there," Ava said as a quiet aside to Carmela.

The vampire gave them a speculative look as he produced a clipboard and proceeded to scan it. "And you are . . . ?"

Like a shadow emerging from a fogbank, Richard Drake loomed in the doorway before them.

"Justin, these charming ladies are my guests," Drake said in rounded mellow tones. He wore an old-fashioned dove gray morning suit complete with vest and long cape. The only thing his Edwardian outfit lacked was a silk top hat and a silver-tipped cane.

"Well, thank you," Ava drawled. She offered Drake her hand, and he obligingly bent forward and kissed it gently.

"This is definitely the party place," Carmela said. She noted that Drake was still gazing at Ava (who was mooning back at him) but hadn't bothered to look at her.

"This is a pop-up party," Drake said finally. "An adult playroom for a close-knit group of like-minded revelers."

"Like the Beastmaster puppeteers?" Ava asked him. "Are you also a puppeteer?"

Drake gave an ambiguous smile. "In a way, but of a different sort."

"Was that a yes?" Ava asked.

"That was a maybe," Drake said. "But where are my manners? Won't you ladies come in and join the revelry?" He led them into an anteroom that was painted completely black and had an enormous silver-gray gargoyle hanging from the ceiling. There were red velvet couches and love seats scattered all around and tall flickering candles in the corners.

As Carmela's eyes grew accustomed to the dark, she could see people seated on the furniture, talking in low voices, and sipping drinks.

"How interesting that we've crossed paths with you again," Carmela said to Drake. "Twice in one day."

He smiled back at her but offered no reply.

Carmela forged ahead. "I trust you suffered no ill effects from your earlier run-in with the somewhat unruly T.J.?"

"That," Drake said, "was most unfortunate. Rowdy behavior is never acceptable in polite company. I do apologize."

"Oh, we didn't mind one little bit," Ava said, fluffing her hair. "Fights are always kind of exciting. Like old-fashioned duels."

"Still, I hope you ladies don't think less of me," Drake said.

"We don't think much of anything," Carmela said. "Because we don't really know you." Deep in her heart lurked the red-hot suspicion that Drake could very well be Devon Dowling's killer.

"Excuse me," Ava said, "but I've been meaning to ask, how do you do that thing where you look like you're gliding on air?"

"Practice," Drake said. He ducked his head down and nuzzled the side of her neck.

"Mr. Drake!" Ava squealed, but she was pleased.

Carmela could see that Ava was vibrating

like a tuning fork.

This is not good. I do not want Ava to get involved with this man.

"Is there a place we can get a drink around here?"

Carmela asked. "A cocktail," Ava said. "I'd love a cocktail."

"Our very own Hellfire Club happens to be right downstairs," Drake said.

"Say what?" said Ava.

"Our bar," Drake said.

"In that case," Ava said.

"You see the stairs over there?" Drake pointed across the room.

"The ones under the glowing bat?" Carmela asked. *Jeez, this place is trippy.*

"That's right. Go ahead and follow them down," Drake said.

"You're not going to join us?" Ava asked, obviously disappointed.

"Perhaps . . . later," Drake said.

The hellfire club might have been a pop-up bar, but it looked like it had been there since the last century. Actually, the century before World War I. An old-fashioned wooden bar stretched across the basement room. Behind it were ornately carved shelves that held an array of glittering liquor bottles and, Carmela was fairly sure, a few bottles of absinthe.

The ceiling was low, the floor was pieced together from shards of slate, and the walls were stacked boulders reinforced with wood pilings. Dim red lights and a few candles lent an eerie glow.

"Creepers," Ava said. "What is this place?"

"I think it really is the Hellfire Club," Carmela said. "I mean, look at this place. It's like something out of a Victorian novel. Or a dungeon that some crazy French nobleman put together in the seventeenth century."

"And everybody is wearing costumes," Ava said. "Except us."

"I guess we didn't get the memo."

"We could at least get a drink."

They stepped up to the bar and glanced around.

"Hah, there's even a drink menu," Carmela said.

"Yeah, but look at the names. Crapple Bomb, Goat's Delight, Atomic Cat, Cement Mixer, Flaming Gorilla. I don't know what these drinks are, and I get around!"

"Help you, ladies?" A bartender was leaning forward on the bar and staring at them. He had a dark widow's peak and bags under his eyes, and he wore his goatee long and braided. His hands and arms were tattooed all the way up to his waffle weave shirt. He could have been thirty or seventy.

"Um, what's good here?" Ava asked. "You got any recommendations?"

"I make a mean Duracell Cocktail," the bartender said. "And if you like to live dangerously, there's always a shot of Fireball to warm your innards."

"I've heard about that," Carmela said. "What is that, whisky?"

The bartender nodded as he reached back and grabbed a bottle of Fireball.

"Cinnamon whisky," he said as he spun two shot glasses onto the bar and poured amber liquid into each of them. "Down the hatch, ladies, my compliments."

"That's a challenge if I ever heard one," said Ava.

She picked up her glass and tossed back the whisky while Carmela took a judicious sip.

"Wheee!" Ava cried out, slamming her glass down onto the bar. "That's like drinking molten lava right from a volcano!"

"Piquant but with a caustic nip," the bartender said.

"Hot and spicy," Carmela said. "But I do like that cinnamon."

"Another round?" the bartender asked.

"Maybe we should get a nice safe glass of wine," Ava suggested. "Instead of going for another Fireball."

"Works for me," Carmela said. Three tiny sips had been enough for her.

They ordered wine, sipped it, and watched as more people arrived downstairs.

"Do you get the feeling something is about to happen?" Ava asked.

"I do," Carmela said. "But I have no idea what."

"Something to do with puppets?"

"Maybe."

"Ooh, don't look now, but Old Scratch is watching us," Ava said.

"Old who?" Carmela glanced around.

"I said *don't* look."

"Okay, I'm not looking. Now tell me again what you just said."

"There's a devil watching us. You know, as in Beelzebub or Mephisto? He's sitting at the end of the bar, kind of peering at us from behind a post."

When Carmela got a chance, she casually glanced that way. And discovered that Ava was right. A man in a shiny red mask with tiny white horns and a slim-cut black jacket was staring intently at them.

"Who could that be?" Carmela asked.

Ava shrugged. "Dunno. But it's weird.

Kooky."

"This whole place is kooky."

"Yeah, it kind of gives me the creeps."

"Holy crap, Ava, now what are those ninja puppet guys doing?"

They both turned away from the bar and watched as a half dozen ninjas formed a circle and grabbed a series of black ropes. Their eyes followed the ropes up to the ceiling where some kind of black, poufy shroud hung in the center of the room.

"What *is* that thing?" Ava asked. "Some kind of weird piñata?"

Suddenly, a man's voice boomed over a loudspeaker.

"Ladies and gentlemen, if you'll please direct your eyes to the center of the room."

"I hope something doesn't pop out at us," Carmela said.

Everyone's eyes were focused on the dark thing that hung suspended from the ceiling. Then, as if a silent command had been given, the ninjas jerked on the ropes, causing the shroud to pull away.

An enormous puppet suddenly dangled in the center of the room.

"It's a woman!" Ava cried. "Wearing an ornate eighteenth-century ball gown."

"But look where her head's supposed to be!" Carmela cried.

The woman's head was completely missing, and red streamers, meant to indicate blood, fluttered from her gaping neck.

"OMG, there is no head," Ava said in a startled voice.

"Ladies and gentlemen," the announcer intoned. "I give you the newest addition to the Beastmaster Puppet Theater. Queen Marie Antoinette!"

"Whoa!" Ava said. "This is beyond creepy."

"But not as creepy as the devil that just got up from his barstool and is heading our way." Carmela grabbed Ava's arm and said, "Let's get outa here!"

They sprinted up the stairs, fighting their way against a tide of people who were coming down, anxious to get a look at the new Marie Antoinette puppet.

"Hurry, hurry," Carmela urged. She continued to pull Ava behind her.

"Oh man," Ava cried, "I knew coming here was a bad idea."

"You did? Really? And you didn't say anything?" They were upstairs now, Carmela hurdling a footstool and losing her grip on Ava. "Come on. Hurry up!"

Ava was right behind her, panting like crazy, her stilettos ringing against the wooden floor like a pair of castanets.

"Just a few more steps and we're home free," Carmela huffed. She slid to a stop, pushed her shoulder against the front door to shove it open, and screamed!

Ava didn't know why Carmela was screaming, but when she heard her friend shriek, she couldn't hold back, either. Together they cowered in front of a tall man who was backlit in the doorway. With the faint glow from a streetlamp, they were unable to see his face.

"Wait. What?" Carmela said. She touched a hand to her chest and let out a gasp of recognition It was Babcock!

"What are you doing here?" Babcock yelled, stunned out of his mind to literally run into them like this.

"What are *you* doing here?" Carmela yelled back. She still wasn't using her indoor voice.

"I was following someone I *thought* was Roy Sultan. But I lost him. He either came in here or ducked down the alley."

"You think Sultan came in here?" Carmela asked.

"Maybe he was the one who was watching us!" Ava cried. "And wearing the devil costume."

"Somebody was *watching* you?"

199

"Old Scratch," Ava said.

Babcock looked puzzled. "He was scratching? You mean like making obscene gestures?"

"No, like coming after us," Carmela said.

"Who is this guy?" Babcock asked. "Show me!"

So the three of them descended to the Hellfire Club and looked around the very crowded room.

"Ye cats!" Babcock said when he saw Marie Antoinette hanging there, sans head. "What the hell is that thing supposed to be?"

"Their newest puppet," Carmela said. "Like it?"

"It's hideous," Babcock said. "Enough to give you nightmares."

"I think that's the general idea," Carmela said.

Babcock surveyed the bar. "Where's your devil guy? Point him out to me."

"I don't see him," Ava said. "He's gone. He must have ducked out."

"Are they selling drinks here?" Babcock asked. "If it's a cash bar, they need a special permit to do that."

Carmela touched his shoulder. "Can you not be a bureaucrat for one minute? Can you maybe just take us home?"

They left quietly and crawled into Babcock's car, which was parked a half block away. Nobody spoke as he drove them back to their apartment complex and pulled into the back alley.

Then Ava clambered out of the back seat and said, "Well, it's been peachy. Thanks for being my wingman, Carmela. Thanks for the ride, Edgar."

In the darkness, Babcock said, "Where did you two go tonight? Besides that weird party."

"Matchmaker," Carmela said.

"I don't know what that is. Explain, please."

"You know, like in *Fiddler on the Roof*. Ava hired a woman to fix her up with a suitable date."

"She needs somebody to fix her up? Ava does?" Babcock chuckled. "Now I know you're pulling my leg."

"It's the truth," Carmela said.

"The kind of truth where you're only a sort-of partner in a wine bar? That kind of stretched-out, bungled-up truth?"

"I wasn't deliberately trying to upset you, really I wasn't." *Dear Lord, he brought up the wine bar again?* "I just thought the wine bar would be a fun thing. A diversion. And then it all got away from me."

"So you're really not a proprietor?"

"Of course not. What it comes down to is this — I'd probably teach one painting class one night a week. And if that works out, then Gabby and I will alternate. So it'd only be every other week."

Babcock gazed at her expectantly.

"And I promise I'll have Quigg change that sign. Remove my name."

"Tonight?"

"Well, more like tomorrow. And if he doesn't, I'll climb up on a ladder myself and slop on five gallons of white paint."

"Promise?" Babcock asked.

"I do."

Babcock's face creased in a smile. "Carmela, those are the words I definitely want to hear from you."

CHAPTER 16

Thursday morning and the French Quarter was flush with blue skies, abundant sunshine, toe-tappin' music, and good feelings.

"I knew Babcock would come around, I just knew it," Gabby said. She and Carmela had hung out their *OPEN* sign and were standing at the front counter sipping cups of strong chicory coffee from their trademark *MEMORY MINE* mugs.

"I promised him I'd only be leading a class now and then. That you and I would be trading off," Carmela said.

"And he's okay with that?"

"He said he was." Carmela looked thoughtful. "You know, I think Babcock's finally learning to trust me."

"That's the most critical element in a relationship."

"Do you trust Stuart?" Carmela asked.

"No," Gabby laughed. "Of course not. I may be sweet, but I'm not stupid."

Carmela nodded. "There you go. The age-old unacknowledged tension between men and women."

Their reverie was interrupted by two women who burst through their front door expectantly.

"We're visiting for the weekend," one of the women announced. "And we were told this was craft central in New Orleans."

"Your information was spot-on," Carmela said. "Come on in and let's see what we can do to get your creative juices flowing."

"We're sisters," the woman said, as if Carmela and Gabby couldn't tell by their nearly identical curly brown hair and wide smiles. "I'm Janice and she's Denise. I'm into painting and Denise is way big into scrapbooking."

"Carmela's our resident painter," Gabby said to Janice. "And I'm pretty heavy into scrapbooking myself." She pointed at their wall of scrapbook paper. "Want to take a look?"

"Do I ever," said Denise.

While Gabby and Denise pored over paper, Carmela led Janice to the back of the store where she had a stash of blank canvases as well as unpainted birdhouses, wooden frames, candleholders, and cigar boxes.

"Cool," Janice said. "You paint on all this stuff?"

"And more," Carmela said. "Plates, rocks, knickknack shelves, canvas bags, you name it."

"I love that cute little cigar box. You think I could give something like that a whirl?"

Carmela grabbed the unpainted cigar box off the shelf and placed it on the table.

"But I'm not sure where to start," Janice said.

Carmela held up an index finger. "Give me a second." She ducked into her office, grabbed a cigar box she'd decorated several months ago, and handed it to Janice.

"Wow." Janice was enthralled. "It looks like an antique box that was crafted during the Renaissance."

"That's the whole idea," Carmela said. "Give it some personality, make it look old. For this box I painted the inside gold and the outside black. Then I rubbed a smidge of black paint over the gold and distressed the outside. Then I scrubbed on just a hint of blue paint and some bronze glaze. And you see how the lock and hinges have a green patina?"

"Nice."

"It's really just paint. The thing is, you can create almost any special effect using paint. And a judicious application of two or three layers is always useful for giving wood a faux aged look."

"And then you added those cute little angel faces," Janice said.

"The painter Raphael's angels. They come as decals."

"I think I'd like to try that," Janice said.

While the two sisters happily crafted their way through the morning, Carmela and Ava waited on several more customers. One woman wanted metallic ribbon and matching brads so she could decorate cream-colored pillar candles for her dinner party.

Another woman wanted charms so she could make her own dangly earrings. Of course Carmela had a rather wondrous stash of charms in the form of dragonflies, keys, Egyptian elements, petroglyphs, and animals.

And, finally, two more regulars, Jill and her daughter, Kristen, wanted a pink album so they could put together a scrapbook for baby Jillian.

Back at the front counter, Carmela signed for a UPS package and skimmed through the morning mail.

"Anything?" Gabby asked.

"A few vendor invoices." She picked up the UPS parcel and shook it. "And I think our calligraphy pens finally arrived."

"I can't believe that tonight's going to be your first painting class next door. You must be excited!"

"More like nervous."

"You? Carmela, you've taught so many craft classes over the years that this should be like child's play!"

"But none of the classes I've taught had Quigg Brevard breathing down my neck. Or Babcock lurking in the wings, waiting for me to fall on my face."

"He wouldn't do that," Gabby said.

Carmela stared at her.

"Well, I think you'll do just fine. Better than fine."

Carmela breathed a sigh. "All we can do is start slow and see how it goes. A paint-your-plate class tonight, miniature canvases next Tuesday."

Gabby smiled. "And then we'll switch off."

"You're sure Stuart's okay with you helping me?" Carmela asked.

"Stuart's a pussycat. I guess Babcock's the one we should worry about after all. There could be . . . what would you call it? Recidivism?"

"He doesn't like me working with Quigg, that's for sure. But he's tolerating it for now."

"The man is a saint."

"Well, I wouldn't go *that* far."

While Gabby rang up a customer at the counter, Carmela slipped into her office and dialed Babcock's number. Gabby's comment about him being a saint was swirling in her brain, and she wanted to make darned sure that things were still copacetic between them.

"Hello?" Babcock said. "What?"

"Don't sound so excited," Carmela said.

"Carmela?"

"You were expecting someone else?"

"In this job I never know what to expect," Babcock said. "We're always on the fine edge of disaster around here."

"And they're talking about making you a chief?"

"Bite your tongue, because I don't want the job. I don't need the headache and hassle."

"How about the status and extra income?" Carmela asked.

"Well . . ."

"Exactly." Then, "I thought we should talk."

"We are talking," Babcock said.

"I mean about . . . you know."

"We're good."

"Did you go back and try to find Roy Sultan last night?"

"No. I think I got a bum tip."

"You were following him because you got a tip?"

"An anonymous tip. Tiresome, isn't it?" Babcock said. There was a burst of loud voices on his end, and then he said, "Sorry, sweetheart, gotta run."

Carmela sat there for a few minutes, thinking about the devil she'd seen last night in the Hellfire Club, wondering who it could have been. When she couldn't come up with any definitive answer, she grabbed a huge cardboard box and carried it out to the craft table. Janice and Denise had since left, and Carmela was anxious to get a jump on her class.

"What have you got there?" Gabby asked.

Carmela reached in and pulled out a tall glass cylinder.

"It looks like you're about to make a terrarium," Gabby said.

"Something like that, only minus the green plants and dirt."

"Ah, this is for your Vacation in a Bottle class. What time's that supposed to start?"

"Two o'clock," Carmela said.

"I can't wait to see what you come up with."

"Neither can I," Carmela said as she dumped a small bag of fine white sand into the glass jar. "After all, I'm breaking new ground here. Literally."

In between helping customers, Carmela worked on her vacation in a jar. She put in a red rubber flip-flop, added some colorful shells, a starfish, and an old pair of sunglasses. She was contemplating what else to add, when, out of the blue, Trevor Jackson — T.J. — walked into her shop.

"May I help you?" Gabby asked. She was standing behind the front counter, ringing up a customer.

T.J. spotted Carmela at the craft table, waved a hand at her, and walked back through the shop.

"T.J.," Carmela said. This was a nasty surprise. What could he possibly want?

T.J. stared at her with eyes that were narrowed and intense. "I need a favor. I need your help."

"Excuse me?" Carmela was completely taken aback since, in her mind, T.J. was still a legitimate suspect. "Help with what? What can I do?"

"Can we talk somewhere privately?"

Carmela sighed as she led him into her office. She had no idea where this was going. Maybe she didn't want to know.

"That was quite a scene you created yesterday," she said as she plunked herself down in her chair. "At the funeral luncheon."

T.J. settled in a director's chair opposite her and did everything but hang his head. "I . . . That was really stupid," he said. "Inexcusable. I don't know what came over me."

I do. You went totally postal.

He rubbed his arm gingerly. "I've even got bruises from tossing that chair and then falling on my ass."

I bet you do. Dummy.

"So what do you want?" Carmela asked. She got right to the point because she was busy. Customers, crafts, a murder investigation. No sense making small talk with some goofball who went ballistic at the drop of a hat. No sense at all.

"I need your help," T.J. said.

"Yes, you mentioned that. In what way?"

In a halting, plaintive voice, T.J. said, "I know you're in tight with Detective Babcock. So I was hoping that maybe you could talk to him, kind of intercede for me, and get this police investigation off my back."

Carmela kept her voice neutral. "I don't think that's going to happen."

"But the police seem to think that *I* killed

211

Mr. Dowling! When I didn't!" T.J. cried.

"They think your quick temper and penchant for getting into fights warrants a serious look."

And by the way, were you the devil last night? Were you the one watching us at the Hellfire Club?

T.J. touched two fingers to the side of his head as if trying to tamp back his disappointment. "It's because I've been so upset these past few days. It's how I deal with grief! I know I'm not the most mature individual in the world . . . I let my emotions run completely wild. But I feel *horrible* about Mr. Dowling being killed. You *know* that!"

"Uh-huh," Carmela said.

"Please. You have to believe me."

The jury's still out, pal.

When Carmela didn't answer, T.J. said, "If you won't plead my case, who will?"

"I'm afraid," Carmela said, "that you're going to have to gut this out on your own."

"Until the police find the *real* killer," T.J. said. He sounded utterly despondent.

Carmela stared at him intently. "Until they find the killer. Yes."

"I wish he hadn't come in here," Gabby said once T.J. had left. "You've told me so many awful things about him that now he kind of frightens me. I kept waiting for something horrible to happen. For him to start knocking over displays or something."

"T.J. can be pretty erratic," Carmela said.

"Didn't Babcock tell you to keep the door locked? Well, maybe we should."

"Maybe."

"We could get one of those discreet doorbells and hang out a sign that says *RING FOR SERVICE.*"

"You mean the kind of snooty little sign that intimidates customers and scares them away?" Carmela asked. But she was half teasing.

"Oh, you. Forget I even mentioned it. Now what was I . . . oh, I know. Mrs. Delachaise called. You remember Mrs. Delachaise?"

"The woman we designed the invitations for," Carmela said. "For her daughter's bridal shower."

Gabby nodded. "She wants to stop by and pick them up."

"We don't have them yet."

Gabby tapped a foot nervously. "When do you think we will have them?"

"How about just as soon as I run down to the printer and grab them?"

"When would that be?"

Carmela glanced at her watch. It was just after eleven. "Now?"

"Thank you," Gabby breathed.

The sun was still shining and the weather was even warmer as Carmela walked down Esplanade Street, headed for Inkspot, one of her favorite printers. A street musician plucked away at a guitar, and a Lucky Dogs hot dog vendor and a mule-drawn cart that sold hand-pulled taffy were both parked at the corner. It was all Carmela could do not to grab a dog and a sticky treat. Even better, a gelato truck was parked farther down the block. *Vesuvius Gelato* was written on the side of the truck in fanciful script, and there was a drawing of Mt. Vesuvius topped with a gelato cone. But Mrs. Delachaise was waiting. And Gabby was on pins and needles.

Carmela swung through the door into Inkspot, inhaling the pungent aroma of hot ink and paper. She had one hand raised, ready to bid hi and hello to Harvey, the owner, but before she could get a peep out of her mouth, she saw Roy Sultan standing at the front counter. He was wearing a three-piece cream-colored suit that made him look as if he was auditioning for the role of Colonel Sanders.

"Carmela!" Harvey called out effusively when he saw her, and he raised a hand in greeting. Which caused Roy Sultan to turn around and stare at her.

Oh boy. Two suspects in one day. To what do I owe this honor?

"Hi, Harvey," Carmela said. "Hello," she said to Sultan. She couldn't exactly ignore him, since he was standing right there at the counter.

"Yes, hello." Sultan was cool in returning her greeting.

And then, because Carmela prided herself on being able to elicit bits and bytes of information from the most reluctant of subjects, she said, "Picking something up?"

"Folders and sales sheets," Sultan mumbled.

"Here you go, Mr. Sultan," Harvey said. He slid two large boxes across the counter.

"Those must be for your big real estate project," Carmela said. She kept her demeanor neutral, hoping he'd forgotten their somewhat nasty run-in yesterday at the funeral.

"That's right," Sultan said. His ego was too big to contain, though, and he was suddenly eager to talk about his fancy-ass project. He opened one of the boxes and pulled out a glitzy folder emblazoned with

SULTAN REAL ESTATE. There was a crest — maybe crossed swords and an eagle? — that hearkened back to the sad demise of the Romanoffs.

Carmela didn't know what the crest was supposed to represent, but she gave an encouraging nod as Sultan continued to show her his finished pieces. There were sales sheets for each of his three different condo models, the Manchester three-bedroom unit, the Marigny two-bedroom unit, and the Magnolia one-bedroom unit.

"Very impressive," Carmela said. "And to think you brought this project to fruition so rapidly."

"Oh no." Sultan shook his head vigorously. "This building has been in the works for a long time. This is what I do, after all. Lease space to tenants, rehab buildings, buy investment properties. Yup, there's good money in real estate."

"I'm sure there is," Carmela said as Sultan gathered up his boxes and hustled out the door.

"Here you go, Carmela," said Harvey. "Your invitations. Rose gold embossing plus we used the hundred-and-twenty-pound cardstock, just as you requested."

"Wonderful, Harvey. Thank you so much." Carmela paused. "Tell me something, will you? When did Roy Sultan put in his order for his folders and sales sheets?"

Harvey's eyes crinkled in amusement. "Are you kidding? It was a super rush job that we had to turn around in less than four days." He wiped a hand on his ink-stained apron. "It's as if the guy woke up one morning and said, 'This is the day my building's going condo.' "

CHAPTER 17

"You're back. And just in time for lunch," Gabby said.

Carmela set the box of invitations on the front counter and glanced at the wall clock. "I'm starving. What did you have in mind?"

"I think I should run out and grab muffulettas from the Merci Beaucoup Bakery. The ones stuffed with capicola, salami, mortadella, and provolone." She smiled at Carmela. "As you might have guessed, I have a craving."

"Okay then, go. But be sure to bring one back for me."

Carmela slid behind the front counter just as a customer came in.

"Help you?" she said.

The woman looked around the shop and smiled. "I hope so. I'm interested in making a collage, but I need some suggestions on how to get started."

"Did you have a theme in mind?"

218

The woman pulled a sheaf of sheet music from her bag. "I have all this old sheet music from the '30s. I thought maybe I could work it in somehow."

"That's a wonderful idea," Carmela said. She pulled out a piece of tagboard and handed it to the woman. "You glue a few artfully ripped pieces of sheet music onto this. Then . . ." Carmela walked over to her display of rubber stamps and pulled out a bird stamp. "You stamp the bird on the sheet music, color it in using colored pencils, add a few paper flowers."

"I love that," said the woman.

"Then go a little crazy. Glue a strip of black mesh or burlap at the bottom, crumple up some more paper and glue it on, then spatter on some paint."

"To create multiple layers," said the woman.

"You can never have too many layers. It's like a good gumbo, you just keep adding ingredients to make it richer."

Carmela rang up the woman's purchases and bid good-bye just as Gabby slipped back into the shop and dropped two white paper bags on the counter along with two large paper cups filled with sweet tea.

Carmela eyed the bags. "I can just imagine the spicy olive salad soaking into that soft muffuletta bread."

Gabby shoved a bag at her. "Then go eat. Don't choke your sandwich down *too* fast, but hurry a little before we get busy again."

Carmela retreated to her office, sank into her chair, and unwrapped the thick sandwich. She took a bite. Mmn. Good and juicy. While she ate, she skimmed through her e-mails. One was a request for her to do a demo for a scrapbooking club in Shreveport. Yes, that might be a lot of fun.

Carmela answered a few more e-mails, then worked on a schedule for upcoming classes. Between honchoing classes at Quigg's wine bar and teaching her own classes, she'd have to noodle around a few more creative ideas. Maybe an eco scrapbook class on going green? Or artistic storytelling?

She'd just clicked Send when Gabby popped her head in.

"Mrs. Delachaise is here for her invitations," Gabby said.

"Great."

As soon as Mrs. Delachaise saw Carmela, the mother of the soon-to-be bride plopped her bright red Longchamp tote on the counter and said, "I'm so excited. I can hardly wait to see them."

Carmela lifted the top of the box and

handed Mrs. Delachaise one of the invitations. She watched as her face changed from anticipation to sheer delight.

"Oh my, these are stunning. Even better than you promised," Mrs. Delachaise said.

"The rose gold embossing worked beautifully on the heavy cream-colored stock," Carmela said. "As you can see, I really pushed the printer to do an extra special job."

"And they did. Thank you."

Carmela placed the cover back on the box and handed it to Mrs. Delachaise. "Enjoy. Have fun sending them out. Let us know how it goes."

"This is why I love working here," Gabby said, once Mrs. Delachaise was out the door. "We get to make someone blissfully happy every single day."

"And don't tell anybody," Carmela said, "but the whole creative process is fun for *us,* too!"

Gabby bobbed her head. "Designing cards and invitations and posters is a total hoot."

At two o'clock on the dot, the bell over the front door ding-dinged and two of Memory Mine's most steadfast crafters came bustling in. Tandy Bliss and Baby Fontaine.

"We're back," Tandy boomed. "Did you

miss us?"

"It feels like ages," Carmela said. "Even though we just saw you darlings two days ago."

Baby gave Carmela a double air-kiss and said, "And look what Miss Skinny Britches brought along for us to nosh on."

"Buttermilk jumbles," Tandy said, dropping a round tin on the craft table. "And are they ever good." She looked around, rubbed her hands together, and said, "I'm ready to dig into this project. After my trip to New York, I've been dying to figure out how to use all the doodads I schlepped home."

Her sentence was punctuated by another ding-ding as three more women piled into the shop. An older woman who introduced herself as Madge and two young women who wore matching green Tulane sweatshirts. Josie and Madison.

Madison pointed a thumb over her shoulder indicating a small backpack. "We brought lots of souvenirs and stuff for class."

"Then let's get started," Carmela said.

Everyone settled in as Gabby placed large glass cylinders in front of each one of them.

"Today," Carmela said, "we're going to turn your vacation treasures into forever keepsakes."

"Wow," Madison said.

"Best of all, we're going to show you a unique way to display them."

There was a spatter of applause, and Carmela held up the sample jar she'd made earlier.

"As you can see, my vacation was at the beach. I started with a base of sand, along with a few shells and pebbles scattered in. Then I added the red flip-flop for color, and the sunglasses for fun, and a little paper parasol that reminds me I had a fabulous time."

Everyone laughed.

Madge said, "If we didn't vacation at the beach, what would we use as a base?"

"Great question. Let's say you visited Paris. You could take a French newspaper and crumple it up. Then add a miniature Eiffel Tower."

Madge still didn't look sure.

"Don't worry about it," Carmela said. "We've got plenty of florist's putty, colored pebbles, hunks of driftwood, and gemstones that can anchor your display."

Tandy held up a hand. "What about for my New York trip?"

"New York is fairly glittery," Carmela said. "So let's put in a few colored gems. Then you can add your rolled-up *Playbill* and . . .

what else have you got?"

"A miniature Empire State Building and Statue of Liberty," Tandy said.

"Perfect," Carmela said. "What else?"

"Some theater tickets and a yellow cab the size of a Matchbox car."

"You're off and running," Carmela said as she moved on to help Madison display a fan, miniature Kabuki mask, chopsticks, and brocade coin purse, all souvenirs from her trip to Japan.

As everyone got busy, munched cookies, and exchanged ideas, Carmela sat down next to Baby, who was arranging mementos from her Hawaiian vacation.

"How you doin'?" Carmela asked.

"Good. Great," Baby said. "This is a lot of fun."

"I was wondering," Carmela said, "if you knew Colonel Barnett Otis? I understand he owns a home in the Garden District."

Baby turned to her with big blue eyes. "He's been my neighbor forever. He and Del play golf together once in a while. Over at Belle Terre. Why the sudden curiosity?"

"Not so sudden. He and Devon had an issue over a piece of art."

Baby put a hand to her mouth. "Oh my gosh, you don't think that Colonel Otis could have . . ."

"I don't know. At least I don't *think* so."

"But you're curious. And worried. I can tell because when you're fretting about something you develop a teeny-tiny line between your eyebrows."

"If this is a pitch for Botox, forget it," Carmela laughed.

"No, it's just . . ." Baby waved a hand. "Never mind. What do you want to know?"

Carmela shrugged. "Whatever you can tell me."

"Well, I know that Colonel Otis is a former stockbroker who collects art, drinks bourbon, and entertains on a fairly frequent basis."

"So he's retired." Carmela hadn't collected art, drunk bourbon, or entertained formally in years. She was always too scattered, too busy.

"And he's older, probably in his early seventies, so I can't imagine he would be able to get the jump on someone." Baby saw the doubt on Carmela's face and added, "But you never know."

"No, you never know," Carmela said. "But thanks for the . . . information."

"Are you going to talk to him?" Baby asked. "Or, better yet, have Babcock question him?"

"I think Babcock already has." Carmela

225

turned the idea of Colonel Otis over in her mind. He was still on her list. But running into Roy Sultan today had moved *him* up a couple notches as well. Somebody was guilty, but nobody was talking.

As the women worked on their jars — with Gabby offering words of encouragement — Carmela grabbed the sample plate Quigg had given her. She decided she'd better paint it to use as an example tonight. But what to paint?

She went into her office, grabbed one of her sketchbooks, and thumbed through it.

There. The butterfly.

She grabbed a set of paints and got to work, swirling on a light wash of blues, green, pinks, and oranges, but letting a little white space show through. Then she painted a swallowtail butterfly, outlining him (or her) in black, and then daubing in green and yellow dots on the wings.

"That's gorgeous!" Baby cried. She'd tiptoed in to see what Carmela was working on.

"Thank you," Carmela said. She stood up and peered out her doorway. "I didn't mean to leave you guys high and dry."

"You didn't," Tandy said, glancing up. "We've been having a merry old time."

"We sure have," Madison said as everyone

else nodded along. "Will you be putting a schedule for more classes on your website?"

"Count on it," Carmela said. She watched as everyone smiled and began tidying their work space. They were getting ready to leave, anxious to carry home their prized vacation in a jar keepsake.

"Carmela," Gabby said. She was standing at the front counter, holding up a finger. "Telephone."

"Good-bye," Carmela said, half walking Josie and Madison to the door. "Thanks for coming. Hope to see you real soon." She hurried back to her office and grabbed the phone. "Carmela here."

"Guess what! I've got a date!"

"Ava?"

"Miss Penelope set me up with a really sweet guy."

"You already talked to him?"

"He called a few minutes ago. And we're going out *tonight.* Carmela, you gotta stop by and wish me luck!"

"Today? Now?"

"Yes!" Ava said. "You're my mentor. My moral compass. My crazy BFF."

"But I've got . . ."

"Please!" Ava squealed.

Carmela glanced at her watch. If she ran fast, hit all the green walk lights, and didn't twist an ankle in the process, she could probably squeeze this in.

"Okay, hang tight. I'll see you in little bit."

Carmela touched a finger to her plate. Good. It was drying. By the time her class rolled around at Blush and Brush, it'd be perfect.

Now all she had to do was . . .

"Carmela."

She whirled around to find Jekyl Hardy standing in her doorway.

"Jekyl! What are you doing here?" Then she smiled and said, "Did you miss my class?" It was meant as a joke since Jekyl was one of the most talented and artistic people she knew. How he kept coming up with all those fabulous designs for Mardi Gras floats, year after year, she'd never know.

But Jekyl was looking serious, not his usual devil-may-care self.

"I've got something for you," he said.

"What's that?"

He arched a single eyebrow. "Information."

"Maybe you better come in and sit down," Carmela said. Jekyl was suddenly looking super serious. When they'd both plunked down in facing chairs, she said, "What's up?"

"You know that Devon lives — well, lived — in the same building that I do."

"Napoleon Gardens," Carmela said. It was a red brick, rehabbed warehouse.

"And that my friend Misty Haworth has the apartment next to him."

Carmela suddenly felt nervous. Like the room was about to tilt on its axis.

"What are you getting at?"

"Misty thinks somebody broke into Devon's apartment last night."

"What!"

"She thinks she heard them moving around inside."

"She *thinks* she did or she really *did*?"

"She did," Jekyl said.

Carmela touched a hand to her forehead. "Holy shit."

"Keep in mind that Misty is also a big believer in ghosts and spooky haunts, so she also thought it could have been Devon's spirit, come back to set things right."

"It wasn't Devon's spirit," Carmela said.

"No," Jekyl said. "I doubt it was." He steepled his fingers together and stared at her. "The thing is . . . why would someone break in?"

"Because they're looking for something,"

229

Carmela said immediately. "Something they didn't find at Devon's shop."

"Such as?" Jekyl said.

Carmela exhaled slowly. "I have no idea."

Carmela knew she should call Babcock immediately and tell him about the possible break-in, but she resisted. Instead, she bid good-bye to Jekyl, said good night to Gabby, and headed out for Juju Voodoo. As she walked along, dodging revelers as well as street vendors, she wondered again what a burglar might be looking for in Devon's apartment. Was it the snippet of Lincoln's coat? Was it a piece of jewelry? Or something else? And could the night visitor have been Sonny Boy Holmes, the burglar that Babcock had told her about?

Everything surrounding this case seemed to be getting mysteriouser and mysteriouser.

Catching sight of Juju Voodoo lifted Carmela's spirits somewhat. The quaint little shop with its wooden shake roof, shiny red door, and window displays never failed to make her smile. From a distance, Ava's shop looked like a charming curiosity shop, but inside . . . Carmela grinned as she pushed open the door . . . that was another story.

Flickering candles in the dim interior were the first thing that intrigued visitors. Along with the click-clack of skeletons hanging overhead was the heady scent of incense and lemon balm with an undertone of Poison by Christian Dior, Ava's favorite perfume. Antique glass cases were filled with talismans, jewelry, bottles of potion, voodoo dolls, and saint candles.

Ava looked up from a display of evil eye pendants, pushed back a hank of dark, curly hair, and smiled.

"You made it!"

"Barely," Carmela said.

"I got a match," Ava said almost shyly. "Can you believe it? That Miss Penelope is a true wonder, a love Svengali. In less than twenty-four hours, she came up with my dream date. This matchup . . . tonight . . . could change my life!"

"Um, possibly." *But probably not.* "So who is this guy? You say you talked to him?"

"He called me early this afternoon and was very polite, a real gentleman."

"And you have a date for tonight. This guy moves fast."

"True love waits for no one," Ava said. "Plus, he told me we'll be attending a concert."

"I'm impressed. Your date sounds cultured."

"Classy."

231

"I hope you have a terrific time," Carmela said.

Ava spun around on her heels. "I think I'm already breathless in love."

"Save a little of that excitement for tomorrow night, will you?"

Ava stopped spinning. "Why, what's up?"

"I'm supposed to help judge the Jazz Fest's Gumbo Cook-Off, and I was hoping you'd come with me."

"I'd love to as long as I'm not out enjoying a *second* fabulous date with Mr. Wonderful."

"Okay then," Carmela said. "Have a wonderful time tonight. While I'm teaching tipsy women how to paint plates, I hope you're listening to a concerto by Bach or Beethoven."

"Oh my God," Ava said. "It really does sound classy, doesn't it? Maybe I should get all primped up and wear an evening gown. I'd better go home early and do a wardrobe check! And thank goodness my bod's in good shape from doing my twerkout workout."

CHAPTER 18

Blush and Brush looked even more elegant than it had yesterday. The lights were turned low, rows of wine bottles sparkled on the bar, ficus trees and wicker baskets filled with ferns had been tucked into every nook and cranny.

Behind the counter, Dewey and Ardice from St. Tammany Vineyards busied about, heating up gumbo and assembling mini sandwiches.

Maybe this evening would be a piece of cake, Carmela decided. Then, just as she started to let herself relax, Quigg snuck up behind her and poked a finger in her ribs.

"Surprise!"

"Hey!" Carmela yelped, her shoulders rising to her ears as she whirled around to face him. "Don't do that."

"Chill out, babe. No need to go all squirrelly."

"Then keep your mitts off me."

Quigg took a step backward in mock surprise. "Or what?"

"Or I'll . . ."

Before Carmela could come up with a really haughty retort, the front door swung open and a television camera pushed its way through. She caught the call letters on the side of the camera. KBEZ-TV.

"Oh man, you called a TV station?" Carmela said.

"Gotta pump up the publicity," Quigg said. "Besides, it's cool. You know these guys."

Quigg was right. Carmela did know them. In fact, she was fairly friendly with Zoe Carmichael, an on-camera reporter, and her cameraman, Raleigh. Best of all, they were good at their job. And not too pushy. Maybe this would be okay after all.

"A little bird told me you got roped into working part-time at this cute little wine bar," Zoe said. She was young, stylish in a black leather jacket and slim-cut khaki slacks, with a mass of reddish-brown hair. Raleigh was Raleigh. Jean jacket, saggy jeans, worn tennis shoes.

"And I see you guys got roped into covering Quigg's grand opening," Carmela said.

Zoe shrugged. "What can you do? Quigg is all buddy-buddy with our station manager. Lets him eat for free at Bon Tiempe."

"Don't you just love old-boy cronyism and graft?" Carmela said.

"Hey," Quigg called out. "Watch it."

Raleigh moved closer and aimed his lens at them. "Let's get started, huh, Zoe? Time's a-wasting. There are two other events we gotta cover tonight."

Zoe clicked on her battery pack and switched to professional mode. "Gotcha. So I'll do a quick fifteen-second intro and then you cut to Carmela and Quigg. Maybe do a two-shot of them standing in front of the bar."

So Carmela and Quigg squished in together while Zoe did her opening piece, flashed a smile at the camera, and then turned to ask them a few questions.

Quigg was over-the-top nervous, jumbling his answers like a chattering monkey. Carmela felt jittery but was outwardly calm and fairly articulate. Zoe saved the day by calling Blush and Brush "a dazzling new wine bar" and "the newest fun spot in the French Quarter."

The only really bad part was when Quigg, gripped by a paroxysm of enthusiasm, slung an arm around Carmela's shoulders and called her the best partner anyone could ask for.

At which point Carmela fought to disentangle herself as her head filled with visions of Babcock catching the news footage, gasping when he saw that hug, and getting so incensed his brains blew out his ears.

Five minutes later, the scene changed dramatically. The TV crew packed up and left, and Quigg's invited guests began to pour in.

Carmela noticed that most of Quigg's guests were women. Good-looking, poufy-haired, dieted-down, well-maintained women. And that Quigg was in his element as he exchanged air-kisses, sprinkled compliments like fairy dust, then led them to the various tables and pulled out chairs for them. Carmela also noticed that amidst all the kissing and shameless flirting, Quigg hadn't bothered to introduce her.

I'm the hired help tonight. The lady with the painted plate. That's why he wanted me? Well . . . jeez.

Then the front door opened again and Carmela couldn't believe her rotten luck.

Oh no!

Glory Meechum, Shamus's horrible big sister, came clumping in. She looked haggard and puffy faced, and wore her trademark brown skirt suit and lacquered gray helmet hair. Tagging along behind Glory was her mousy cousin Millicent.

Glory was the one woman Carmela knew would be a sullen holdout to Quigg's charms. She and Millicent brushed past Quigg with barely civil greetings and settled at the table nearest the door. Then Glory's head swiveled like a periscope and her hard eyes landed on Carmela.

Carmela lifted a hand in greeting. "Hi," she said in a small voice. Then, reluctantly, she went over to say hello to Glory.

"You," Glory said by way of greeting.

"Nice to see you again," Carmela said from between gritted teeth. Glory had never, *ever* been cordial to her.

"What are you doing here?" Glory demanded.

"Would you believe I'm the brush in Blush and Brush?"

"*You're* going to lead the plate painting class?" Glory asked.

"You catch on fast," Carmela said. She was determined not to let Glory get under her skin.

"I remember you," Millicent said. "From the wedding." With her frizzled hair and dowdy purple-gray dress she looked like a cross between Miss Havisham and the Piper Laurie character in the movie *Carrie.*

Glory pounded the table with her fist. "A

year," she said. "I predicted that Shamus and Carmela's marriage would only last a year. And then it blew up after only six months. You see how right I was? How clever I am?"

"Do you really want to beat a dead horse?" Carmela asked. *Damn. I should have grabbed one of Ava's voodoo dolls when I had the chance.*

"I gave you and Shamus silver salt and pepper shakers for a wedding gift," Millicent said.

"Do you want them back?" Carmela asked.

Millicent thought for a few seconds. "No, that's okay. I'm sorry it didn't work out."

"So, Carmela, what are you doing here?" Glory asked.

"Knock, knock," Carmela said. "Painting? You drink some wine and I show you how to paint a plate. Couldn't be simpler."

"You're a mean little trollop," Glory snarled.

"The pot calling the kettle black," Carmela said. "I'd love to hang around and catch up on old times, maybe paint our nails and braid each other's hair, but I've got work to do."

Quigg had just started gesturing to her like mad.

"What?" Carmela hissed at him.

"We're a hit!" he crowed. "A goldarned hit!"

Carmela glanced around the wine bar. Everyone was happily sipping wine while Ardice served small bowls of crab gumbo along with pork pop biscuits. The pork pops were tasty little mini biscuits stuffed with cheese, bacon, and andouille sausage. The stuff of dreams in New Orleans.

"They do look happy," Carmela allowed. "Let's give them a few more minutes to feed their little faces and then we'll pass out the plates and paint."

"Good thinking," Quigg said. "Glad you're on top of this."

Painting plates turned out to be an even bigger hit than the wine and food. The women dabbled, daubed, spattered paint, and howled with delight. Once Carmela had explained the setup and showed her sample plate, there was no stopping them.

Plates were soon adorned with free-form swoops of color, floral motifs, hearts, birds, cats, and more. A few would-be painters tried to mimic Carmela's butterfly, and one creative genius even painted a mermaid on a half shell.

Carmela admired each plate as it was

finished and instructed the women about letting their plate dry and coating it with sealant. Several asked for her business card, which was a terrific sign that the event — and the plate painting — had been extremely well received.

"Next week we'll be painting miniature canvases," Quigg told his audience as he slipped from table to table. "And I'm taking reservations *now.*"

Carmela tiptoed over to Glory and Millicent's table and was surprised at Millicent's plate. It was a bunch of yellow and orange flowers that looked surprisingly elegant. Glory's plate, on the other hand, was just dibs and dabs. She'd obviously concentrated on the wine drinking portion of the evening rather than the plate painting. Oh well.

Then Quigg made the colossal mistake of joining them.

"What lovely plates," he enthused.

Which caused Glory to glare at him and mutter, "Whatever."

Quigg pointed at Glory's plate. "What is that you painted there? A Rorschach blob?"

"You don't know a sunset when you see it?" Glory asked.

"Would you care for another glass of wine?" Quigg asked, still trying to ingratiate himself with Glory. He knew darned well who sat on the board of directors at New Orleans's largest bank.

Glory ignored Quigg and focused on Carmela. "Does that poor cop you've been dating know what's going on between the two of you?" She moved a finger back and forth, from Quigg to Carmela.

"Nothing's going on, our relationship is strictly business," Carmela said.

"Business," Quigg echoed.

"Hmph." Glory wasn't buying it.

"Really, have some more wine," Quigg offered.

"Only if you decide to trot out the good stuff," Glory snarled.

Just when Glory couldn't get any more annoying, Shamus showed up to drive his sister and cousin home.

"Everybody having fun?" Shamus asked, favoring Glory with a huge smile.

"Hmph," Glory said again.

"Good. Great," Shamus said, bobbing his head and winking at Carmela. He looked like the kind of goofy bobblehead doll they passed out at ballparks.

"Can you please get her out of here?" Carmela asked under her breath.

"What? *Problema*?"

"Kind of."

241

And there'll be an even bigger problema if Babcock decides to stop by on a whim and sees me here with both Quigg and Shamus. Whatever will he think then?

"Hey, have you heard the crazy news?" Shamus said. "I've been asked to take part in the Most Eligible Bachelor Auction tomorrow night!"

Carmela gave a delicate snort. "You're still considered an eligible bachelor? Even after being married to me?"

"Technically, I'm a bachelor, yes. When they asked, I couldn't turn them down. It's a fund-raiser for a really good cause."

"What's the cause? The indolent rich guys club?"

"Naw, it's something to do with children's literacy."

"Even so, this has to be a major ego trip for you," Carmela said.

"Oh yeah, for sure. I'm counting on some really big bucks being spent on little old me."

"If you receive the winning bid for Most Eligible Bachelor, what is it you have to do?"

Shamus shrugged. "Go on a date with some chick, I guess. Somebody who'll pay buckets of cash for the pleasure of my company." He winked again. "Win-win."

Glory drained her wineglass, tried to stand

up, and then dropped back into her seat. Both Shamus and Millicent quickly pulled Glory to her feet, and then the threesome toddled out of the wine bar.

Good riddance, Carmela thought. Time to go home.

Carmela staggered into her apartment, tired, happy with her presentation, unhappy about the scene with Glory and Shamus.

The Meechums had a nasty habit of popping up in her life when they were least expected. Tonight was one of those nights.

Oh well.

Carmela roused Boo, Poobah, and Mimi and clipped leashes to their collars. Then they were outside and rushing across the courtyard, Carmela grasping the three leads like a Roman charioteer.

The night was cool and refreshing with a breeze (slightly pungent with dead fish) off the Mississippi River. Their pace was brisk, but the dogs kept dancing around one another and repeatedly tangling their leashes. Carmela had no sooner untangled Poobah and Mimi, when Boo would dart in front of little Mimi and the tangling would begin anew.

After a while, Carmela gave up and let the dogs have their cat's cradle of leashes. They wandered down Baronne Street, went around the block, and then came down the back alley.

Halfway down, Carmela started to get a funny feeling, a tickle in her stomach, that she was being followed. She listened carefully and, yes, there were definitely footsteps crunching in the gravel behind her.

Really?

She kept moving but listened carefully again. Yes, someone seemed to be shadowing her.

What to do!

With just the brick wall of an apartment building on her right and a row of garages on her left, there was no place to duck into, no place to get help. So Carmela urged her pups to walk faster. Tangled leashes or not, her only hope was to get home fast.

Hurrying, feeling a blip of panic now, Carmela stumbled on a hunk of loose pavement. She flailed, struggling to right herself, and, in so doing, dropped Poobah's leash.

He immediately spun around and ran off. Started barking.

"Poobah! Come on!" Carmela kept going, figuring the dog would hear her call and come running.

Not Poobah.

From out of the darkness Carmela heard

a deep-seated growl, then the sound of jaws and teeth snapping together. Whoever had been on the receiving end of Poobah's snap let out an angry "oof" and ran down the alley.

"Poobah, come! Good dog!"

By the time Carmela got to her apartment door, she was winded and scared out of her mind. Fearing that a hand would drop on her shoulder at any moment, she unlocked the door, hustled herself and the dogs inside, and slammed the door. The dead bolt was thrown and the chain put on for good measure!

CHAPTER 19

Not thirty seconds after Carmela threw the lock and heaved a shaky sigh, there was heavy banging on the door. *WHAM, WHAM, WHAM!*

Oh no!

"Boo, Poobah, get your furry butts over here and try to look fierce!" Carmela rasped. "Poobah, do your snapping thing again."

The two dogs gazed at her, looking incredibly bored, not a whisker twitching. Obviously, Boo was no guard dog and Poobah had already shot his wad.

"Mimi, can I at least count on you?"

But Mimi was sprawled on a fuzzy rug, paws up, her little pink tongue lolling out the side of her mouth.

Just my luck.

And still the banging didn't stop! And then, whoever was outside and wanted to get in grasped the doorknob and actually shook the door!

"What to do, what to do?" Carmela muttered to herself.

She crept up to the door, expecting it to be split open any minute by a crazed ax-wielding maniac.

"Who is it?" Carmela shouted, not opening the door (no way!).

"It's me!"

"Who's me?" she called out in what she hoped was a sharp, authoritative voice.

"It's your nosy neighbor who just returned from her date from hell."

"Ava?" *Really?*

Leaving the chain on, Carmela creaked open the door and pressed one eye to the narrow gap. And there, dear Lord, stood Ava. She was dressed in a frilly pink blouse and black leggings, perched on silver stilettos. She carried a matching silver purse that was roughly the size of a bread box.

"Were you just in the alley before?" Carmela asked.

"Before what?" Ava asked. She looked upset and a little bedraggled. One of her false eyelashes seemed to have come unglued. Actually, Ava looked a little unglued.

"Never mind." Carmela undid the chain and let Ava in. "Say, missy, why are you darkening my doorstep and scaring me half to death when you're supposed to be out with . . . Wait one hot minute, did you just say date from hell?"

Ava touched a hand to her forehead as if trying to figure out a response or stave off a migraine.

"My date," she said. "My date was beyond horrible. In fact, he broke new ground in the annals of horribleness."

"What are you talking about? Wait, would you like a drink?"

"I'd like my own bottle." Ava stepped over Mimi and followed Carmela into the kitchen.

Carmela grabbed a bottle of wine and a corkscrew.

"So what happened? What caused your evening to go off the rails so badly?"

"First of all, the guy's nickname was Tank. That alone should tell you something."

"He was an oil field roustabout? An automotive worker?"

"No, I think he was on permanent sabbatical from any kind of meaningful employment. And he rode a motorcycle."

"That explains your windblown look." Carmela popped the cork on a bottle of Sauvignon Blanc, poured out two glasses of wine, and handed one to Ava.

Ava took a long sip, then said, "You see my hair?"

"It's cute. Kind of a messy bun."

"It didn't start out messy. But when you're riding on the back of a 1200cc Harley, you're at the mercy of the elements."

Carmela fought to stifle a grin. "So what else went wrong?"

"Oh, she wants to hear more," Ava said. "How about this? Tank's knuckles practically dragged on the ground when he walked, and beneath his Day-Glo green shirt and puka shell necklace, I had the feeling his body was incredibly hairy."

"What about the concert?"

"The concert was some broke-down rock band called the Four Wheezers. It was basically a bunch of swamp rats and a goat."

"A goat, really?"

"The goat was metaphorical. But, *cher*, they were awful. Even Auto-Tune couldn't have saved those guys."

"Huh, and you'd so hoped that your date — Tank? — was the cultured sort."

"I'm afraid the only culture in Tank's life is a moldy carton of two-year-old banana-kiwi yogurt that's undoubtedly stuck in the bottom drawer of his refrigerator." Ava took another sip of wine. "And then we went out to eat."

"How was that?"

249

"Ever been to Bonzo's Diner?"

Carmela shook her head. "Never. What's it like?"

"They oughta rename it the Road Kill Grill. From your grill to ours."

"I'm sorry your evening didn't work out as you'd hoped."

But Ava was wound up and ready to vent.

"Tank also criticized my choice of clothes. He said I wasn't dressed up enough."

"You've got to be kidding. That pink frilly blouse is straight out of, um, Frederick's of Hollywood?"

Ava tossed her head and gave an affirmative nod. "So I said to him, 'Pardon me if I don't look all spiffy like Kate Middleton going to Ascot.'"

"Then what?" Carmela asked. Listening to Ava was fascinating. Almost as good as a really nasty political dustup on *The View.*

"Just that I'm disappointed that Miss Penelope turned out to be such a fake and a fraud," Ava spat out. "She got me to shell out twenty-nine ninety-five plus tax and I ended up with nada."

"That's all she charged?"

"It was still a rip-off!"

"Come on into the living room and sit down," Carmela urged. "Try to relax."

Ava plopped down on the leather chaise

lounge. "I'm *trying,* believe me."

"Maybe a matchmaker isn't the best way to go," Carmela said.

Ava bobbed her head. "That's what I'm beginning to think. Shit happens when you put your trust in the wrong people." She gave a wan smile. "I think that's a direct quote by Kierkegaard. Or maybe it was one of the Kardashians. Anyway, I was thinking maybe I should try Spindr?"

"Use a sketchy dating app?" Carmela was horrified. "You'll end up with an ax murderer!"

"Couldn't be any worse than tonight's date."

"Oh yes, it could."

"Well. Maybe." Ava drew in a deep breath and let it out. Shook her head like Poobah when he came in from the rain. "There. I hope I've exorcized all the icky bad karma."

"Nothing like a good exorcism to set you straight again."

Ava settled back with her wine. "How's your investigation coming? Anything new I should know about?"

"Not really. T.J., Roy Sultan, and Richard Drake are still my main contenders, but I can't seem to get a handle on any concrete evidence."

"It can't be Drake," Ava said.

"Actually, it could be. *You* just don't want it to be him. But what I'd really like to do is talk to Colonel Otis again. Really hold his feet to the fire."

"*Pourquoi?* Why?"

"I get the feeling that Otis was more than a little disgruntled with Devon. That he didn't relish learning that an expensive painting he'd purchased was actually stolen merchandise. So . . . maybe there's something there?"

"Maybe," Ava said as she pulled a Hostess Ding Dong out of her bag and started to unwrap it.

"You're going to eat that?"

"When I'm nervous I snack."

"And wash all that sugar and fat down with a forty-dollar bottle of wine?" Carmela said as her phone rang. She grabbed her phone and said an off hand, "Hello?" She was fully expecting it to be Babcock.

Instead, she got the surprise of her life.

"I gotta talk to you," a voice rasped. A voice she didn't recognize, but one that carried an urgent, slightly nasal tone.

"Who is this?" Carmela asked.

"My name is Sonny Holmes."

"Sonny Boy Holmes?" Carmela yelped. *Holy shit, it's the art thief!* she mouthed to Ava.

"Hang up!" Ava cried in between bites.

Carmela shook her head at Ava and said to Sonny Boy, "Why do you want to talk to me? Wait a minute, was that you in the alley before?" She wished she could somehow record this conversation so Babcock could hear it, too.

"Alley?" Sonny Boy sounded confused.

"Never mind," Carmela said. "What do you want?"

"Everything's gotten completely out of hand," Sonny Boy said. He sounded like he'd just run a four-minute mile with a bad head cold.

"Excuse me, but I'm seriously not following you," Carmela said. Her heart was blipping a million miles an hour. Was she right now talking to Devon's killer? And what could she do about it? How could she somehow lure Sonny Boy in so Babcock could question him? Or maybe even apprehend him?

"That safecracking thing . . . at Dulcimer Antiques?" Sonny Boy said. "That's on me. Okay. That was a job I did. But murdering the poor antique guy? Definitely not my style. I'm a second-story guy, not a stone-cold killer!"

"What are you . . . ?" Carmela began. Her mind was in a spin.

"I can't explain this over the phone."

"Wait. You're telling me you *didn't* murder Devon Dowling?"

"I swear I didn't touch a single hair on that man's head." Sonny Boy's breath was coming in faster gulps now. "But I . . . I know who did."

"Then tell me!" Carmela cried.

"I can't. Not like this. You have to meet me somewhere."

"He wants to meet us," Carmela whispered to Ava.

Ava shook her head. *No way.*

"Why me?" Carmela asked. "If you're as innocent as you claim, why not go to the police? You could talk to . . ."

"That won't work," Sonny Boy countered. "Ain't no way I'm going to the police. I got a record that could land me back in Dixon Correctional. But I read about you in the paper and then I asked around. I know you're real close with that Detective Babcock."

"Let me get this straight. You want to meet me and tell me who murdered Devon Dowling." Carmela's brain was racing, trying to figure out a next move. Sonny Boy sounded on the up-and-up. On the other hand, this could be a horrible, twisted trick. A trap. *Come into my parlor said the spider to the fly.*

"The thing is, I ain't gonna be anybody's puppet anymore."

Carmela could almost feel her brain lighting up like a pinball machine as she immediately thought of Richard Drake. Was that who Sonny Boy was referring to when he said puppet? After all, Drake hung out with the Beastmaster Puppet people . . .

"I don't want to talk to your Detective Babcock face-to-face, but I need to get an important message to him," Sonny Boy said. "There's a whole lot he needs to know!"

Carmela was scared, but she pulled it together and listened carefully as Sonny Boy gave her explicit instructions.

"Well?" Ava said when Carmela got off the phone.

"He wants to meet with us."

"Us?" Ava said.

"Well, me," Carmela said. "Tonight."

"I suppose he set up a meeting in a sleazy bar somewhere."

"He wants to meet in St. Louis Cemetery. Over in the Garden District."

Ava's eyes got big. "No way."

"Listen to me, Ava. Sonny Boy Holmes wants to spill the beans about something."

Carmela could barely contain her excitement — or was it fear?

"I think Sonny Boy Holmes knows exactly

who killed Devon!"

"It could be a trap," Ava said.

"That's why I need you to come with me."

"Well jeez, Carmela." Ava looked both nervous and undecided.

Carmela picked up her car keys and jangled them. "If you're not coming, I'll go alone."

Ava groaned as she brushed a few crumbs off her blouse and stood up. "This goes against my better judgment. But this entire evening has been against my better judgment. So . . . what are we waiting for?"

The wrought-iron gates of St. Louis Cemetery loomed like a sentinel in the darkness.

"Spooky," Ava said.

"Cemeteries usually are," Carmela said. *Especially this one with its ancient mausoleums and cracked-oven tombs. It's not a place I relish walking through at night.*

Ava stuck a hand out. "Hold my hand?"

Carmela grabbed Ava's hand as they walked through the gates and were immediately swallowed up in darkness.

"There's nothing to be afraid of," Carmela said as they crunched along a gravel path with large tombs on either side of them. She knew she was whistling in the dark, and Ava knew it, too.

"Only the fact that thousands of people are buried here, the place is absolutely haunted, and it's supposed to be where the vampire Lestat is buried," Ava said.

There was a strange rustling sound and then a faint noise just above their heads. A soft *who-woo*.

"What was that?" Ava asked. She wasn't just jumpy, she was all atingle.

"Probably an owl."

"Well, I don't like it."

"Try thinking about something else," Carmela said.

"I am," Ava said. "I'm remembering that this exact cemetery was featured on the Travel Channel's *America's Most Haunted Places*."

"Maybe not that kind of something else."

"Why are there so many clouds overhead?" Ava asked. "Why isn't there moonlight shining down so we can see where we're going?"

"I don't know." Carmela looked up and saw only a roil of gray bubbles in the sky.

They picked their way past an enormous mausoleum that featured stone pillars, elaborate wrought-iron bars, and two glass windows.

"Is that set up so people can see in or to keep people out?" Ava asked.

"Both," Carmela said. It was true. Many of the old mausoleums had locked gates and glass windows. If you got up the nerve to brush away the dust and grime and then pressed your nose against those windows, you could peer in at decades-old moldering wooden coffins.

"Where exactly are we supposed to meet this Sonny Boy?" Ava asked as they stumbled along.

"He said to come in the main gate, walk straight ahead, and then turn when we got to the winged angel tomb."

"I think that's the angel tomb up ahead."

"I think you're right," Carmela said. Her nerves were twanging like guitar strings now. She was scared but hopeful that something might come of this encounter.

"Now what?" Ava was staring up at an angel with a bowed head and chipped wing.

"Now we're supposed to follow the circular path around to the obelisk tomb."

"That's where we're going to meet him?"

"Supposedly," Carmela said.

"Okay. But I sure hope this guy is a charmer."

"Ava, you can't date him!"

"Couldn't be any worse than Tank," Ava muttered.

Clutching each other even tighter, Carmela and Ava tiptoed past tilting tombstones and gaping crypts. The wind had picked up, and the night air felt as though it were alive with spirits.

"Over there?" Ava asked. They could just make out the obelisk straight ahead, its needlelike spire plunging skyward. "I don't see anyone."

"Maybe we're early," Carmela whispered as they approached the tall tomb.

"Maybe Sonny Boy's not coming."

"Oh, he'll be here."

They tiptoed toward the obelisk, scared out of their wits and moving oh-so-slowly.

Just as they drew to within ten feet of the obelisk, the clouds slowly parted and a shaft of moonlight shone down like a key light on a darkened stage.

"Do you see anything?" Ava asked as they stared at the obelisk that was now iced in moonlight.

Carmela blinked. Were her eyes playing tricks on her? "I think he's . . ."

Sonny Boy was there all right. He was sitting on the grass, his back resting against the tomb and his legs sprawled out to either side of him.

And even though Sonny Boy was staring straight ahead at them, it was quite obvious that his throat had been slit from ear to ear.

CHAPTER 20

Her teeth chattering so badly she could barely control her nervousness, Carmela immediately called Babcock's cell. When it jumped to voice mail, she hung up.

"Voice mail," Carmela said.

"Try another number!" Ava cried.

She hurriedly punched the button. Thank goodness she had Babcock's office phone on speed dial.

The phone rang and rang, adding to her trepidation. Finally, when Carmela was about to give up, someone picked up and said, in a disinterested voice, "Officer Radcliffe."

Carmela fought to keep her words from becoming jumbled. "I'm trying to get hold of Detective Babcock, please. It's an emergency!"

"Who's calling?"

Carmela gritted her teeth to stop herself from screaming. "Please, this is his fiancée,

Carmela Bertrand, and it really, really is an emergency."

Radcliffe must have lowered the phone to his chest because his voice sounded muffled when Carmela heard him call out, "Any of you guys seen Babcock?" This was followed by a few mumbled voices and one "Not lately."

"You're sure?" Radcliffe asked the group. "This chick says she's his fiancée and that it's an emergency."

"It sure is," Carmela muttered to herself.

Radcliffe lifted the phone to his mouth. "Sorry, ma'am. I've just been informed he's in with Chief Montoya and can't be disturbed. Can I help you?"

Carmela was beside herself. Here she was, standing in a dark cemetery next to Sonny Boy's corpse with Ava completely flipping out.

What's wrong with this picture?

To top it off, Carmela had no idea where the killer might be (still!) lurking, and she couldn't seem to get in touch with the one person she absolutely needed.

What can I say to this officer so he'll run and grab Babcock and perp-walk him to the phone?

"Miss? Are you still . . . ? Oh, wait . . . I think he . . . Here he is now."

Carmela listened hard as Radcliffe informed Babcock of his emergency call. And she practically wept with relief when Babcock picked up the phone and said, "Detective Babcock."

In fact, she did start to cry. "Edgar, it's me! Something awful happened. Please, you've got to come right away!"

When Ava saw that Carmela was crying, tears started dribbling down her face, too.

"Carmela? Calm down," Babcock said. "Tell me what's wrong."

Where to start?

"There's all this blood!" Carmela cried.

"Are you injured?" Babcock's voice was filled with alarm. "Was there an accident? Should I send an ambulance? Talk to me, Carmela, tell me what's going on!"

"No, it's not me. I'm about to go nuts but I'm not hurt. It's . . . it's Sonny Boy Holmes."

"What!" Babcock screamed in her ear.

"Ava and I were supposed to meet him in St. Louis Cemetery. He . . . he had some information he wanted me to pass along to you. But before we . . ."

"Holy shit!" Babcock yelped. "You're in the cemetery with Sonny Boy Holmes? And he's injured? Let me talk to him!"

"I can't because he's dead!"

"Dead? So you're there with his *body*?"

"Yes, we . . ."

"Stay on the line, Carmela. I'm going to pass the phone back to Officer Radcliffe, and I want you to remain on the line so we know you're okay. I'm dispatching two squads right now, and I'm coming as fast as I can. Okay? You got that, sweetheart?"

Carmela nodded into the phone. She knew Babcock couldn't see her, but the lump in her throat was so large she wasn't able to squeak out any more words.

Carmela and Ava huddled together in the shadow of the obelisk, not saying much to each other, but keenly aware of every little creak and crack that sounded around them.

"Were those footsteps?" Ava whispered.

"I think it's just branches scratching against a tomb," Carmela said.

"Do you realize how creepy that sounds? How Alfred Hitchcock?"

"Ava, do you see where we are right now? It *is* like a scary movie."

"With zombies shuffling after us?"

"I think we'd do better to think positively," Carmela said. "Babcock's on his way, after all. A couple of squad cars, too."

"And he didn't even yell at you."

"Don't hold your breath, I'm sure the yelling portion of the evening is still to come. And maybe we'd feel better if we moved away from the dead body?"

They shuffled a few steps away and waited.

"Hallelujah," Ava said when they finally heard the thin, distant wail of a police siren. "Somebody's coming."

"Probably an ambulance," Carmela said.

"A hearse would be more useful."

"I bet Babcock's bringing half the NOPD with him. This is one creepy setup. Murder in a cemetery."

"Gives me a new case of shivers and the shakes just thinking about it," Ava said. Then, "I wonder what Sonny Boy wanted to tell you."

"Now we'll never know."

Ava glanced around quickly, sneaking a look at Sonny Boy's body, and said, "Unless there's some sort of clue."

"What do you mean?"

"You know, like in the movies when the killer drops a pop can with his DNA on it."

Carmela thought for a few moments. "Hmm, you make a good point." Suddenly she wasn't quite as scared anymore.

And even as a rising cacophony of sirens drew closer and closer, their curiosity jumped into overdrive.

Ava was the first one to tiptoe up to Sonny

Boy's body and take a really good look.

"Just look at him," Ava said. "If you can overlook the bloody trachea and glazed eyeballs, Sonny wasn't a bad-looking dude. Kinda scrawny, but better-looking than Tank was, that's for sure. Probably more polite, too."

"Sonny Boy *was* polite on the phone," Carmela allowed. "Even though he sounded scared to death."

"And see," Ava said, pointing to a brown paper bag that was sitting on the ground next to Sonny Boy. "He looks like a planner. It would appear Sonny Boy brought along a snack. Maybe he suffered from low blood sugar or something."

Carmela gazed at the crumpled brown bag. "A snack? No, I don't think so."

"Then what?"

The sirens were almost on top of them now as Carmela crept forward to inspect the bag.

"You're gonna look inside?" Ava asked in hushed tones.

Carmela snatched up the bag and held it for a moment. Then she stepped over to a flat tomb and turned the bag upside down. They both stepped back as if expecting a copperhead to come slithering out to attack them.

What slithered out was a piece of black cloth, a diamond bracelet, and a small blue velvet pouch with a half dozen loose diamonds inside.

"Crackers!" Ava cried. "What is all this stuff?"

"I think it's the stuff that was stolen from Devon's safe!"

"Do you think Sonny Boy brought this stuff along so he could give it to us?" Ava asked. She cocked her head to one side and sighed. "Maybe Sonny Boy was trying to turn over a new leaf and never got a chance. That's so sad." She shook her head. "Poor Sonny Boy, he was trying to reform, to be a good citizen."

"I don't know, Ava. Sonny Boy said he wanted to *tell* me something, not *give* me something. It's possible we weren't the only meeting he had scheduled for tonight."

"But what . . . ?"

Ava's words were interrupted by loud shouts. Then footsteps crunched on gravel and flashlight beams bobbed in and around the darkened rows of mausoleums and tombs. Suddenly, a bright circle of light flashed directly in Carmela's face. She squinted and raised a hand to shield her eyes from the glare.

"They're over here!" the man aiming the

flashlight shouted.

More footsteps pounded toward them from all directions, then blue-clad bodies emerged from the darkness. The first one Carmela recognized was Bobby Gallant, Babcock's right-hand man.

"Bobby," Ava said. There was a distinct purr in her voice. She'd always had a thing for Bobby. "We've got to stop meeting like this."

Gallant was cool and laid-back. "Carmela, Ava, we need you to wait over here." Without being pushy, Bobby walked them to a mausoleum and had them stand with their backs against it. "Just wait right here, please." He turned away and said to the nearest uniform, "What's the ETA on Babcock?"

"Central said he just got out of his car," the uniformed officer said. "Figure a minute or so. Crime Scene just rolled in." He gave a nod. "They'll set up a perimeter and flood the area with lights. We'll have one hundred percent scene control in under three minutes."

Carmela bounced on the balls of her feet. She couldn't wait for Babcock and his reassuring hug.

THWACK! THWACK! THWACK! Three light stanchions went up in quick succession, and within seconds, 100,000 lumens of light flooded the area, making it look like high noon on a summer day.

"Eeew," Ava said, squinting. "Sonny Boy doesn't look so good now under those killer lights."

"Like a bad autopsy," Carmela agreed as her eyes searched the first responders who continued to pour in. She was looking for Babcock. When she finally spotted him, Carmela gave a little finger wave and said, "Edgar, over here!"

Babcock ignored her. Instead, he made a beeline for Bobby Gallant and Charlie Preston, the Crime Scene tech.

"Whaaat?" Carmela said, taken aback.

"Maybe Babcock didn't see you," Ava said.

"He saw me."

Babcock was kneeling down now, taking a cursory look at the body. Then he walked over to the flat tomb where Carmela had laid out Sonny Boy's bag of goodies.

"Is that the so-called scrap of coat?" he asked.

"Don't know," Charlie Preston said. "But I can't wait to get it into the lab and analyze it."

Babcock shook his head, walked back to confer with Bobby Gallant again, and then came over to Carmela.

"Did you see . . . ?" Carmela began.

Babcock steamrollered right over her.

"Have you completely lost your mind?" he shouted. "What are you doing in a cemetery, after dark?"

"I told you," Carmela said. "I was supposed to . . ."

"Meet Sonny Boy Holmes," Babcock finished. "Are you looking for trouble? Agreeing to meet up with a known criminal? A criminal who's on our short list for murder?"

"Sonny Boy was on your short list?" Ava asked.

Babcock ignored her. "This has to be the most absurd, nonsensical, harebrained scheme you two have ever cooked up. Have you taken leave of your senses? Do you know that it could be one or both of you lying in the pool of blood over there?"

Babcock's voice grew louder and more forceful with every word. Many of the officers and Crime Scene techs glanced up from what they were doing to watch the commotion.

"Edgar, I can explain," Carmela said.

"Don't 'Edgar' me. I am a detective in the NOPD investigating a homicide. *You* have no role here whatsoever."

"Edgar, just listen . . ."

"Excuse me, what's my name?"

"Detective Babcock." Carmela had never seen him this angry before.

"Excuse me," Ava said. "If I might . . ."

"Might what? Stick up for your coconspirator when she is absolutely in the wrong on all counts?"

Ava shook her dark curls and took a deep breath. "Carmela was only trying to help. She loves you even more than I've ever loved anyone. Well, maybe except for Coco, my favorite teddy bear, but I tragically lost him during a camping trip in Buzzard Roost Park. Anyway, *you* are the love of Carmela's life. If you can't see that . . . well." Ava shrugged. "There's just no hope at all."

Babcock was silent for a moment as he fought to draw a few calming breaths. "Just tell me, what possessed you ladies to come here tonight?"

"Sonny Boy called me out of the blue and asked me to meet him," Carmela said. "He wanted me . . . begged me . . . to deliver a message to you. He was willing to admit to the robbery of Devon's safe, but he said he didn't want to get tagged for the murder. He wanted you to know that he isn't . . ." She glanced over at the body. "That he *wasn't* the killer."

270

Babcock shook his head. He wasn't buying Carmela's story.

"Maybe Sonny Boy wanted to get *you* out of the way," Babcock said to Carmela. "Did you ever look at it that way? Maybe he figured out that you were running your own shadow investigation."

"You think he wanted to kill *me*?" Carmela cried. The notion stunned her.

"And me?" Ava asked.

"It's certainly possible," Babcock said.

Carmela put a hand on either side of her head as if she was trying to remember something.

"No," she said. "There's more to it."

"What?" Ava and Babcock said together.

"Jekyl paid me a visit earlier today. He said that someone was bumbling around inside Devon's apartment last night," Carmela said.

"Bumbling around how?" Babcock asked.

"Like . . . looking for something," Carmela said. "Breaking and entering."

"Could it have been Sonny Boy?" Babcock asked.

"I don't know. Maybe. But I have a funny feeling it was someone else," Carmela said.

"Maybe the person who slit Sonny Boy's throat tonight?" Ava said.

Babcock squinted at Ava. "Hmm."

"There's something else," Carmela said.

"There's always something else," Babcock said.

"This is important. When I talked to Sonny Boy on the phone, he made the comment that he wasn't going to be anybody's puppet anymore."

"Do you think he was referring to Richard Drake? Because of his association with the Beastmaster Puppet Theater?" Babcock asked.

"Maybe," Carmela said. "That was my first thought."

"The only good thing about tonight is that losing Sonny Boy narrows down my list," Babcock said.

Carmela held up a finger. "Remember Colonel Otis?"

"The rich guy who was unhappy with Dowling's appraisal," Babcock said.

"He lives, like, two blocks from here."

"Holy smokes, Carmela, Colonel Otis could be the killer," Ava said.

"The man has a fairly sterling reputation," Babcock said.

"So what?" Ava said.

"You're telling me Colonel Otis might have killed Devon Dowling *and* Sonny Boy Holmes?" Babcock said. "Sounds awfully far-fetched."

"Sounds possible to me," Ava said.

"You have no say in this," Babcock said to Ava. "You're the wacky sidekick who followed my crazy fiancée here on the pretext of exchanging information."

"We *were* going to exchange information," Carmela said.

Babcock just gazed at her. "I've got to get back to the scene. But you two . . . I'm ordering you to head straight home."

"Be truthful," Carmela said. "Haven't I been just a teeny bit helpful?"

"Not one bit. Not even a minuscule amount." Babcock lifted an arm and waved over a uniformed officer. "Please escort these two ladies out of the cemetery immediately. And for God's sake, don't listen to any of their crazy theories, answer any questions, or, under penalty of death, allow them back in." He spun on his heels and walked away.

"He's scary when he's mad," Ava said.

"Tell me about it," Carmela said.

"Ladies?" the officer said. "Shall we move it along?"

He led Carmela and Ava to the front gate of the cemetery, glanced around, and said, "Is that your car over there?" He indicated Carmela's little red Mercedes, a long-ago gift from Shamus.

"Yes."

"Better hop in and drive home like the man said."

"Will do," Carmela said.

But she'd just spotted an aqua blue sign kitty-corner from where they were standing. A sign that glowed like a beacon in the night and said COMMANDER'S PALACE.

Carmela smiled at Ava. "Could you use a drink?"

"I thought you'd never ask," Ava said.

Once inside the venerable restaurant, with its warm glow, tinkle of glasses, and gentle hum of conversation, Carmela said, "It's amazing, but I kind of feel better already."

"Wait until you glug down a nice relaxing glass of wine."

As they turned into the bar, a man came barreling out and nearly crashed into them.

"Watch it!" Ava cried.

"You!" Carmela yelped as she took a step back.

It was Peter Jarreau, NOPD's media liaison. He looked positively frantic as he stared at them, then immediately checked his phone.

"I think you might have another PR disaster on your hands," Carmela said to him. "Sonny Boy Holmes was just murdered across the street."

"I know, I know, I just got the call!" Jarreau looked shaken by this newest crisis. "I'm headed over there right now. Doggone, I sure don't need this!"

As Carmela watched Jarreau fly out the door, she said, "New Orleans doesn't need this."

CHAPTER 21

Gabby was standing behind the front counter, scanning the front page of the *Times-Picayune* newspaper and looking a little bug-eyed.

"I can't believe you were actually, physically, *there* last night at the murder scene," Gabby said. "I mean, once again, Carmela, you were right there at ground zero. And this time in a *cemetery*!"

"That's me, the town jinx. I show up . . . you know some poor soul has been murdered."

"And this guy Sonny Boy Holmes really had his throat slit from ear to ear?"

"Gabby." Carmela put her hands on her hips. "Do you really want to know all the gruesome details? The stuff they didn't dare put in the newspaper because everyone would lose their breakfast?"

"I suppose not. But do you think this Sonny Boy Holmes was the one who murdered Devon Dowling?"

Carmela shook her head. "My very strong hunch is that it was someone else."

"Then how does Sonny Boy fit in?"

"I know this sounds kind of strange, but I think somebody was manipulating him."

"You mean like mind control? So he would kill people?" Gabby looked terrified.

"Not like a zombie or anything. And not necessarily for the purpose of killing. But maybe to steal artwork. Or steal . . . something." She thought about the intruder in Devon's apartment. "I don't know. But I have a strong feeling that a dangerous character is still lurking in the background somewhere."

"You mean the killer."

"Yes."

"But you don't know who it is."

"No," Carmela said. "But I'm going to make it my mission in life to find out. For Devon's sake. And for Mimi's."

"Mimi," Gabby murmured. "That poor little dog. I wish you would have brought her along today."

"Mimi's fine. She's happy staying home with Boo and Poobah."

"I suppose by now they've formed their very own little doggy posse."

■ ■ ■

Friday mornings were always hectic at Memory Mine, and Carmela was kept busy sorting through new papers — marbled paper, Shizen Pastel Paper, and banana fiber paper — and helping any number of customers.

Two women came in looking for ideas on Bible journaling, and Carmela found them a lovely album, some rubber stamps depicting crosses, praying hands, doves, and even a die-cut of Noah's Ark.

Another customer wanted to decorate white Chinese takeout boxes for her daughter's birthday party, so Carmela found some fabulous dragon stamps, blue and white Chinese beads, and gold tassels.

Then Mrs. Delachaise, of the bridal shower invitations, came into the shop and looked around expectantly.

"Mrs. Delachaise," Carmela said. "Is everything okay? Your daughter liked the invitations?" *Is there a problem here?*

"Oh yes," Mrs. Delachaise said. "She loved the invitations."

"Well . . . whew."

"Now she wants to know if we can create matching place cards for all the guests."

Carmela's brain was already spinning. "Let's see now, the invitations were cream-colored cardstock with rose gold ink. So . . ." She slid open a flat file and pulled out a piece of heavy cardstock. "This should match up perfectly. And, as you can see, this sheet is already perforated for place setting cards. All you have to do is hand-letter the guests' names or print them out on your computer."

"Hand lettering would probably look best," Mrs. Delachaise said.

"Then I'd suggest using one of our special pens. It lends a lovely calligraphy effect, but it's really just as easy to use as a regular marking pen. And the pen comes in gold, copper, and rose gold."

"Rose gold, of course," said Mrs. Delachaise.

"And if I could suggest one more thing," Carmela said. "We have some adorable little organza bags that you can fill with flower petals. To give away as favors."

"Real flower petals?"

"More like silk petals."

"Do you stock those, too?"

"We've got gold and silver organza bags as well as pink rose petals."

Just when Carmela was up to her ears sorting through rubber stamps, Quigg came charging through the front door. He smiled at Gabby and said, "I've gotta talk to Carmela!"

"About the murder?" Gabby asked.

"No, no. About last night's paint and sip." Quigg suddenly froze in his tracks, and a puzzled expression came across his face. "Wait, there was a murder?"

Carmela pursed her lips. "Current events are not exactly Quigg's forte," she told Gabby.

"Somebody got killed?" Quigg asked. Then, dismissively, "Well, never mind about that. I just wanted to thank you for lending your expertise last night. And for making opening night such a rousing success!"

"I'm glad everything worked out," Carmela said.

"No, it was better than working out. It was phenomenal. That footage that KBEZ shot? The interview with you and me? It was featured prominently on the ten o'clock news!" Quigg puffed out his chest. "Just from that quick, forty-second sound bite, people are already calling Blush and Brush to book an evening. Entire clubs of women!" He chuckled and pretended to tilt an imaginary glass to his lips. "And you know how much wine those book club ladies drink!"

"I'm happy for your success," Carmela said.

"*You* helped make it happen," Quigg enthused. "Things couldn't have worked out any better."

Clearly the latter part of your evening was far better than mine.

"Hey, go take a look outside," Quigg said.

"And what would I be looking for?" Carmela asked. *I hope he didn't put my name in lights or something gaudy and horrible like that.*

"It's just a little something to show how much I care about you."

Carmela held up a hand. "No. The thing is, Quigg, you *don't* care. You *can't* care."

"I just wanted to give you a little thank-you gift, a token to show my appreciation. I can do that, can't I?"

"Depends on what it is," Carmela said. "A bottle of wine would be acceptable. A Tesla would probably be over the top."

"He put out ginormous pots of flowers," Gabby called from the front desk. "I already looked."

"Aw, you spoiled the surprise," Quigg said.

"Sorry," Gabby said.

Carmela walked to the front door and peeped out. Sure enough, there were now two terra-cotta pots filled with flowers —

281

bounteous, riotous flowers — flanking her front door.

"Nice," she said. "Thank you very much."

"Pink Ruffle azaleas and Louisiana peppermint camellias," Quigg said. "My favorites." He followed her back inside and then kept moving closer and closer to Carmela, looking as if he wanted to give her a hug. Which forced her to keep backing up. Another few feet and she'd end up in the alley.

Up at the front counter, Gabby was looking out the window when her sharp eyes spotted a familiar someone bobbing along the sidewalk.

"Uh-oh," she said.

Carmela caught the note of worry in Gabby's voice. "What?"

"Babcock alert."

Carmela's blood ran cold. "What? Now?"

Gabby's voice rose in panic. "Babcock's coming down the street, and I think he's . . . yup, I'm pretty sure he's headed this way."

"You're like some kind of homing beacon," Quigg said, grinning at her.

"And you're persona non grata in Babcock's eyes. We've got to get you out of here. Fast!"

"Back door!" Gabby shouted.

"Right." Carmela grabbed Quigg's arm

and tugged him toward the back door.

"You're giving me the bum's rush?" He was suddenly irritated.

"If the shoes fits, yes."

"Okay . . . but . . ."

Carmela slid open the door to the dock, shoved Quigg out, and yelled, "Go! Begone with you!"

She slammed the door shut just as Babcock stepped into the shop.

"Thanks for the pickup," Carmela called out. "Let me know when I can stop by and do a press check." Then she turned around, flashed an enormous smile at Babcock, and said, "Well, hello there."

"Why do you look so guilty?" Babcock asked.

"Guilty? Me? Nooo."

"We've been frantically busy all morning," Gabby said, trying to deflect any kind of suspicion that might be fizzing in Babcock's mind. "So many customers. I guess it's because of the big influx of folks in town for Jazz Fest."

Babcock knew something was fishy, but he wasn't sure what. He pointed a finger at Carmela and said, "We need to talk."

"About?"

"You know what."

So they sat in Carmela's office, Carmela

trying to remain cool and blasé while Babcock ticked off about a million points that all dealt with the mistakes Carmela had made last night.

"When are you going to learn not to run off to meet strangers in cemeteries?"

"I don't know," Carmela said. It was an honest answer but one that didn't sit well with Babcock.

"This isn't a laughing matter, you know. This isn't some Nancy Drew mystery you're out to solve. There's no tolling bell, no twisted candles. This is reality."

"I'm aware of that. And I feel terrible that Sonny Boy was murdered. He really did want to give me some critical information regarding Devon Dowling's killer."

"You still believe that?" Babcock asked.

"Yes, I do. When Sonny Boy first called, he sounded scared. Frightened out of his mind, actually. And like I told you last night, he wanted to use me as a go-between. He wanted his information to get to *you*."

But Babcock wasn't convinced. "I don't know. It sounds awfully convoluted."

"Because it is. I agree."

Babcock stared at her, his eyes searching, his mood still dark. "I'm a little bit angry with you. First the wine party last night . . ."

Carmela waved a hand. "That was noth-ing."

"No, it was *something.* I don't like it, but I'm not stupid enough to forbid you from working with that sleazy Brevard fellow. That's all the incentive you'd need to . . ." He hesitated.

"To what?" Carmela asked.

Babcock rubbed the back of his hand against his chin. "I don't know."

Carmela reached over and took his hand. "Edgar, I love you. I'm not going to do anything to mess that up."

"Promise me?"

"Yes, of course."

"Then why don't you . . ."

"Shop for a wedding gown?" Carmela said. "I've got an appointment Amour Couture this afternoon."

Babcock's face brightened instantly. "You do?"

Not exactly. I just blurted that out to stall you. But I could. I could call Amour Couture and haul my body over there for a fitting.

"That's wonderful," Babcock said. "That's the kind of forward progress I've been hop-ing for."

Carmela just smiled.

"And what's this I heard about you being on TV?" he asked.

285

Carmela stopped smiling. "Just a quick sound bite," she said hurriedly. "Not even worth mentioning."

"Detective Babcock?" Gabby called out. "You have a visitor."

Seconds later, Peter Jarreau crowded into Carmela's office, his pungent aftershave filling the air.

"I've liaisoned with print media as well as broadcast concerning the events of last night, but I'm getting pushback," Jarreau announced to Babcock. "They're still demanding details. How much do you want me to release?"

"Don't tell them anything," Babcock said.

"That's going to go over like a lead balloon," Jarreau said.

"Too bad. That's how it has to be," Babcock said.

Jarreau made a quick note on his iPad. "Okay. Got it." Then he switched his focus to Carmela. "I wanted to speak with you, too."

"With me? What about?" Carmela asked.

"I wanted to make sure you weren't talking to the press," Jarreau said. "Giving any statements."

Carmela stared back at him. "Why would I do that?"

Now Babcock had to stick his two cents

286

in. "Oh, I don't know, maybe for the same reason you've insinuated yourself in the middle of our murder investigation?"

"Hey, I'm interested because my friend was killed!" Carmela cried. "And because I was there — almost there — when it happened." *Do they not understand this?*

"You have to leave the investigating to us," Babcock said.

"To the professionals," Jarreau said, his reply a little too sharp for Carmela's liking.

"Sure. Okay. Got it," Carmela said. In her mind she'd already blown off Peter Jarreau. "But I do have a quick question."

"What's that?" Babcock asked.

"Did you question Richard Drake again?"

"Not necessary," said Jarreau.

"But he's still a person of interest?" Carmela asked.

Babcock shrugged. "Maybe."

Jarreau shifted back and forth, then said, "Okay boss, I've got to get going."

"Don't call me boss," Babcock said as Jarreau hurried out of the shop.

"Aren't you the boss?" Carmela asked.

Babcock shrugged.

"I'm positive they're going to offer you that position as chief."

"They already did."

"Wow. What would that mean? More responsibility?"

"More time on the job," Babcock said.

"More time away from us," Carmela said.

There was a loud crackle, then a squawking sound. Not Babcock's cell phone but his radio.

He grabbed it off his belt and keyed in. "Yeah?"

The dispatcher rattled off a series of code numbers that Carmela didn't understand, then finished with ". . . tip on a Colonel Barnett Otis."

"Uh-huh," Babcock said. "Go on."

There was a string of loud crackling and then a garble of words that finished with ". . . possible owner of the knife that killed Sonny Boy Holmes."

Carmela leaned back in her chair. *What?*

But Babcock was already on his feet. "I gotta move on this," he said.

"Call me!" Carmela cried as he dashed out the door.

CHAPTER 22

Carmela was on pins and needles, waiting for Babcock to call back about Colonel Otis. This could be the big break they'd all been hoping for. Maybe, finally, Devon's murder would be solved and justice would be served.

After wolfing down a shrimp salad, Carmela waited on several customers, and now had time to put some finishing touches on the new menu she'd designed for the Praline Parlor café.

Because the Praline Parlor was located in a rehabbed cottage over in the Bywater area, she'd given the menu a quasi-French-Caribbean look. The name Praline Parlor was at the top, surrounded by an oval wreath of herbs and flowers. To the left of the wreath were two fancy forks, to the right were a knife and spoon. The menu would change daily, so Carmela had basically created a template that the restaurateurs could

use to feature their changing array of start-
ers, salads, entrées, and desserts.

Carmela added a floral motif at the bottom and then sat back to study her design.
She decided it was looking pretty good.

More and more, Carmela and Gabby had
been expanding Memory Mine from a
scrapbook shop into crafting and graphic
design. And it was starting to pay off big-
time. They'd already gotten design projects
from Tea Party in a Box, Bozwell Antiques,
and the French Rabbit Gift Shop.

"That menu design looks great," Gabby
said from over her shoulder. "It's got that
perfect bistro look. A little French, a little
New Orleans."

"Thank you. I just hope Liz and Jeffrey
like it." They were the owners of Praline
Parlor. Two thirty-somethings who'd
ditched their nine-to-five jobs, cashed in
their 401(k)s, and taken the terrifying leap
to become newly minted restaurateurs.

"They'll love it," Gabby promised. "And
what's with all the little tins?" Carmela was
surrounded by a small arsenal of empty Al-
toids tins, lip gloss tins, tea tins, and some
small round metal tins that she'd ordered
online.

"I'm thinking of teaching a class on
decorating tiny tins. So many people are

into the solid perfume trend."

"They sure are," Gabby said. "I even know a woman who makes solid perfumes right in her own kitchen. She does all kinds of natural scents like jasmine, rose, lily, honeysuckle, and mimosa."

"Sounds as if we should incorporate her know-how into our class."

"She'd probably be tickled." Gabby picked up a small tin that Carmela had covered with Japanese washi paper. "How'd you do this?" The paper was pale green, made from banana fiber, and scattered with tiny chrysanthemums.

"Nothing to it. First, I cut two small circles of washi paper, leaving a little bit extra to overlap. Then I sprayed glue on the top and bottom of the tin and placed the paper over each piece."

"Then you just pleated and folded the paper so it fit nicely," said Gabby, studying the tin. "Very few wrinkles, too."

"Luckily that type of paper is very forgiving."

An hour later, Carmela finally got the phone call she'd been waiting for.

"Well?" Carmela said to Babcock. "What happened? Did the tip pay off?"

"Colonel Otis has a rather extensive knife

291

collection. Spanish daggers, bowie knives, curved blade Japanese knives, Israeli knives, and even something called a *jambiya* knife from North Africa. You name it, he's got it."

"But?" Carmela said. She was hanging on Babcock's every word.

"But they're all in a large display case mounted on green velvet. And it doesn't appear that any of the knives are missing or have even been moved recently."

"So the bottom line is?" Carmela asked.

"That we couldn't pin a single thing on Colonel Otis. His only contact with Devon Dowling seems to be the art appraisal."

"Did you ask Colonel Otis where he was last night? Did he have an alibi?"

"Claims he was sitting at home, watching TV. The National Geographic Channel, something about coral reefs. His wife vouched for him."

"They could be in this together," Carmela said.

"I thought about that. I really did," Babcock said. "After all, the man only lives a block or two away from St. Louis Cemetery."

"Proximity is important," Carmela said.

"It is except for the fact that we received an anonymous tip about his knife collection. A typed letter that was stuck on the windshield of Bobby Gallant's car. And I rarely put much stock in anonymous tips."

"Do you think the note was a deliberate misdirection?" Carmela asked.

"I think that's exactly what it was."

"So now what? You're saying that talking to Colonel Otis was just a wild-goose chase. That somebody set you up?"

"Maybe they set me up and maybe they tried to set up Colonel Otis. I don't know, but this kind of thing makes me a little crazy," Babcock said.

"It's serving to intensify the search," Carmela said. "So that's good."

"No, things are too intense as it is. I just received a call from the mayor, and he wants to hold a press conference to announce that we apprehended Dowling's killer last night."

"Technically, you didn't apprehend him," Carmela said. "All you found — or, rather, I found — was another dead guy. Who may or may not be connected in a tertiary way."

"This whole case has become very tricky. Everybody wants to spin the story a different way." Babcock paused. "Including the mayor."

"That doesn't sound good. Can you convince the mayor to hold off on his press conference?" Carmela asked.

"Maybe. Hopefully. I'm going to try my

darnedest."

"Do the police have anything? Anything at all?" Carmela asked.

Babcock hesitated. "No. It's all smoke and mirrors and PR right now."

"And wishful thinking."

Silence spun out for a few moments, then Babcock said, "I thought you had an appointment to look at wedding gowns today."

"I do. In fact, I'm leaving in a few minutes," Carmela lied.

"Have fun, sweetheart. I'm sure you'll look beautiful in all of the dresses."

Feeling a tinge of guilt, Carmela hung up the phone and immediately called Ava.

"What are you doing right now?" she asked when Ava answered.

"Um. Unpacking my new line of organic voodoo dolls?"

"Is Miguel working today?" Miguel was Ava's assistant.

"He's here."

"Can you bug out early?"

"What is this, twenty questions?"

"Here's the deal. I kind of told Babcock I was going wedding gown shopping today."

Ava screamed so loudly that Carmela was forced to hold the phone away from her ear.

Wedding gown shopping?" Ava screeched again at the top of her lungs, sounding like an injured banshee.

"It brings you that much joy? Or was that a cry of pain? Another single lady bites the dust?"

"No, I'm totally thrilled!" Ava said. "Be still my heart. This is big . . . no, this is huge! I'm in. Where are we headed, *cher*?"

"I thought maybe Amour Couture over on Dumaine Street. Do you think you can peel yourself away from your voodoo dolls and meet me there in twenty minutes?"

"You got it, chickadee!"

Gabby was staring at Carmela when she hung up the phone. Her eyes sparkled, her nose fairly quivered.

"You're really going to shop for a wedding gown?" Gabby asked. "Really?"

"That seems to be the consensus. Should we close early so you can come along? You know I'd love your opinion, even if you are the calm, rational one."

"Yes, I want to go!" Gabby cried. Then she threw up both hands and waved them in the air. "Wait, no! I shouldn't. I can't." She pursed her lips and made a lemon face. "You know what, Carmela? The truth is, I'd rather wait and be surprised. I want to hold out until the big day arrives. Then I can gasp at the full cinematic effect when you finally walk down the aisle."

"That's very sweet of you. But what if there's not a traditional aisle to walk down? What if Babcock and I don't get married in a church? What if it's — oh, I don't know — a riverboat?"

"Please don't do that," Gabby cried. "Please think about the dead fish and the disruptive tugboat toots."

"Okay, no boat. I promise."

"But the walking-down-the-aisle thing, that's no problem, Carmela. I'm sure you'll find the perfect venue. And I'm totally overjoyed that you're *finally* taking this wedding seriously."

"You're sure you don't want to come along?"

Gabby shook her head. "I'm seriously into delayed gratification. But if you want help picking out earrings or veils or even a venue, you know I'm happy to lend a hand!"

Amour Couture was a small, elegant jewel box of a shop. Lot of shiny black accents against white carpets, white walls, and (obviously!) white dresses. Even the sales lady, who welcomed them and introduced herself as Greta Mignon, was wearing a sleek, size two, black skirt suit. With her blond hair scraped back into a tight chignon accented with a black bow, Greta appeared practically ageless, anywhere from forty to sixty.

"Congratulations," Greta said to Carmela. "Welcome. It's always an honor to help a new bride select her bridal gown." She sat Carmela and Ava down in white club chairs, gave them each a glass of champagne, and said, "What type of ceremony do you have planned?"

"That's still up in the air," Carmela said.

Clearly, Greta was familiar with this type of on-the-fence answer from a would-be bride, because she segued skillfully into her second question: "Then what kind of bride are you, my dear?"

"Nervous?" Carmela said.

Greta laughed merrily. "Of course you are. You're taking a huge step. What I meant was, do you picture yourself as a barefoot, on-the-beach, bohemian bride? Or perhaps a classic church-and-country-club bride? Or is your style more romantic or sexy or even trendy?"

"Sexy," Ava said. "Definitely sexy."

"Romantic?" Carmela said. She wasn't sure what that meant, but it sounded nice. Like something Babcock would approve of.

"Spoilsport," Ava muttered.

Greta beamed at Carmela. "And what style of dress do you want to try on? Are

297

you looking for a ball gown, a fit and flare, perhaps a mermaid style, or . . . ?"

"Ball gown," Ava said. "But extremely low-cut."

"Mmn, something simple and elegant," Carmela said.

"She means boring and conservative," Ava said. "Carmela's not exactly an edgy leather and lace chick. But since I'm gonna be her maid of honor, you can count on me to add a dash of cheekiness to the ceremony."

"I'm sure that will be lovely," Greta said.

Carmela went into the dressing room and tried on a poufy ball gown–style dress. When she saw her image in the mirror, she laughed out loud and said, "This is way too over-the-top. I look like I should be climbing into a pumpkin coach at midnight."

"It reminds me of that creepy Marie Antoinette puppet," Ava said.

"Then get me out of this thing!" Carmela cried as Greta rushed to help.

"I never thought I'd say this, *cher,* but you do gotta go a lot simpler," Ava said.

But the cream-colored A-line dress Carmela tried on was too simple, and a blush-colored fit and flare was just too weird.

"This is starting to feel like 'Goldilocks and the Three Bears,' " Carmela said to Ava when Greta dashed off in search of more dresses. "One's too hard, one's too soft. Hopefully, there'll be one that's just right."

"You'll find the perfect dress," Ava said. "I know you will. But while we're at it, I did a little digging of my own." She hastily produced a purple floor-length gown festooned with tiers of cheetah print ruffles. "What about this for my maid of honor dress?"

"It's great if you don't mind being mistaken for Miss Kitty at the Long Branch Saloon," Carmela said. "Ava, honey, if you're going to be my maid of honor — or even my maid of dishonor — you've got to look halfway weddingish."

Ava gave a thumbs-up. "Gotcha. I guess we need to kind of meld our styles."

"Something like that, yes."

Ava pulled out a red halter dress with a beaded waist. "Now this one's totally gorgeous. Very Grecian."

"Which is wonderful if we're going to dance to bouzouki music and smash plates. But we're not."

"Still too much?"

Carmela nodded her head in the affirmative.

"Are we having any luck?" Greta asked from the doorway of the fitting room.

Both Carmela and Ava shook their heads.

"Why don't you try this?" Greta said, handing a gown to Carmela. "It's very romantic in its styling. Very popular with brides today."

But when Carmela put it on, Ava laughed out loud at the puffy sleeves and high lace neck.

"*Cher,* you look like one of those spooky old-fashioned dolls. You know the ones that come alive and try to strangle you?"

"Thanks a lot," Carmela said.

It was a good thing Greta stepped in to save the day.

"I don't know if this is exactly your style," Greta said, "but I've got a wedding gown that's . . . shall we say, rather special?"

"More special than this one?" Carmela asked. Even she had to laugh at the lace insets and flowing sash.

"Let's see whatcha got," said Ava.

Greta's choice turned out to be a backless halter dress with a touch of lace on the bodice and a free-flowing skirt.

"I like it," Carmela said once she had it on.

"It's a little bit Marilyn," Ava said. "Plus, it's always nice to show a hint of skin."

"This is more than a hint," Greta said.

Carmela positioned herself in the three-way mirror. "It's glam, but not revealing in a bad way."

"Do you think you'd want to wear a long veil?" Greta asked.

Carmela shook her head.

"How about adding a bustle," Ava suggested. "Give Carmela a touch more booty."

"No, thanks," Carmela said.

"I think maybe . . . a blusher veil?" Greta said as she slipped a small ivory headpiece onto Carmela's head. "It's literally called a tulle birdcage veil. And, as you can see, this one's sprinkled with small crystals."

Carmela stared at herself in the mirror. The dress looked absolutely gorgeous, and the tulle veil, which barely covered her eyes and nose, lent the perfect accent.

"Ooh!" Ava squealed. "I love how that veil adds a special hint of mystery!"

Mystery? Me? Carmela thought.

"You look very beautiful," Greta said to Carmela.

"You do," Ava said. "It's perfection."

Carmela glanced at herself in the mirror, checking every angle. Then she nodded her head slowly as a beatific smile spread slowly across her face. "You're right, it's perfect."

CHAPTER 23

Carmela watched as Ava poked and prodded her way through an assortment of paints, powders, eye shadows, and lipsticks that she'd dumped out on top of her dining room table.

"Where's that scintillating lipstick I bought at my friend Tinsley's makeup party last week?" Ava asked as her fingertips danced across a dozen golden tubes. "The one called Infrared?"

"You sure we have to get all glammed up?" Carmela asked. "Can't we just dab on a little bit of mascara? Or skip it and go au naturel?"

"Au naturel means boring and bland, cupcake. Don't you want to convey a sense of fabulosity when you judge the gumbo cook-off tonight?"

"You really think a bunch of gumbo foodies are going to care what I look like?" Carmela asked. "Won't they be too busy stuffing their faces and demanding more okra?"

"And then there's the Most Eligible Bachelor Auction afterward," Ava reminded her in no uncertain terms.

Carmela winced. She'd forgotten about that. Tried to forget anyway.

"The Bachelor Auction. Crap. I suppose I should try to look a little better than whatever poor, unsuspecting woman is the high bidder for Shamus."

"Frankly, I don't know who'd even *want* to bid on Shamus. It's not like he's a prize catch or anything," Ava said.

"It's all about the money," Carmela said. "Shamus has that air of *eau de bankroll* wafting about him."

"Yeah, that can be a potent draw. But, seriously, is Shamus even technically a bachelor?"

"He is for charitable purposes. He's going to be someone's tax deduction."

"Maybe Shamus's bad boy reputation will precede him and nobody will bid on him," Ava said. "Or *you* can turn the tables and bid on him." She gave a wicked cackle.

"Been there, done that," Carmela said.

"But if you won, you could force Shamus to do all sorts of odious chores. You know, like defrost the freezer or clean the vegetable drawer. Pick up dog poop."

"Let's get back to the makeup," Carmela said.

"Gotcha."

Ava smoothed foundation over Carmela's face, then applied a light dusting of powder.

"I'm giving you a slightly darker look," she said. "To make you look a trifle exotic."

"Just don't use that baby blue eye shadow on me, okay? Last time you made me up I looked like some kind of weird cross between a Stepford wife and a Dresden doll."

Ava gently smoothed eye shadow onto Carmela's lids with a finger.

"I'm using a color called Serpentine Green," Ava said.

"Sounds weird."

"No, it's gorgeous and very blendable. Now hold perfectly still while I apply a touch of mascara."

Carmela held still. She felt the mascara go on and then something like spiders touching her lashes. Was it a second coat of mascara?

"What is that?" she asked.

"Big surprise," Ava said.

"I'm not really in the mood for surprises." Carmela reached for a hand mirror, held it up, and gasped. "Ava! What did you do?"

"Like it?"

"My eyes look like tarantulas!"

"No, no, sweetie, they look magnetic. Because they *are* magnetic."

"What?"

"They're the newest, hottest beauty trend. Magnetic eyelashes. You see? There are two sets of lashes, each with tiny magnets in them. You just snap them on over your own scraggly lashes and, voilà! Instant sexy bedroom eyes."

"And these will stay on?"

Carmela was studying her eyelashes in the mirror and (strangely) starting to get used to them. They did make her eyes look huge and exotic. Maybe that was a good thing?

"They'll stay on just fine," Ava said. "But because they're magnetic, maybe you shouldn't get too close to a metal door-frame. Or a power line. Or hold a fork near your eye. Just in case. You know what I mean?"

"Ava!"

"Kidding. I'm kidding. See, I'm wearing them myself and they look fabulous." Ava batted her lashes at about fifty flits a second. "Okay, let's move on to your wardrobe."

"Camel sweater and beige slacks?" Carmela said.

Ava stuck out her tongue and made a gagging sound. "Good thing I brought along a wardrobe bag stuffed full of goodies."

"But nothing too outrageous." Ava had once convinced Carmela to wear a sequined zebra-striped dress. It had taken months to live that fashion disaster down.

"I'm thinking va-va-voom combined with a bit of down home."

"I don't know what that means," Carmela said.

"A gold sequined jacket paired with blue jeans," Ava said.

"Really?" Carmela wasn't exactly blown away. In fact, it sounded like a weird combo.

But Ava was insistent. "Try it. For me."

So Carmela did. She dug out a pair of soft, faded, light blue denim jeans, added a black tank top, and then put on the sequined jacket. The pairing looked . . . amazing.

"Wow," Carmela said as she stared at herself in her smoky mirror and saw a very fashion-forward girl looking back at her.

"You see how cute you look?" Ava said. "Very high-low. All the celebs are doing it. I'm forever seeing photos in *Star Whacker* magazine. Blue jeans with a Dior jacket. A plain white T-shirt with silk pants and Manolo heels."

"Are you going to do this high-low thing, too?" Carmela asked. Right now, Ava was wearing skintight white silk slacks with a low-cut black top.

"I'm going to do high-high," Ava said. She reached into her bag and pulled out a red leather jacket. When she put it on and snapped two buttons closed, the jacket snugged her like a kid glove.

"You're not going to be able to snarf down all the different gumbos if you're wearing *that* outfit," Carmela said. "It doesn't look like you can even breathe."

Ava shrugged. "How many entries can there be?"

That question was answered the moment they entered the Enchantment Ballroom at the Marquis Hotel. The mingled aroma of shrimp, crab, okra, sausage, Cajun spices, bay leaves, thyme, and filé gumbo powder hovered in a roiling cloud of foodie perfume. Gigantic pots of gumbo steamed like slumbering volcanoes as samples were doled out by proud chefs wearing crisp white jackets and toques.

"Good gravy," Ava cried. "Looks like the gang's all here."

At first glance they saw that Bayou Betty's, Bing Bang's Gumbo, Black Bottom Gumbo, and McTooth's Café were all represented. And there were lots more restaurant booths scattered throughout the room.

"I wonder if Quigg is here, too?" Carmela said. Quigg's chefs served up some mean gumbos at all three of his restaurants.

"He's a serious player so he has to be here," Ava said. "And take a look at this crowd. Lots of pretty people all jammed elbow to armpit."

Carmela gazed out over the enormous, jostling crowd. People shuffled from booth to booth, tasting gumbo, drinking beer, greeting friends, and having a generally raucous time. In one corner of the room, a zydeco group stood on a raised bandstand and pounded out traditional rhythms.

"Helen told me this was a major Jazz Fest event," Carmela said. "How is it we never hit this up before?"

Ava shrugged. "Dunno. But we're here now, so let's dig in."

"Carmela! Oh, Carmela!"

Carmela turned to find Helen McBride, the editor in chief of *Glutton for Punishment,* making a beeline for her. Her orangey-red hair was usually frizzy, but today the frizz was supersized due to the industrial-strength humidity hanging in the air. Helen's mouth was turned down in a frown, she'd bitten off all her lipstick, and she was dressed in her usual go-to sports gear — a hoodie top and yoga pants.

308

"Helen," Carmela said.

"There you are." Helen touched a hand to her forehead in a theatrical gesture. "Thank goodness. I need to round up my judges and get this party started."

"You remember my friend Ava?" Carmela said.

"Ava. Sure," Helen said. "In fact, I got something for you." She shoved a wristband into Ava's hands. "Snap this on, honey, and then you won't need to buy any tickets for the gumbo or beer tastings."

"Hot dang!" Ava said.

"And you, my little kumquat," Helen said, grabbing Carmela's arm and pinching it hard. "You need to come with me."

Helen dragged Carmela through the crowd toward a judges' table in the corner.

"Nancy!" Helen called out.

A blond woman in a black body-con dress turned and smiled.

"Carmela, meet Nancy Eggers," Helen said. "Nancy does restaurant reviews on KLEZ radio. Freelances with us sometimes as well."

"Hi," Carmela said as she shook hands with Nancy. "Nice to meet you."

"Carmela here is a local entrepreneur and foodie. She's a partner in that new wine bar with Quigg Brevard."

309

"Actually, I'm just helping him out," Carmela said. "No strings attached."

"Lovely to meet you anyway," Nancy said.

"And where is . . . Oh, there you are," Helen said. "Roy, get your behind over here, will you?"

A silver-haired man turned to face them, and Carmela recognized his jowls instantly. It was Roy Sultan, the real estate developer.

Carmela and Roy stared at each other for a few long moments, until Helen began barking orders.

"Here are your badges, judging sheets, and clipboards," Helen said, handing them a packet of materials. "And first things first, please stick on your shiny bright *OFFICIAL JUDGE* badges."

Everyone complied.

"Now remember the golden rule of gumbo." Helen held up an index finger. "It has to have the consistency of stew, not soup. If it's soupy, it's out!"

The judges nodded and Roy Sultan made a move to start for the restaurant tables, but Helen reined him back.

"Do not forget," Helen said, "that gumbo is Louisiana's state cuisine. So it's imperative that we recognize only the very best of the best and do Louisiana proud!"

There were mumbled okays from the three judges.

Helen cocked a knowing eye at them. "Some of the gumbos represented here are Cajun gumbos and some are Creole gumbos. Do you people understand the major difference?"

This time the mumbles were indistinct.

"Tomatoes," Helen said, enunciating carefully as if she were doing after-school remedial instruction to a class of dummies. "Creole gumbo includes tomato, Cajun does not. Got that?"

Everyone understood.

"One last thing," Helen said. "I want you to cast your personal preferences aside for now. I don't care if squirrel meat makes you puke, or crab or Gulf shrimp gives you a case of hives. You are here to judge the overall quality and flavor of each dish without any personal bias. Is that clear?"

Carmela had the sudden urge to salute.

"And remember our judging parameters. Hot, spicy, and zingy." Helen clapped her hands together. "Now let's get out there and do this!"

Carmela started out at Bluefish Bob's Booth. Here the gumbo was piquant and spicy, a dark, flavorful roux filled with seafood and sausage. On a scale of one to ten, she rated it an eight.

Moving on to La Belle Bistro, Carmela found herself tasting a wonderful duck and sausage gumbo. This gumbo was served with a side of rice. Probably a nine because she was so fond of duck, although she wasn't supposed to let her personal preferences enter in. But how could she not?

Carmela continued to methodically work her way from booth to booth, tasting every gumbo and marking her scores. It was warm, noisy, crowded, and getting even more crowded in the ballroom, so she was pleased to be wearing her *JUDGE* sticker. No pesky waiting in line!

Ava came up and nudged Carmela while she was sampling a spoonful of Bayou Betty's gumbo.

"How you doin'?" Ava asked. She waved a hand in front of her mouth. "Need a Pepcid AC yet?"

"I'm getting there," Carmela said. She'd tasted something like fourteen gumbos and still had thirteen more to go.

"Me, I'm cooling my gumbo afterburn with a few sloshes of Abita Beer."

"Lucky you," Carmela said.

"Have you tried Quigg's gumbo yet?" Ava asked.

Carmela shook her head. "No. Is he here?"

Ava glanced to her left. "I don't see . . . Wait. Yes, I do. He's not only standing inside the Mumbo Gumbo booth, he's waving at us to come over."

"You don't need to taste all those other gumbos," Quigg said to Carmela when she approached his booth. "Ours is hands-down, smack-yo-momma the best. One taste and you can't help but give us the trophy." He paused. "What's wrong with your eyes?"

"Nothing," Carmela said. "Eye makeup, that's all."

"It looks weird."

"Can we just taste the gumbo?" Ava asked.

"Whatever," Quigg said as he turned to his chef, a behemoth African American man named Bernie who'd been named a top chef several times by the food critic at the *Times-Picayune*. "Bernie, let's give these ladies a bowl of gumbo, shall we? And let's supersize 'em."

"I only need a taste," Carmela said.

"That's all it takes," Bernie said with a wink. "One taste and you'll be hooked for good."

"You want me to hold your clipboard while you eat?" Quigg asked, trying to read what she'd written on her scorecard. "Here, hand that puppy over."

"No way," Carmela said. "You'll cheat."

Quigg gave her an injured look. "Me? Never."

"Yes, you would!" Carmela and Ava cried out together while Bernie just chuckled.

Carmela finished making her rounds, winding up at Black Bottom Gumbo for her final tasting. She was sampling their sausage and okra gumbo just as Roy Sultan lurched up, bumped into her, and almost caused her to spill her bowl of gumbo.

"You done yet?" Sultan asked her. "Made it to every booth?" He was red-faced and sweating, clearly struggling to get through the tastings.

"All done," Carmela said, trying to keep her voice even.

"I got one more to go. This one." Sultan accepted a bowl of gumbo, then set it down on the counter, untouched, as he mopped his brow with a hanky and rolled his eyes. "Hope it's not too hot. All these spices and peppers give me dyspepsia. You know there's actually a pepper called a Carolina Reaper? And one called a Trinidad Scorpion?"

"Guess so," Carmela said. She'd finished her tasting and was now marking scores on her sheet, trying to ignore him.

"You don't like me much, do you?" Sultan edged in closer, his voice tinged with disdain. "You don't trust me."

"Why would I?" Carmela said. "After you tried to oust Devon."

Or maybe you were the one who killed him.

Out of the corner of her eye, Carmela saw Ava sneaking up on them. Ava had an evil grin on her face as she reached out, grabbed a bottle of Bayou Blow Torch Hot Sauce, and squirted a giant helping into Sultan's bowl of gumbo.

"I'm a good judge of character, girly," Sultan snarled. He turned back to his bowl, picked it up, and shoveled an enormous spoonful of gumbo into his mouth. "I suppose you think you're a smart . . ."

That was all Sultan managed to get out. The rest of his words turned into a cacophony of piteous gags and urps.

Perspiration rolled off his forehead, his face took on a pinched, severely pained expression, and his voice rose three octaves to a high-pitched rasp. "Holy flaming balls of . . . aaagh!"

Sultan clutched at his throat with both hands and staggered away as Carmela and Ava stood there and laughed themselves silly.

CHAPTER 24

"That was a good one, huh, *cher*?" Ava asked. She was still laughing as they headed for the judges' table. "Roy Sultan looked like he was about to blow a gasket."

"He was acting like a real jerk, so the hot sauce was a timely move on your part," Carmela agreed. "Thank you."

"That's what friends are for."

Helen saw them coming and said to Carmela, "Did you visit every booth? Taste every single gumbo? Do you have your scores ready?"

"Here you go," Carmela said, handing over her score sheet. "And, cross my heart, I tasted every one of them."

Helen quickly scanned Carmela's score sheet. "This is quite interesting," she said. "Your marks pretty much jibe with what Nancy thought, too. I think we might end up having a clear winner." She looked up, frowned, and said, "Where the hell is Roy

Sultan? Why hasn't he turned in his scores?"

"I think he might be indisposed," Ava said, which sent her into a fit of snorts and giggles.

Helen set off in search of the elusive Mr. Sultan and returned five minutes later with his score sheet.

"You weren't kidding when you said he was indisposed," Helen said. "Holy cow, I had to go and . . . well, never mind all that. I've got his scores now." She grabbed a pencil, made a few marks, and did some quick addition. "Yup, good, it's pretty much a consensus."

"So whose gumbo is the grand prize winner?" Ava asked.

But Helen had already grabbed a large gold trophy and was marching purposefully toward the bandstand. She drew a hand across her neck in the universal "cut" sign, and the band immediately stopped playing. Helen jumped onstage and grabbed the microphone.

"Ladies and gentlemen," her voice rang out. "On behalf of *Glutton for Punishment,* New Orleans's favorite webzine for all things fabulous and foodie, I want to thank you all for coming here tonight to support our Roux the Night Gumbo Cook-Off."

The crowd, stuffed to the max with beer,

gumbo, and bonhomie, cheered wildly. A few people whistled, and someone in the back of the room let loose a wild man howl.

"I especially want to thank our intrepid judges who made it . . . well, most of them did anyway . . . to all twenty-seven of our outstanding gumbo booths."

Ava nudged Carmela's arm. "Hah."

"And to all our restaurant participants, we are so thrilled to have you here to share your unique gumbo recipes with us. Now, without further ado," Helen said, "I'm delighted to present our grand prize trophy to Bayou Betty's, who received an overall perfect score of thirty points!"

There was more loud cheering as Betty Martine, of Bayou Betty's, hurried up to the bandstand to accept her trophy.

"Now can you have a drink?" Ava asked Carmela. "Or is your tummy too full and urpy?"

"I definitely need something cool to soothe my throat and innards," Carmela said. She waved a hand in front of her mouth. "I do believe that was the most servings of gumbo I ever ate at one time."

"Say now," said Ava. "I *parlez-vous'd* with a couple of sous chefs from Black Bottom Gumbo, and they were asking if we'd like to get together and have a drink with them later. Whadya think?"

"Seriously?"

"Hey, I'm just asking. I'm just the messenger."

"Black Bottom boys no, hit the bar yes," Carmela said as they pushed their way through the throng, finally ending up at a busy three-sided bar.

"How can I help you ladies?" asked one of the bartenders. He wore a white shirt, black vest, bolo tie, and a name tag that said FRANKIE.

"Whatever's cold and wet," Carmela said.

"Ditto," Ava said.

"We got Abita, NOLA Blonde, Crescent City Pilsner, and Turbodog," Frankie said.

"Gimme a Turbodog!" a voice called out.

Carmela glanced sideways and immediately saw T.J. standing there. He was swaying slightly and looked like he'd been hammering back drinks all night long.

"Three Turbodogs," Carmela told Frankie. Then she turned and said, "T.J. How do."

"Ayup," T.J. said, nodding at her, his eyes slightly glazed.

"What brings you here, cupcake?" Ava asked as Frankie slid three bottles of beer across the counter to them. She tossed down a twenty and told him, "Keep the

319

change."

"T.J.," Carmela said as she passed out the beers. "You look a little down in the mouth." Actually, T.J. looked incredibly despondent and depressed. But maybe that's because he'd been drinking? He didn't seem to have much capacity to hold his liquor.

"You'd be feeling down, too, if you'd just been fired from your job," T.J. said, his tone slightly aggressive.

"You mean at Dulcimer Antiques?" Ava asked.

"Mr. Dowling's brother has decided to close the shop for good. I told him we could relocate and I could run it, that I had all the necessary skills, but he said no."

"Just no? Just like that?" Ava asked.

"Well, it was 'no, thanks,' but a very indifferent 'no, thanks,' if you ask me," T.J. said. "I don't think he minded putting me clean out of a job. Maybe he even enjoyed it."

"I'm sorry to hear that," Carmela said.

Am I really? Maybe yes, maybe no.

"What's going to happen to all of Devon's beautiful merchandise?" Carmela asked.

T.J. took a swig of beer and let his shoulders droop. "It's all going to be transferred to a shop owned by one of Devon's friends, Charles Chittendon of Victoriana Antiques."

"Oh, sure, I know Charles," Carmela said.

"Is there any chance you could get a job with him?"

T.J. shook his head. "Nope, already tried. Interviewed with Mr. Chittendon and everything, but it's a no-go."

"That's a tough break," Ava said.

"Anyway," T.J. continued, "Mr. Chittendon will be selling all of Mr. Dowling's pieces on commission. These last couple of days, I've been working my fingers to the bone, sorting and packing objects like crazy. Trying to find any descriptions and paperwork that Mr. Dowling might have kept on the various objects." He took another swig of beer and swayed slightly. "Mr. Dowling wasn't the best record keeper." T.J. squinted at Carmela. "And that guy who was helping with the judging tonight? Mr. Sultan, the landlord?"

"What about him?" Carmela asked.

"He's been on my ass telling me to hurry up and clean up the place. You have no idea how much clutter there is. I mean, just the paper alone!" T.J. slapped a hand against his forehead. "Devon was a collector of . . . well, I guess a dedicated scrapbooker like yourself would probably call it ephemera."

Carmela's ears perked up. "Is that so? Ephemera? Really?"

"You can't imagine all the paper and

321

labels and old maps and foreign postage stamps and wrapping materials that Mr. Dowling had saved over the years he'd been there," T.J. said. "I'm afraid he was a bit of a clutter bug. To my eyes, it's all trash can worthy."

"You know, I'm teaching a Paper University class next week, and I'd love a chance to go through all of that paper stuff before you toss it in the Dumpster," Carmela said.

"Come over tomorrow afternoon then," T.J. said as he wandered away. "You're welcome to it. Oh." He hoisted his beer. "Thanks for the beer."

"Holy macaroni," Ava said. "That kid is really bummed."

"Maybe he's got a guilty conscience."

Ava lifted an eyebrow. "You think?"

"I don't know. I wish I knew, but I don't."

"You'll figure it out, you always do," Ava said. "In the meantime, we need to go spy on Shamus."

Carmela smiled. "That auction might be good for a laugh or two."

A tuxedo-clad man with shaggy gray hair and a walrus mustache greeted them at the door of the River Vista Room.

"Good evening, ladies. And welcome to our Most Eligible Bachelor Auction," the man said. "The bidding just started a few minutes ago, so there are still many fine gentlemen available."

"How many guys in total?" Ava asked.

"A dozen of New Orleans's finest young men," the man said, giving them a wink. He handed them numbered voting paddles and programs with bachelor bios, and then said, "That'll be twenty dollars. Each."

"You mean we have to *pay*?" Ava asked.

"It's a fund-raiser," the man said.

Carmela and Ava paid their entry fee and stepped into the room.

"Holy crap," Ava said under her breath as they gazed about. "This reminds me of a middle school dance."

"Boys on one side of the room, girls on the other," Carmela said.

Only in this case, there was a line of uncomfortable-looking bachelors seated behind a podium and about three dozen predatory-looking women sitting in the audience. The auctioneer was a tall, dark-haired woman in a slinky black dress. Her name was Monica something, and Carmela recognized her from her time on the French Quarter Arts Board.

"This is gonna be interesting," Ava said as they slid into seats in the back row. The room was fairly dark and moody, except for overhead spotlights aimed at the podium and the row of waiting bachelors. One bachelor was already up for auction.

"That's Sugar Joe," Carmela said. Sugar Joe Panola was one of Shamus's good friends.

"As you can see," the auctioneer said, "our bachelor is not only handsome, he's very well turned out."

At that, Sugar Joe stuck his hands in his jacket pockets and negotiated a jaunty little spin.

"Our bachelor, Mr. Joe, enjoys football, fishing, and fine dining," the auctioneer said.

"The three F's," Ava said.

"Shall we start the bidding at one hundred dollars? Do I hear one hundred?" the auctioneer asked.

A smart-looking middle-aged blonde in the front row stuck her paddle in the air and said, "One hundred dollars."

"One fifty," another woman called out just as Carmela's phone burped in her purse.

She pulled it out and said, "Hello?"

"Carmela?" It was Babcock.

"Hey there," she said, happy to hear his voice.

"How'd the gumbo judging go?"

"It was actually kind of fun," Carmela

whispered into her phone as the bidding on Sugar Joe continued.

"No ill effects?"

"I feel full, if that's what you mean."

"Carmela?"

"Um, yeah?"

"Where are you? It sounds like there's some kind of auction going on."

"It's nothing, believe me," Carmela said. "Can you drop by my place tonight?"

"Can't, sweetheart. I'll have to call you tomorrow."

"Absolutely." Carmela clicked off, feeling slightly guilty about being at the auction. Oh well, it was for amusement purposes only. Nothing serious with Shamus, that's for sure.

"Was that Babcock?" Ava asked.

"Yup."

"Did you tell him where we were?"

"Nope."

"Smart girl," Ava said as she scanned her bachelor bio program. "Hey, you'll never guess who bachelor number five is."

Carmela answered, "Vampire man. Richard Drake."

"How'd you know that? You haven't even looked at your program."

"Don't have to. I'm staring at him right now."

325

Ava blinked, focused her eyes on the line of bachelors, and made a sound somewhere between a giggle and a simper. "Drake is so delish. I think maybe I should bid on him."

"On Drake? Are you crazy?" Carmela hissed. "What if he's the one who killed Devon? Do you really want to end up in a scary dark place with him?"

"You think . . . not?" Ava said.

"I think . . . never."

"Is *everybody* a murder suspect?" Ava muttered to herself. "Aren't there any guys left to date? Well, I suppose T.J.'s too much of a boozehound, and I wouldn't wanna date Roy Sultan, because he's an old billy goat, but . . ."

Carmela lifted a hand to shush Ava. "Pay attention, it looks as if our dear sweet Shamus is up next."

Looking confident and rich-boy languid in a tuxedo with black satin lapels, Shamus strutted across the stage.

"Next up, Shamus Meechum," the auctioneer said. "And, ladies, this bachelor's a rather good catch. Vice president at Crescent City Bank and owner of a luxury condo in the up and coming CBD, the Central Business District. Mr. Shamus is also a connoisseur of fine wines and a member of the

Pluvius krewe. Shall we start the bidding at . . ."

"Two bits," Ava called out.

The auctioneer laughed it off, but Shamus's face darkened to a deep red.

"Surely, we can do better than that," the auctioneer said in a light tone. "Do I hear one hundred?"

A young woman in a pink tweed Dior jacket stuck her paddle in the air and called out, "Five hundred dollars!"

"Five hundred dollars," the auctioneer gushed. "That's an amazing opening bid!"

"Six hundred dollars," another woman called out.

There was a stir of excitement throughout the room, and the bidding continued, going up in fifty-dollar increments, until the woman in the Dior jacket finally raised her paddle and said, "One thousand dollars!"

"Sold!" the auctioneer said as she slammed her gavel down on the podium.

"Crap on a cracker!" Ava cried. "Who'd have guessed Shamus would fetch that kind of money?"

"He didn't," Carmela said.

"But that woman just . . ."

"She's his girlfriend," Carmela said.

"What!"

"One of three women that he's currently

juggling. Which means she's a ringer," Carmela said. "I'll bet anything that Shamus gave her the money to drive up the bids on him. A *lot* of money so he was guaranteed not to lose face."

"It's like Louisiana politics," Ava said. "The fix is always in."

CHAPTER 25

"We're all dressed up and it's Friday night, the tenderloin of the weekend," Ava said. "So what's our next stop? Kizzy's or Baby Blue's should be jumping and bumping for Jazz Fest. Either of those clubs sound good to you?"

Pulling her two-seater Mercedes away from the curb, Carmela said, "I have a better idea."

A block later, Ava drummed her nails on the dashboard and said, "I'm still waiting. What's this 'better idea' of yours? Is it gonna blow my socks off? Oh, are you thinking about that new place on Frenchmen Street? I hear it's a rather divine meat market."

"I thought we might take a drive through the Garden District."

"Whuh?" Ava shook her head. "You don't fool me, mama. I know that tone of voice. You're up to something sneaky."

"Truth be known, I've still got my eye on

329

Colonel Otis," Carmela said.

"We're all dolled up and you want to fritter away our gorgeousness stalking some old fuddy-duddy?"

"It's not stalking . . . exactly. It's just a drive-by. And he *is* a suspect, after all."

Ava plucked at her white slacks. "Well . . . maybe. As long as we can go someplace super glitzy and glam afterward."

But when they turned the corner onto Chestnut Street, they were shocked to see Colonel Otis's antebellum house lit up like a Christmas tree.

"You're sure this is the right address?" Ava asked.

"Pretty sure. I looked it up on the Internet."

"Hot damn, looks like the old fuddy-duddy is really a party animal in drag."

Carmela stopped her car even with the house. Every time a new car pulled to the curb, a red-jacketed valet ran out to assist the guest and then park the car. And gazing through tall windows swagged with velvet drapes, they saw a jostle of guests hoisting glasses while tuxedo-clad waiters offered hors d'oeuvres from silver trays. Bursts of loud music exploded outward every time the front door opened.

"This changes everything," Carmela said.

"I agree," Ava said. She rubbed her hands together. "You wanna crash?"

Carmela thought about this idea for all of one second. With a party this big, would a couple of extra guests be noticed? Perhaps it was time to find out.

She pulled her car around the corner and slid into a parking spot. Two minutes later, Carmela and Ava were tiptoeing down a shrubbery-lined alley. From there it was just a simple matter of easing themselves through a tangle of magnolias and onto the crowded back patio. Smiling, grabbing flutes of champagne from the tray of a passing waiter, they mingled with the crowd.

"This is fun, *cher,*" Ava said. "Like crashing a wedding, only better. You don't have to do a stupid dollar dance and stick money in the groom's pants pocket. I think we should do this party crashing thing more often." She glanced around. "It might be an excellent way to meet men." She took a sip of champagne. "I mean besides clubbing and cocktailing."

Being practically anonymous in the midst of all these partygoers had emboldened Carmela. She gazed around an elegant garden with its flaming tiki torches, string quartet, slow-dancing guests, and bar that was professionally staffed.

This is how the other half lives, she thought to herself. *A little bit . . . decadent.*

Then again, this was New Orleans, also known as "The City That Care Forgot." Money, liquor, rich food, trust funds, and crazy partying led to some truly bad behavior.

Carmela nudged Ava. "Let's take a look inside and see what's shakin'."

As they walked through a set of French doors into an enormous living room, Ava let loose a low whistle.

"What's shakin' is greenbacks dropping out of the proverbial money tree," she said. "Will you look at this place? Can you say palatial? With a touch of splendor? Your Colonel Otis must have spent a fortune on décor!"

The interior of the house was indeed stunning. Cream-colored walls displayed a superb collection of oil paintings, while large bronze sculptures rested on white marble cubes. There were two twelve-foot-long contemporary gray suede sofas along with clusters of traditional high-backed chairs covered in rose-colored silk fabric. A crystal chandelier hung from the ceiling, a stone fireplace with enough room to roast a wild boar sat at one end of the room, and a large dining room could be seen through a doorway that was flanked by panels of Egyptian wood carvings.

"Yeah, I could live here," Ava said. "I'm not averse to a little sumptuousness. Heck, I could be the queen of sumptuousness if you gave me half a chance."

Carmela's eyes were immediately drawn to the collection of paintings. "Every painting here is a collector's dream," she said as she stepped closer to take a look. "Museum quality."

"That so?" Ava said.

"Just look at this landscape. You see the artist's signature? It's Thomas Cole."

"The only Cole I know is Kenneth Cole," Ava said. "Mr. Fabulous Shoes himself."

"And this one's a Thomas Hart Benton. Amazing."

"You think some of this stuff could be stolen?" Ava asked. "That Colonel Otis makes it a habit to work with underhanded dealers?"

"I thought that might be the case at first, but now I don't think so. These pieces are all by well-known artists. If they were stolen, there's no way they'd be on display like this. They'd be hidden away in a secret room where only Colonel Otis could drool over them."

"What about the painting he brought to

Devon Dowling?"

"It could've been a fluke. The only one that had a checkered past."

"Huh," Ava said. "So nothing here."

"Well . . . Colonel Otis is also supposed to have a rather extensive knife collection," Carmela said.

Ava made a face. "Why does that sound so barbaric?"

"It's slightly creepy, I agree." Carmela finished her champagne and set down her empty glass. Did she want to see the knives for herself? Did she want to scratch that itch? Yes, she guessed that she did.

"Babcock said the knives were on display in his library," Carmela said.

"Lead the way. I guess," Ava said, looking somewhat reluctant.

They walked past an enormous, laden buffet table where guests helped themselves to fabulous food, and stepped into a small anteroom where waiters had stacked extra plates and silverware. That led to a long corridor hung with more paintings and a lovely blue and red Persian carpet underfoot. Luckily for them, there was nobody in sight.

"The coast is clear," Carmela said. "Let's hurry up and take a look."

"Maybe in here?" Ava said. She opened a door and stuck her head in. "Nope, TV room. That big honker of a JBL is a dead giveaway." She gazed at Carmela. "Ha ha, *dead* giveaway."

"Not now, Ava. Keep looking."

A blond woman in a tight red dress suddenly popped out from behind one of the closed doors. She smiled mysteriously, put a finger to her lips, and said in a whisper, "Are you hiding from Freddy, too?"

"We might be," Ava said, looking interested.

The woman giggled and started to tiptoe away. "He's such a dog," she said.

"Excuse me," Carmela called after her. "The library? Do you know where it is?"

"Second door on your left," the woman said as she scampered off.

Carmela walked down the hallway and eased open the door.

In the dim light, the library looked like something out of an English movie. Floor-to-ceiling shelves stuffed with books, a rolling ladder, a large desk with a glowing green lamp, leather chairs with hobnail accents, a floral brocade love seat strewn with pillows.

"Thank goodness it's not *ocupado,*" Ava said as they stepped inside and closed the door behind them. "No Freddy. Whoever he is."

"This place is amazing," Carmela said.

She realized that, under the right circumstances, she could probably spend a lifetime in here. All these marvelous leather-bound books, plus little nooks and crannies to curl up in. All she needed was . . . well, she'd need the red-hot deed to Colonel Otis's house.

"Hello there," Ava said in a casual tone of voice.

Carmela spun around fast, her heart catching in her throat, wondering who on earth Ava was suddenly talking to.

But it was a cat. A lovely tiger cat with the most expressive green eyes.

"Aren't you a pretty kitty," Ava said as she scooped the cat into her arms and began petting it. The cat cuddled up against her and began to purr rhythmically.

"You made a friend," Carmela said.

"Isn't he sweet?" Ava ruffled the cat's fur. Then she glanced around and said, "Where are the . . . ?" at the exact moment her eyes fell on a large display case that hung on the far wall. "Oh. There."

"The knife collection," Carmela almost whispered.

Slowly, almost cautiously, the two women approached it until their noses were practically pressed against the glass case. The knives were arranged in rows, according to size, on a backdrop of green velvet. In the dim light, the bright blades looked ominous and dangerous. And a little mysterious, as if they could become animated at any moment.

"Look at that curved knife," Ava said. "The one with the ivory handle."

"Looks Middle Eastern. Maybe Turkish. And do you see that one?" Carmela squinted, trying to read the label. "An Israeli combat knife."

"Scary stuff," Ava said.

"This is some amazing, extensive collection though."

"Doesn't it seem weird that a guy who loves beautiful art would also be gung ho for these wicked-looking knives?" Ava asked.

But Carmela didn't hear her. She was focused on something else. A knife appeared to be missing from Colonel Otis's collection. There was a faint outline of a long, curved knife, as if it had been pressed hard against the green velvet. The small white label was there, but no knife.

"One of them is missing," Carmela said.

"What?"

"See, there's an outline, but no knife."

"Gulp."

Carmela frowned. "I wonder when . . ."

Loud footfalls echoed in the hallway.

"Somebody's coming!" Ava hissed.

"Hide!" Carmela whispered back.

They dived behind a pair of heavy green velvet draperies just as the library door opened with a click.

"Oh shit," Ava whispered. "What do we do now?"

"Pretend we're looking for a lost earring?" Carmela whispered back. But, no, that probably wouldn't work. They were too far into their deception. So what to do except try to stay hidden?

There was the sound of someone stepping into the room. Walking one, two, three steps in.

"Hello?" a man's voice called out.

They both shrank against the window, holding their breath and hoping they could remain undetected.

"Is someone in here?" the voice called out. "If you are, I'm going to find you."

As his footsteps came closer, the knot in Carmela's stomach tightened.

Suddenly, Ava bent sideways and dropped the cat onto the floor. She gave it a little shove and a soundless admonition to *scoot.*

The cat shot across the room and jumped up onto the desk. Then it arched its back and let loose a loud meow.

"Cat," the man chuckled. Then he turned

and walked out of the room. Pulled the door closed behind him.

Carmela and Ava both breathed a huge sigh of relief.

"That was close," Ava said. "I was afraid I was going to sneeze. Kind of dusty back there."

"Still, hiding and then releasing the cat was smart thinking on your part," Carmela said.

"Who do you think that was?"

Carmela shrugged. "Colonel Otis?"

"Or Freddy. Whoever he is." Ava let loose a nervous laugh. "Oh man, my heart's pumping like a steam engine. Thank goodness we're off the hook."

"But maybe Colonel Otis isn't."

"Because of that missing knife?" Ava said. "Jeez, you don't think he's the one who slashed Sonny Boy's throat, do you?"

"I don't know. Babcock didn't think so. And he took a look at the collection just this afternoon."

"And now one is suddenly missing. Maybe we should watch out . . ."

"For our own throats?" Carmela said. "Because we've been investigating all over town. Sticking our noses in . . ."

"Don't go there, *cher*!" Ava suddenly looked terrified. She crossed herself and

339

said, "Say a prayer. Right now. Say a quick prayer and the angels will help take it back."

"Okay, okay. Relax."

"Never, *ever* tempt fate."

Carmela knew that's exactly what they'd been doing for the last few days. But to keep Ava calm, she said, "Okay, cross my heart, I promise I'll be more careful."

Ava dug in her bag, pulled out a lipstick, and applied it shakily. She leaned forward and shook out her hair. When she stood up, she actually looked a little more pulled together.

"Now what?" Ava asked.

"Are you hungry?"

"Famished."

Carmela glanced around. There was nothing more to do here. She shrugged. "Something tells me we should probably go investigate that twenty-foot-long buffet table."

CHAPTER 26

The buffet table was dazzling even by Garden District standards. A long trestle table covered with a pristine white linen tablecloth was laden with sterling silver chafing dishes filled with crawfish étouffée, braised short ribs, Creole salmon cakes, crab-stuffed shrimp, jambalaya, and fried catfish. Enormous platters held raw oysters, cheese-stuffed portobello mushrooms, sweet potato fries, and hot water corn bread.

Ava's eyes lit up like twin beacons. "Can you believe this spread? If I weren't such a Southern lady, I'd go facedown."

"Go for it," Carmela said.

"No, no, I'm going to graze. Exercise restraint and have a tiny taste of everything."

"That's the spirit."

Carmela, on the other hand, definitely intended to go light. Almost had to after slugging down all that gumbo. She told herself she'd just have a single stuffed

341

shrimp, a small salmon cake, and perhaps a few oysters. They'd slide down like nobody's business.

Ava's voice was suddenly a hot whisper in her ear. "Don't look now, *cher,* but there's . . ."

Carmela jerked bolt upright. The spoon she'd been holding clattered back into the silver chafing dish. "There's *what*?" Had Colonel Otis spotted them? Did he have security working the party? Were they going to be unceremoniously escorted out by a pair of goons?

"There's a dessert bar," Ava squealed.

"You wicked woman, you," Carmela said. "You scared me half to death."

"Didn't mean to." Ava sighed as she helped herself to a giant scoop of sweet potato galette. "Oh man, if only my bank balance was as high as my daily caloric intake."

"Come on, let's fill our plates and head out to the patio."

"Good idea, the lighting is nice and dim out there. Nobody will notice us."

But somebody *did* notice them as they scooted out the door, reaching out to grab another flute of champagne on the way.

"What on earth!" Baby Fontaine shrieked. Her hands flew up in the air, and a wide grin spread across her face. Then, "Kittens, what are you *doing* here?"

"We crashed the party," Ava said.

"No," Baby said. She was adorable in a short black cocktail dress and a diamond teardrop necklace.

"Oh yes," Carmela said. "You didn't really think we were on the guest list, did you?"

"You mean you just waltzed in the front door like nobody's business?" Baby asked. "That's hysterical."

"It was more like creeping through the crepe myrtle," Ava said.

Baby walked with them to a quiet corner of the patio where they all sat down at a white wrought-iron table.

"So," Baby said, "I take it you two are here on some sort of sleuthing expedition."

"You could call it that," Carmela said. "We're still trying to crack the mystery of Devon Dowling's murder."

"So sad," Baby said. She reached over and put a hand on Carmela's arm. "But you're good at ferreting out clues. You and Ava." She leaned closer. "So tell me, what have you discovered? Why are you here?"

"For one thing, there's a knife missing from Colonel Otis's collection," Carmela said.

"And you think . . . what?" Baby asked.

"Well, there was a murder last night in St. Louis Cemetery," Carmela said. "A man who admitted to robbing Devon's safe got his throat slashed."

"Sonny Boy Holmes," Baby said. "I read about him in this morning's paper. You think Colonel Otis did it?"

"It's a possibility," Carmela said.

Baby leaned forward, nervous but a little interested. "So the plot thickens."

"Along with my waistline," Ava said. "If I eat one more bite of this étouffée I won't be able to zip my pants tomorrow."

But Baby wanted to hear more. "Tell me more about the missing knife," she said.

"The weird thing is, Babcock looked at Colonel Otis's collection earlier today, and it was completely intact. Now, tonight, there's a knife missing," Carmela said.

"What do you think that means?" Baby asked.

"I don't know," Carmela said. "Colonel Otis could have just sent it out for repair. Or maybe he removed it from the case to show it to one of the guests."

Baby's eyes burned into hers. "Or . . ."

Carmela met her gaze. "Or he intends to use it on someone."

Ava held up an index finger. "Really?

344

Then, *excusez-moi,* but maybe we should *leave?*"

Rather than exiting via the front door, Carmela and Ava retraced their steps through the magnolias and fumbled their way down the dark alley to Carmela's car.

"I don't know when I've had so much fun," Ava said as she pulled her seat belt across. "I mean, hiding out in the library, getting scared silly, stuffing my fat face, running into Baby . . . that was really great."

"Then you, my dear, are easily amused," Carmela said as she started her car and pulled away slowly from the curb. "Because the whereabouts of that missing knife still sticks in my craw."

"And that kitty. What a sweetheart. I wanted to take him home with me."

"I know what you mean." Carmela knew there was no sense in pursuing the subject of missing knives with Ava. Not tonight anyway. "Every time I see a stray dog in the French Quarter, I want to scoop the poor thing up and rescue it."

"That's what we should do," Ava said. "Pool our money and buy a big old house where we can take care of rescued cats and dogs. Help them find forever homes. There's even a place over on Coliseum Street that's for sale right now. It's kind of dilapidated and clunky-looking. And the yard is bare and scruffy, but we could . . ."

"Ava. I think we're being followed."

"Plant some grass," Ava said. "Like that hardy straw-like stuff the maintenance guys plant alongside freeways. Grass that's resistant to oil and gas and . . . *What did you say?*"

Carmela was gazing into her rearview mirror as she drove. "There's a pair of headlights that's been following us steadily for the last few blocks."

Ava squirmed around. "Are you sure? I don't see anything."

"I've made two turns, and that same SUV has made them, too. He keeps his distance, stays about a half block back, but he's definitely on our tail."

"But I wanna go home. I need my beauty sleep."

"We can't do anything until we lose this guy. We sure don't want him to follow us home."

"Who do you think it is?"

"No idea," Carmela said.

"Somebody from the party?"

Carmela shrugged. "I don't know. But hang on, I'm going to make a tight left turn and accelerate across St. Charles. If we're lucky, he'll get caught on the red light."

The Mercedes flew across St. Charles, just clipping the red light. The SUV came on through, still following them.

"Dang!" Carmela cried. She clutched the steering wheel as she took them down St. Charles, speeding up as she paralleled the streetcar track.

"Now what?" Ava asked in a quavering voice. "I don't like this chase business. After all I ate . . . my tummy's feeling kind of rocky."

"I'm gonna catch up to that streetcar that's ahead of us. Then nose ahead and cross directly in its path. Try to block this guy," Carmela said.

She gunned her engine, came up on the green and red streetcar that was peacefully rumbling along, then pulled ahead. At the next cross street, she made a hard right turn, passing directly in front of the streetcar with only inches to spare.

Ava screamed as the streetcar driver rang his bell furiously. "Holy buckets! We almost ended up a tangled jangled mess!"

"Tell me about it." Carmela was grim faced and growing tired of playing tag with this jerk.

Ava scrunched around in her seat. "But . . . did your foolhardy maneuver

347

work? Did we lose him?"

"You tell me."

"No, damn it, I think that's him behind us."

It was like waving a red flag in Carmela's face. She trounced down hard on the gas and flew down the street. She squeaked through yellow lights, blew completely through two red lights.

And still the SUV kept coming.

Carmela figured to lose him at the river. She hit Napoleon Avenue, turned left, and really poured it on. Only problem was, the road was completely pitted with potholes!

"They haven't fixed these roads since Huey Long was in office!" Ava cried as they jounced along.

Carmela swerved left, then right, then left again, trying to avoid the dips and blips and minimize the damage they were doing to her tires and undercarriage.

"Can you see what color that SUV is? Or the make? Or the license plate?" Carmela asked.

Ava squirmed around. "No, it's too dark. Well, maybe it's blue." She gazed out the side window. "Jeez, it's dreadful scary over here."

They were flying past block after block of dark, deserted warehouses. To their right, an enormous seawall rose up to hold back (hopefully, anyway) the muddy Mississippi River.

"Is there a method to this madness?" Ava asked. She was hanging on for dear life, her long fingernails practically slicing into the upholstery.

"If we keep playing hare and hound, I figure I can lead this jerk right down Tchoupitoulas. From there we hit Canal Street and take him right into the craziness of the French Quarter."

"Bright lights, big city?"

"Something like that," Carmela said. "If we get to a spot where there's lots of people around, maybe we can figure out who we're dealing with."

Carmela's plan worked. Sort of. Right up until the point where they led the SUV on a merry chase down Canal Street and tried to cross Chartres Street.

"Watch out! There's a hot dog cart coming up on your right!" Ava shouted.

She rolled down her window to warn the vendor, but he pushed his red and yellow cart out into the street just as Carmela tapped her brakes and swerved. But it was too late and ill-timed. Carmela's right front fender clipped one end of the hot dog cart and sent it spinning. The cart jerked and wobbled and looked like it was about to tip over.

"Is he okay?" Carmela screamed as she kept going. She was terrified she'd killed the poor guy and crashed his cart. "Is the hot dog guy okay?"

He was. His cart was another story.

The SUV, following close on their tail, smashed into the hot dog cart like a Sherman tank hitting the broad side of a barn. The cart exploded with an ear-shattering, metal-grinding *CRASH.* Shards of glass, a rubber tire, dozens of hot dogs, and a gush of pickle relish and ketchup flew through the air. Hot dogs plip-plopped down on the pavement, splatted against shopwindows, and even landed at the foot of a Great Dane on a leash who promptly licked his chops and snatched up a couple of the wayward dogs.

At the same moment, Ava let out a blood-curdling scream.

"I'm hit! I'm hit!"

Her plaintive cries pierced Carmela's heart like a barbed arrow.

"Dear Lord, you got *shot*?" Carmela was gobsmacked. She hadn't heard any shots fired. Had the SUV driver used a gun with a silencer? A suppressor?

Carmela hit the brakes as hard as she

could. Her tires squealed and pedestrians scattered as she spun in a jouncing half turn and finally rocked to a stop.

"Where, honey, where?" Carmela was out of her mind with fear and worry, practically hysterical. "I didn't hear any . . ."

"Help me!" Ava cried, her voice growing fainter.

Carmela wrenched herself around to help Ava. "Where are you hit? Show me!"

"I think . . . I don't know." Ava flopped back in the passenger seat. "Just get me some medical help! Give me CPR, or call 911, or pour me a shot of Grey Goose!"

Carmela grabbed for her cell phone to call 911. "Are you in terrible pain?"

Ava nodded. "It's pretty bad."

"Show me exactly where it hurts!"

Ava moaned and pointed a finger. "There. Right at my waist." She unsnapped her leather jacket and peeled it open. "Look! All over my slacks. I'm bleeding like a stuck pig!"

Carmela stared for a second, then reached over and touched a finger to the smear of red. Something about it seemed familiar. She leaned forward, gave a sniff, and said, "Ava, that's ketchup."

Ava gulped. "You mean I'm not shot?"

"I don't think so."

"I'm not going to die?"

Carmela sighed. "Ava, you're going to be fine. You just got a little overwrought, that's all." She glanced around. The blue SUV was nowhere to be seen. Her blood pressure was off the charts.

Ava sat up in a kind of daze. "Oh. Sorry. But your car. Is it okay?"

"I think we blew out a tire when we hit the curb back there. And there's probably a dent. And that poor hot dog guy . . ." She started to dial her phone. "I gotta call Babcock."

"Because of a dent?" Ava asked.

"Because of the dirtbag that was chasing us," Carmela said.

Babcock and two squad cars showed up a few minutes later. He scanned the accident scene, inspected the damage on Carmela's car, talked to the terrified hot dog vendor, and then listened tight-lipped and grim faced to Carmela's story: crashing the party, the knife collection, the chase. Finally, when all was said and done, when Ava had showed him her almost-gunshot-wound, Babcock said, "Besides breaking about two dozen laws, you ladies hit some kind of a trip wire."

Carmela squinted at him with one eye. "A whatchit? A trip wire? What does that mean exactly?"

"It means you stumbled upon something you shouldn't have."

"That's why some jackhole chased us?" Ava said. "Why I almost got shot?"

"You didn't get shot," Carmela said.

"I could have."

"Thank goodness, you didn't," Babcock said.

"Can you put out some kind of APB?" Carmela asked.

Babcock shook his head. "On a blue SUV? You know how many of those vehicles there are in New Orleans? In Louisiana proper?"

"A lot?" Ava asked.

"Here's the thing, you poked a stick in a den of snakes, and now you're paying the price," Babcock said.

"What are you talking about?" Carmela asked. Although she kind of knew.

"Someone — probably Devon Dowling's killer — knows you're onto him," Babcock said.

"But I'm not onto him," Carmela said. "I have no idea who it is. Or who was chasing us tonight."

"Doesn't matter," Babcock said. "Whoever the killer is, you've got him extremely agitated."

"Oh my gosh, that's so exciting," Ava cried.

Dumbfounded, both Carmela and Babcock turned to stare at her. Finally, Babcock said, "It's not exciting. It's *terrible!*"

Chapter 27

After the craziness of last night, Carmela and Ava decided to treat themselves to a nice, leisurely brunch at Antoine's.

"Wait a sec," Ava said, as they stopped under the wrought-iron balcony that shaded the entrance to the iconic restaurant. "I gotta straighten my wig."

"Why are you wearing a wig when your own hair is perfectly gorgeous?" Carmela asked.

"Naw, it was all frizzled this morning, but this Sassy Girl model gives me a headful of fun, bouncy curls."

"And a white skunk stripe, I might add."

"Never you mind about that. And by the way, ma'am, why are *you* trying to sneak that little dog into a fancy-pants restaurant like Antoine's?"

Carmela glanced down at her oversized pink nylon tote bag. Mimi was snuggled inside and being quiet as a mouse.

"I thought it might be good for her to make a return trip to Devon's shop."

Ava lifted an eyebrow. "So she can find closure?"

"Maybe. Plus, I sensed that Mimi needed a little time away from Boo and Poobah. They can be a bit much."

"Hah!" Ava said. "*We* can be a bit much."

They walked through ornate glass doors and into an elegant entry where diners had been welcomed for the last 127 years. A maître d', wearing a bow tie and perfectly tailored jacket, greeted them immediately.

"*Bonjour.* Good morning. You have a reservation?" he asked in honeyed tones.

"Not today," Carmela said. "Is that a problem?"

"Not at all," the maître d' said. He picked up two menus and led the ladies into a large dining room where soft music tinkled and cream-colored walls and brass fixtures lent a feeling of old-world elegance. Mark Twain, Tennessee Williams, the Duke and Duchess of Windsor, and five U.S. presidents had dined here.

"A quiet table, if you've got one," Carmela said.

"Certainly." He led them to a discreet corner table, pulled out two bentwood mahogany chairs, and seated them.

"This table would be perfect if you were a private eye on some kind of stakeout," Ava said. "You can see the whole room from here."

"But it's also fairly inconspicuous," Carmela said as she slid the bag holding Mimi under the table.

Ava scanned the menu, then picked up the wine list. "Water isn't going to do it for me today."

The waiter was immediately at their table. "An aperitif?" he asked.

"More like wine," Ava said. "Mmn, what have you got in a light rosé?"

"May I recommend a glass of our Côtes de Provence Rosé?"

"Perfect," Ava said. "Carmela?"

"Ditto," Carmela said.

"Very good," said the waiter.

"It better be," Ava said.

Carmela studied the menu. "No gumbo today."

"No gumbo for a while," Ava decreed. "I had to lay flat on my bed this morning to button these jeans."

"So just a salad?"

"Maybe . . . although everything here is so nice and tasty."

The waiter brought their wine and took their orders. Carmela opted for the eggs

Sardou, a house specialty, while Ava hemmed and hawed, but finally ordered the rather lavish crab cakes with Creole horseradish sauce.

When the waiter brought their luncheon entrées, Ava waited until he'd left and then said, "That was some crazy shit that went down last night, huh?"

"I had nightmares," Carmela said. Her dreams had been filled with images of flashing knife blades, driving through fog her headlights couldn't pierce, and the terrible screech of metal against concrete.

"I dreamed I bought a new jumpsuit but it didn't fit," Ava said.

Carmela took a delicate bite of egg and artichoke. "I'm still puzzling over who chased us last night. Clearly, it had to be one of our suspects."

"Or somebody who was at the party?"

"Somehow I don't think Colonel Otis left his guests so he could get his jollies by terrorizing us."

"Then who?" Ava asked.

"T.J.?"

"We'll be seeing him in a little while. Maybe he'll look guilty as sin and it'll be case closed."

"Roy Sultan's still in play," Carmela said. "Or it could be . . ."

"Please don't say Richard Drake. Honestly, *cher,* could a vicious killer look that handsome?"

"I see your point, I really do. But it *could* be him."

"If I got to know him better, I could do a little espionage for you." Ava batted her lashes.

"Don't you dare. I can't afford to lose my BFF."

Ava scraped up a bit of sauce with her fork. "On another note, is Babcock still steamed at you?"

"I haven't talked to him today, but you make an excellent point." Carmela pulled out her phone and speed-dialed his number. "Let's find out."

He answered on the first ring. "Babcock."

"You sound tense," Carmela said. "I may have a cure for that."

"Just as long as it doesn't involve a high-speed chase," Babcock said.

"Say, thanks bunches for getting my tire fixed."

"It's just one of the complimentary concierge services available from the NOPD."

"Really?"

"Of course not. We'd rather just bash you over the head with a rifle butt and haul you into jail."

"I heard that," Ava said. "Tell him I heard that."

"What are you up to today?" Babcock asked. "Staying out of trouble, I hope."

"Ava and I are having brunch, then she's going to help me dive into a pile of old paper and stamps. I'm on the hunt for some ephemera." Carmela didn't mention the fact that the old paper was at Devon Dowling's antique shop. "What are you doing?"

"Right now, I'm pacing up and down the corridor outside the mayor's office. I've been here for more than an hour with no end in sight."

"Impressive. You two must be best buds," Carmela said. "You got him to hold off on that press conference yesterday, so he must really trust you."

"You're kidding, right? All I got was a stay of execution. The mayor still plans to hold a press conference tonight to announce that Dowling's killer has been apprehended. He thinks residents as well as tourists will relax when he tells them the 'French Quarter crisis' is over."

"I don't get it. Shouldn't he be announcing that Sonny Boy Holmes was found dead?"

"He's kind of glossing over that part."

"How do you gloss over a dead body?"

Carmela asked.

"Chalk it up to myopic politics?" Babcock said.

Ava aimed a fork at Carmela. "Tell him I heard that, too."

Carmela couldn't hide her confusion. "But do *you* think Sonny Holmes was Devon's killer?"

"To be honest, I don't know what to think right now. All I know is that I have to convince the mayor to hold off on his press conference for a little while longer until I get this thing figured out."

"Are you? Will you?" Carmela asked.

"That remains to be seen. On a related note, we got the results back from the lab on that fabric snippet."

"You mean the piece from Abraham Lincoln's coat?"

"More like Joe Lincoln's coat."

"You mean it's a fake?" Carmela asked.

"Turns out the fabric's not old enough. The lab techs found traces of synthetic fibers."

"So everybody's there working away?"

"Not quite. It being Saturday, most people are at home enjoying their weekend," Babcock said.

"Poor sweetie. So you're the only one walking around on pins and needles?"

"Right now, yeah. But I'll eventually call Bobby Gallant and my PR guy in. Bobby can help me brainstorm while Jarreau tries to whip up a more convincing story for the media."

"Okay, call me if . . ." But Carmela's phone had suddenly gone completely dead.

"Crap!"

"What's wrong?" Ava asked.

"My battery's dead. What with all the excitement, I forgot to recharge last night. Babcock's gonna think I hung up on him."

"No, he won't, sweetie. That man worships the eggshells you walk on."

Forty minutes later, luncheons devoured, bill paid, tip left, and Mimi still snuggled in Carmela's tote bag, they stood up and walked leisurely toward the front entrance.

"Next time I think I might order the petite filet," Ava said. "I think the red wine sauce and mushrooms are . . ."

She stopped dead in her tracks as Richard Drake burst through the doorway of the Hermes bar. As if propelled by hurricane force winds, he planted himself firmly in front of them, quivering with rage and indignity.

"You two are the worst, the absolute worst troublemakers I've ever met!" Drake shouted.

"Us?" Ava managed to squeak out.

"Accusing *me* of murder! How dare you!"

"Slow down," Carmela said, raising both hands in a calming gesture. "What are you talking about? What happened?"

"A certain detective named Babcock came gunning for me, that's what happened," he spat out. "I'm sure you're well acquainted with him."

Carmela cringed inwardly. Of course she'd pointed Babcock in Drake's direction. On the other hand, Babcock had pointed Babcock in Drake's direction.

Drake clenched his teeth so hard it looked like his jaw would pop out of its socket. "Someone threw an accusation of guilt directly at me. And I'm guessing it was the two of you!"

Carmela started to deny it, then stopped. Why bother?

"You have no idea what I've been through," Drake railed. "Hours of questioning by incompetent detectives. Every one of them trying to trip me up, catch me in a lie."

"Look," Carmela said, "we're all upset by what happened to Devon Dowling. And people are naturally suspicious."

"Upset? Suspicious? That doesn't begin to

cut it!" Drake screamed.

Carmela gazed past Drake's left shoulder and saw a bartender staring at them intently. He was clearly upset by the noisy disruption.

"Maybe we should take this outside," Carmela suggested.

"No!" Drake cried. "The police searched my house, searched my car, and completely infringed on my rights." He stopped abruptly, looking as if he had something more to add. Then he snapped his mouth shut, turned, and walked away. Stormed right out of the restaurant.

Ava watched him go, then whipped her head back toward Carmela. "Do you think this hurts my chance of having a meaningful relationship with him?"

"You don't want to date that guy," Carmela said. She put an index finger to her head and twirled it. "He's too crazy and hotheaded."

"I'm hot-blooded," Ava said.

"I think . . . I think I need to call Babcock back. Let me borrow your phone for a minute."

"Sorry, I left it in the car."

"Then can you take Mimi outside while I run back and find a pay phone? There has to be one somewhere."

"Got it," Ava said as she grabbed Carmela's tote.

Carmela walked back through the dining room and turned down a long hallway carpeted in green and hung with photos of past Mardi Gras parades and fancy balls. This restaurant was so old, so brimming with nostalgia, that they must have an old-fashioned phone booth here somewhere. Didn't they?

Carmela spotted an alcove but was disappointed to find only a silver wine cooler stuck in it. Farther down the hallway she found a half-open door. The sign on it said *MANAGER'S OFFICE*. Maybe she could borrow his phone?

Carmela knocked, then pushed the door farther ajar. She called out, but no one answered. She stuck her head inside to find a desk strewn with papers. And a telephone sitting next to a closed laptop.

Perfect.

She decided to take a chance and tiptoed inside, grabbed the phone, and called Babcock.

When he answered this time, he sounded tired.

"It's me again," Carmela said. "I just had a nasty run-in with Richard Drake."

"You *what*?"

"Did you get some kind of tip on Drake?"

"Yeah, we did. Yesterday afternoon. I found a note stuck on my windshield. A typed note."

"You mean as opposed to handwritten?" Carmela asked.

"I mean actually typed on an old-fashioned typewriter."

Carmela wondered who would still have a typewriter. Maybe someone . . . older and more traditional? Like Roy Sultan or Colonel Otis? She filed that bit of information away in her brain. Babcock might not consider it a relevant clue, but she did.

"So it was typed," Carmela said.

"Same as the last one. You didn't put it there, did you? To goad me into looking at Richard Drake again?"

"No! Of course not! I'd never trick you like that."

"Well, once we got the note, we had to take it seriously. And now we've probably wasted another ten or twenty man-hours chasing after the wrong guy."

"So you think Drake is the wrong guy? That he's innocent?"

"He couldn't have a better alibi. As it turns out, he was with three dozen of his vampire friends all day long and into the evening."

"They vouched for him? He was definitely in someone's sight the whole time?" Carmela asked.

"Hell, yes. After the parade they all went to Buddy Preston's Smokehouse Grill. I guess it was some kind of vampire club party. Probably all sat around drinking beer and eating ribs."

"Wouldn't vampires prefer kabobs?"

"You mean steak on a metal skewer?" Babcock laughed. "Carmela, you are too much. You gotta give your brain a rest."

As Carmela hung up, she could hear someone walking down the hallway. It could be the manager — or someone else. Either way, she was caught red-handed. Bummer. In her mind she hastily concocted a heartfelt apology for entering the office without permission . . .

Until the door was suddenly pulled shut!

What? Who did that?

Carmela lunged for the doorknob, grabbed it, and tried to turn it. And found it was stuck tight.

Why is this doorknob not moving? Because someone is standing on the other side grasping the doorknob and hanging on to it?

Bending forward, Carmela put her ear against the door and listened. She could hear faint, shallow breathing. Someone was definitely standing on the other side!

Who would do that? Was Richard Drake so wacked-out that he'd ducked back inside to settle a score with her? That didn't quite make sense.

Still grasping the doorknob with one hand, Carmela banged hard against the door with her other hand. *WHAM! WHAM! WHAM!*

"Let me out!" Carmela yelled.

Not a sound came from the other side of the door.

Carmela felt the first blip of panic. If she grabbed the phone again and called for help, she'd have to release her hold on the door. But what if the person on the other side — who clearly wasn't particularly friendly — came barreling in? And then what would happen? Would he shoot her? Stab her?

Carmela shivered, suddenly remembering the missing knife in Colonel Otis's collection. What to do? What to do?

Fighting down her panic, she heard a faint voice. And another set of footsteps approaching. Someone else was coming down the hall.

"*¿Qué estás haciendo?*" a voice called out.

Instantly, the doorknob loosened in Carmela's hand and she heard footsteps hurrying away.

Carmela drew a deep, fortifying breath and pulled open the door. A sous chef carrying a tray piled with soft-shell crabs was standing there, looking at her with a curious look on his face.

But there was nobody else.

Whoever had been holding the doorknob had disappeared.

CHAPTER 28

"Who do you think it was, *cher*?" Ava asked. "Someone playing a joke on you?"

"Whatever it was, it was a pretty rotten joke," Carmela said as she knocked on the front door of Dulcimer Antiques.

"You don't think Richard Drake came back after his little hissy fit, do you?"

"I don't know, Ava. But it certainly would have been convenient for him." She knocked a second time. "Nobody home? T.J. was expecting us. At least I hope he remembered that he invited us over."

"He's probably hungover." Ava banged on the door so hard the glass panes rattled in their frame. *BAM. BAM. BAM.*

From deep inside the shop, T.J. yelled, "We're closed. Go away."

That only caused Ava to bang harder.

Finally, T.J. jerked open the front door and yelled, "Didn't you hear me? I said we're . . ." His anger and frustration diffused abruptly when he saw who it was. "Oh, it's you guys. Man, you're noisy." T.J.'s eyes looked swollen and puffy, and he wore the same shirt he'd had on last night.

"Rough night?" Ava asked in a snarky tone.

T.J. put a hand to his head and smoothed back a shock of unruly hair. "Yeah, kind of."

"Do you remember inviting us to look through Devon's collection of old paper?" Carmela asked. She hoped they weren't wasting their time here.

"I guess." T.J. opened the door wider so they could step inside.

ARF! ARF!

T.J. gave Ava a funny look. "Did you say something?"

Mimi's head popped up suddenly as she peered over the side of Carmela's tote bag. Her eyes were bright and shiny, and she seemed to be giving everything a curious look.

"Oh, the dog," T.J. said.

"She knows she's back home," Ava said. She gave the dog a commiserating look and then added, "It's kind of sad, isn't it?"

But Mimi was eager to get out and explore familiar territory. So Carmela lifted her out of the tote bag and set her on the floor. Mimi wasted no time in rushing around the shop to sniff at everything.

"Cute," T.J. said, but in a disinterested way.

Carmela glanced about the shop. The front window was still boarded over, and cardboard boxes were piled everywhere. It looked as though T.J. really had been busy and that half the antiques had already been packed. She also noted that a white residue — fingerprint powder? — still clung to the doorframes and the front of a large oak secretary with a pull-down front. Fragments of yellow crime scene tape still hung from the window.

T.J. rubbed his forehead and yawned. "I'm gonna need about a gallon of coffee to get me started today."

"But it looks like you've made some forward progress," Carmela said. "I mean with the packing."

"Yeah, but it's a complete pain," T.J. said. "I gotta put that plastic bubbley stuff around all the fragile pieces and then pack them in boxes filled with plastic peanuts."

"Life's tough," Ava said.

"Thank goodness this is the last of it," T.J. said. "After I get done, hopefully this weekend, I'm out of here."

"We just had lunch at Antoine's," Carmela said to T.J. She figured that if he'd been the doorknob holder, something might register on his face.

Nothing did. T.J. just stared at her, looking sleepy eyed. "That's a nice place. Real fancy."

"This one time a really rich older guy took me there on a date," Ava said. "And he ordered snails for both of us, but I couldn't eat them. I know they're French and gourmet and everything, but to bite into such a creepy-crawly thing . . ."

"Uh-huh," T.J. said. Because Ava continued to rattle on, he looked to Carmela for help.

"About Devon's paper stuff," Carmela said. "Where would we find that?"

T.J. nodded and scratched his stomach. "Back room. Help yourself."

"I guess we always do," Ava said.

They walked into the back room, which was even more of a mess than the front of the shop. Devon's desk and large worktable were mounded with an array of crumpled paper, mismatched cups and saucers, broken pocket watches, vintage glass jars, old Christmas decorations, and assorted tchotchkes.

T.J. lifted a hand. "Some of the old papers you might be interested in are scattered around that big table there. And there's plenty more stuff stashed in boxes. Just look around and help yourself to whatever. Oh, and be careful of those ugly Chinese pots, they're kind of tippy."

"I like the one with the pouncing dragon," Ava said.

T.J. wrinkled his nose. "Ugh. You could probably buy it for a song. So . . . I'll be in front packing if you need me."

"Right," Carmela said. She was eager to get started.

Ava put her hands on her hips. "What a mess."

"But every mess holds a potential treasure," Carmela said. "Just look at this." She picked up a newspaper that was folded accordion style and had bright red type.

"Wrinkled old paper. So what?" Ava said.

"It's a Chinese newspaper that was probably used as packing material. It'll make a terrific background for someone's travel scrapbook."

"What about this old calendar?" Ava asked. "And these certificates of authenticity?"

"Perfect. It's all perfect."

Mimi wandered in and Carmela picked her up and gave her a kiss. "How are you doing, sweetheart?"

"She looks sad," Ava said.

"All pugs look a little sad to me," Carmela said. "Because of their eyes. But I suppose Mimi spent so much time here she still might have deep-seated feelings."

"Or anxieties," Ava said. She spotted a blue dog bed and said, "Maybe she'd be more comfortable in her little bed?"

Carmela carried Mimi to her bed and slowly set her down on the tufted mattress. Mimi sighed and closed her eyes.

"Perfect," Carmela whispered. Then she sat down at the worktable and tried to decide how to organize the mounds of paper. "Ava, grab a couple of boxes, will you?"

Ava walked out front, rustled around, and returned with two cardboard boxes.

"Now what?"

Carmela picked up a felt-tipped pen. "I'm going to label them *Background* and *Ephemera.*"

"How do I know which is which?"

"We'll put all the stuff like the Chinese newspaper in the Background box and items such as stamps or fancy labels into the Ephemera box."

Ava dug into one of the nearby boxes, ripping out folded-up paper. "Got some maps here. Looks like Norway . . . Nope, I've got it upside down. Italy."

"Perfect! When you're talking vacation scrapbooks, maps make great backgrounds."

"And here's some packing paper from Germany . . . or is it France? What would Deutsche Post be?"

"Definitely Germany."

Ava continued to rummage through the large box, pulling out the occasional unique piece. "I thought this would be drudge work, but it's actually kind of fun."

"T.J. was right when he said these papers might be interesting," Carmela said. "Some of these pieces are going to be perfect for my classes. Fancy European labels and stamps . . . oh, and a bill of lading from Paris. Look at this miniature Eiffel Tower stamped in the corner."

Ava leaned across the table. "Looks old."

"Because it is."

"Devon was a real pack rat, huh?"

"I like to think of him as a collector."

Carmela and Ava worked for a good couple of hours, poring through a dozen boxes, sorting, smoothing, unearthing treasures as they went along. T.J. looked in on them once but wasn't much interested in their paper hunt.

But what they discovered was gangbusters! They found gallery invitations, business cards, handwritten receipts, old photos, antique advertising, and some vintage paper watch faces — all of it a unique bit of history.

"Our two boxes are completely stuffed," Ava said. "I'm going to have to start a third one." She hoisted the box marked *Background* and struggled to move it out of the way. "I think we need . . ."

The corner of Ava's box bumped up against a green Chinese vase that was sitting on a narrow rosewood stand. As the vase began to tip precariously, Ava cried out, "Oh no!" and Carmela made a dive for it.

It was too little, too late. The vase wiggled and wobbled and then tumbled to the floor.

CRASH!

Shards of hundred-year-old ceramic flew everywhere while the rounded base with the dragon motif rolled under the table.

"What was that?" T.J. cried out. Footsteps hurried toward them and then he appeared in the doorway, looking startled.

"Sorry!" Ava cried. "So sorry! I didn't mean to break it." She looked like she was ready to cry.

T.J.'s eyes roved the floor and spied the dozens of shards. "Oh, *that* stupid thing," he said disdainfully. "Not to worry."

"Really?" Ava said. "Because I can pay

for . . ."

But T.J. had already disappeared and gone back to his packing.

"Whew." Ava blew a hank of hair out of her face. "I sure didn't mean for that to happen. Maybe I should grab a broom and try to . . ."

"Ava, shhh." Carmela held a finger to her mouth.

"Huh?"

When part of the vase had rolled under the table, a brown paper package had spilled out and struck one of Carmela's feet. Now, curious, she leaned down and scooped it up. Though it was loosely tied with string, she pushed a corner of the brown paper wrapping aside and peered in. And couldn't believe what she saw.

White. Loosely shaped and wrapped in plastic. It looked like a brick of cocaine!

Holy shit! Is this even possible? Cocaine hidden in Devon's shop? How could that be?

Carmela studied it again. Yes, it was possible.

Ava stared at her with trepidation. "What, Carmela? What is it?"

"We have to go," Carmela said, standing up fast.

"Now? Shouldn't we clean up all these broken pieces?"

Carmela scooped Mimi into her tote bag and grabbed one of the cardboard boxes. "Change of plans. We have to go now. Can you manage that other box?"

"Yeah, but . . ."

Though she was burdened like a pack animal, Carmela swept into the front of the shop.

"T.J., thank you *so* much. This paper stuff is absolutely wonderful."

T.J. looked up from where he sat cross-legged on the floor, wrapping an amber glass lamp. "So you salvaged some interesting pieces, huh?"

"Great stuff, interesting stuff," Carmela said as she blew past him.

"Thanks," Ava said, following closely in Carmela's footsteps. "Sorry about the vase."

"Quick," Carmela said once they were outside. "Get in the car."

Ava wedged her box in the back seat of Carmela's car. "You gonna tell me what's going on or . . . ?"

"Just get in the car." Carmela had already jumped in and started the engine. As soon as Ava's passenger door clicked shut, Carmela accelerated away from Dulcimer Antiques. She swerved down Royal, turned at St. Louis Street, and pulled over to the curb.

"What's going on?" Ava cried.

Carmela glanced around quickly, then reached into her handbag and pulled out the brick of cocaine. Handed it to Ava. "You tell me."

Ava looked stunned. "Holy cats, is this what I think it is?"

"I think it is."

"Like . . . a special delivery from El Chapo himself?"

"I'm right, huh?" Carmela asked. "This is a packet of drugs?"

"Unless I'm mistaken, this is cocaine, honey. Blow. White Lady. California Cornflakes."

"How do you know so much about this?" Carmela asked.

"Because I'm a devoted reader of *Star Whacker* magazine. They're always doing huge exposés on celebrities who've been caught red-handed with drugs. Or who are just coming out of rehab." Ava snorted as she reached up and adjusted her wig. "As if *that* ever works."

"Do you think Devon Dowling could have been dealing drugs?"

"Devon? No way," Ava said.

"What about T.J.?"

"With his appetite for getting high, I don't think he would have left a pound of cocaine just lying around unopened."

"It wasn't just lying around. It was in that Chinese vase you tipped over."

Ava frowned. "In the vase? How do you think it got there? Who put it there?"

"No idea."

"Where'd it come from? Where was it headed?"

"Again, I don't know," Carmela said.

"I'm thinking we should get this stuff to Babcock. Like, right now!" Ava said. "I for one don't want to get locked up in some dank jail cell for possession! I don't want to submit to a body search, work on a chain gang, or play a supporting role in *Orange Is the New Black.*"

"You watch too much sensational TV," Carmela said. "We *found* the drugs, we didn't *buy* them. It's not like we're actual drug traffickers."

"Try telling that to the guys in the black helicopters from the DEA."

"Of course we'll turn the drugs in. But aren't you curious as to how these drugs ended up in Devon's shop? And do you think they might be connected to his murder?"

"You think Devon's killer was really after drugs?" Ava asked. "And he killed Devon because of . . . these drugs?"

"I don't know, but it's a very strange co-incidence."

"Two crimes in one small antique shop," Ava said slowly.

Carmela looked at the brown paper the drugs were wrapped in. "There's no name on here, just an address. No postage stamp, either."

"So what does that mean?"

"They had to be delivered by someone. A courier or private messenger."

"Drug mule?" Ava volunteered. She wiggled her fingers. "Here, let me take a look at that."

Carmela passed her the package.

Ava studied it. "Yup, this was probably hand delivered directly to Devon. Look at the address, it's 715 Royalton Street."

Carmela shook her head. "That's not right, Devon's address is 715 *Royal* Street."

"So it's a little off," Ava said. "You're talking three extra letters. So what?"

"There's something really wrong here. There's no Royalton Street in New Orleans," Carmela said.

Ava scratched her head. "Then where is it? Is there a Royalton Street somewhere else or is this address just a complete screwup?"

"Give me your phone."

Ava handed over her phone and watched as Carmela Googled "715 Royalton Street Louisiana."

"Anything?" Ava asked.

"I'm looking, I'm looking. A lot of ads for Royal Street restaurants are clogging the page. Wait . . . yes. It's an actual address in New Iberia. There's definitely a 715 Royalton Street in New Iberia."

"You think some coked-up drug mule dropped the cocaine off at the wrong address?" Ava asked.

Carmela stared at her. "And then the person whom these drugs were intended for dropped by and murdered Devon? Because Devon was being a good guy and was about to turn the drugs over to the police?"

Ava's eyes widened in surprise. "Is that what happened?"

Carmela pursed her lips and sucked in air. "Dear Lord, Ava, I think that's exactly what happened."

"So who's the jackhole cokehead who lives at 715 Royalton Street in New Iberia?" Ava asked.

But Carmela's brain was already spinning. "There's only one way to find out."

CHAPTER 29

Before Ava could catch her breath, Carmela hit the gas and they were barreling out of New Orleans, headed west.

By the time they flew through Gretna, Mimi had started to whimper.

"Slow down, would you? Even the dog is scared," Ava said.

Carmela, always a speed junkie, was energized by both the freedom of the lightly trafficked highway and the possibility of getting a bead on Devon's killer. With her adrenaline pumping, she ignored Ava's pleas and continued to race west on U.S. 90.

Towns became fewer and smaller as they drove through Terrebonne Parish and then St. Mary Parish. Louisiana swampland hugged both sides of the road.

"Pretty out here," Ava said. "Lots of birds." She lowered her window slightly and was greeted with a cacophony of soft coos and caws. "What are *those* guys?" she asked as a flock of large birds flew gracefully across their path.

"Blue herons," Carmela said. "Probably flying home for the night."

"Which is what we should be doing. Instead of chasing our cute little tails."

"You think this is a waste of time?" Carmela asked.

"I . . . I don't know. Maybe. But I suppose it's worth a shot."

"Thank you."

The sun was sitting low in the sky and sparkling off the dark waters. Bald cypress poked their trunks up everywhere as well as black gum trees and willows. The palette of greenery was amazing — bright yellow marsh marigolds surrounded by light green spike rush. In other areas, the brackish green of floating fern and water spangles covered the murky water.

"Remember the plant material that was found in Devon's shop?" Carmela asked.

Ava gazed out the window at bayous and swamps that stretched as far as the eye could see. "Lots of plant material out here."

Ava's phone chimed. She dug it out of her bag and said, "Hello?"

Carmela glanced at Ava. Her lips were pursed, and she did not look pleased.

"Who is it?" Carmela whispered.

"It's my date from hell."

"The Miss Penelope date? Hang up."

But Ava was talking to him now.

"Thursday?" she said. "Not a chance. When, you ask? How about never — is never good for you?"

She hung up, smiled at Carmela, and said, "So that's that."

"Good for you. Pull out that road map, will you?"

Ava opened the glove box, pulled out a Louisiana state map, and unfurled it. She studied it for a moment, frowned, and then turned it right-side up.

"Uh-oh," she said.

"What?"

"I'm not very skillful at map reading. I'm no Magellan."

"If Google Maps is correct, we don't go all the way into New Iberia," Carmela said. "We need to turn south on Darnall Road. Do you see that anywhere on the map?"

Ava squinted at the map. "Nope."

"Keep looking."

"I am."

"Because we're getting pretty close. Have you seen any road signs that indicate a Darnall Road?"

Ava lifted her eyes from the map and scanned the road ahead. "Um. Yeah."

"Where?" Carmela asked.

"Right here! Turn!"

Carmela hit the brakes, skidded across two lanes of traffic as angry drivers honked their horns. She made her turn, but just barely.

"Ava! You have to give me more warning than that!"

Ava had let the map slip to the floor as she cuddled Mimi in her lap. "I apologize. My faux pas. I'm just glad you've got grippy tires and excellent reflexes."

Carmela let out a shaky breath. "Me too."

They drove down a macadam road littered with potholes and lined with bald cypress trees dripping with gray-green Spanish moss.

"This is more like it," Ava said.

"More like what?"

"More like a hiding place for a notorious drug ring."

Carmela drove across a rickety wooden bridge and onto more broken blacktop. The road twisted along, skirting groves of tupelo trees and marshes redolent with sea lavender.

"Are you sure we're headed in the right direction?" Ava asked.

"Not exactly. But if that's the town of Lydia up ahead, we're at least in the general vicinity."

"It is Lydia. We just passed a dilapidated sign that said 'Beautiful Downtown Lydia, point six miles.' Maybe we should stop and ask for directions?"

"I think that's an excellent idea," Carmela said. She slowed down as she drifted past a couple of small wooden houses. The exterior wood shingles were weathered and silver from continued beatings by the rain, wind, sun, and occasional hurricane.

"I see lights," Ava said.

Carmela turned into a rutted driveway as Ava started bouncing in her seat.

"It's a honky-tonk. We can ask for directions and maybe have ourselves a nice, refreshing beverage."

Carmela gazed at the pitted stucco building that may or may not have been a rehabbed gas station. The low-slung roof held a solitary string of holiday lights — most of which had burned out. A white tin sign with faded black letters spelled out *BUMPERS.* It hung tilted and haphazard from the roofline.

"Directions, yes. Drinks, no," Carmela said. "We're not here to barhop and mix with the local gentry. In case you forgot, we're on a secret mission to track down a possible drug dealer."

"Spoilsport," Ava said. But she seemed okay with Carmela's decision.

Carmela parked her car between a rusted-out Chevy Silverado and a shiny new Ram Laramie. A few motorcycles — mostly Harley-Davidsons — were parked in the lot as well.

"Should I bring Mimi in?" Ava asked as she pushed open the car door. "For protection?"

"Why not." Carmela gazed at the little pug Ava was cradling. Mimi didn't exactly inspire confidence as a guard dog, but she did have her charms.

As they pushed open the front door of Bumpers, the smell of beer, whisky, and vapes quickly overpowered the humid swamp air.

A wooden bar ran the entire length of one wall. It was scarred from years of bottles, glasses, ashtrays, and maybe even skulls being slammed against it. The walls were hung with trucker caps — or gimme caps, as they were more often called. The caps were emblazoned with logos from the New Orleans Saints, Cajun Navy, LSU, Louisiana National Guard, and even a few slogans such as "Wassup?" and "Who dat?"

Two men who'd been shooting pool straightened up and their eyes widened at

389

the sight of the two pretty ladies who'd just waltzed in. One of the men, a tall, good-looking blond guy in plaid shirt and faded jeans, walked over to Ava and gently bumped his hip against hers. "Welcome to Bumpers, pretty lady."

Ava grinned and bumped right back. "Sorry, honey, but I'm above your pay grade."

The other pool shooter suddenly looked interested and started over to join in the game. Heads turned and throats were cleared by the other half dozen denizens in the bar.

But Carmela had already grabbed Ava and pulled her away from Plaid Shirt. "Directions, remember?" she hissed.

They turned toward the scuffed bar where the bartender, a short, round man in a grimy white apron, leaned forward to greet them.

"Dogs aren't allowed in here," he said. His voice was high and slightly hoarse.

"That's not a dog, it's my purse," Ava said.

The bartender shrugged. "In that case, what can I get for you ladies? We got a two-for-one special on Hand Grenades."

"Say what?" said Ava.

The bartender grinned and squeaked out, "Vodka, gin, rum, grain alcohol . . ."

"And melon liqueur," Plaid Shirt said. He'd come over to join them.

"Shaken not stirred?" Carmela asked.

The bartender cocked a finger at her. "Sassy. You're right with the program."

"What we really need is some help with directions," Carmela said.

"Where you goin'?" Plaid Shirt asked. "What's your hurry?" He eyed Mimi carefully.

Carmela focused on the bartender. "I'm trying to find a friend who lives on Royalton?"

"Come to the right place, you have," the bartender said. He pointed to a skinny guy in blue and white ticking stripe overalls who was hunched over his beer at the bar. "Slaney there worked at the post office for a while."

Slaney looked up from his drink. "Mostly during the holidays. When the regulars couldn't keep up." His eyes drifted back to his beer, and a look of sadness came over his face. "Course that's all changed. Now it's all texts and e-mails."

"But you could direct me to Royalton?" Carmela asked.

"I could drive you," Plaid Shirt offered.

"Ooh," Ava squealed. "Or we could stay and have a drink?"

Carmela raised an eyebrow until it quivered. "What do you think?"

"No?" Ava turned to Plaid Shirt. "I guess that's a no. Sorry, big guy. We'll try to make it back some other time."

Carmela huddled with Slaney, listening carefully, trying to commit his directions to memory while he mumbled on about following Weeks Island Road and passing Stumpy Bayou.

"Those guys were nice," Ava said when they were back in the car. "And friendly."

"That they were," Carmela said as she pulled back onto the road.

"So you know where we're going?"

"I think so. We follow this road for a few miles, then hang a right on Shell Road."

"And you know where that is?"

"Somewhere past Stumpy Bayou and Warehouse Bayou," Carmela said as she clicked on her brights.

"How do they come up with those names?" Ava wondered.

It was full-on dark now. And lonely as sin as they hurtled down a narrow road that got even narrower the farther they ventured into the bayou.

"Scary out here," Ava said. "Lonely. A UFO could crash-land, and nobody would be the wiser."

"We're okay, just keep your door locked."

"We could have had a nice strong man to guide us . . ."

"Here's Shell Road," Carmela said. She slowed way down and made a cautious right-hand turn.

"This isn't really an actual road," Ava said as they crawled along, dirt and rocks clunking against the undercarriage of the car. "This is nothing but a dirt track."

"Or in highway department lingo, unimproved," Carmela said.

"It *needs* to be improved. This road is starting to jostle the fillings loose in my teeth."

They drove deeper and deeper into the bayou, the road closing in on both sides with thick, dark foliage. They crossed a shaky single lane wooden bridge, dipped down a hill, and, just like that, their headlights shone on a morass of mud directly ahead.

"Are you sure your car can make it through all that muck?" Ava asked.

"I'm giving it my . . . ugh . . . best," Carmela said as they lurched and twisted through the sticky pit of mud. The car's back wheels spun and whined noisily.

Ava groaned. "Please don't tell me

that . . ."

"We're stuck," Carmela said as the car shuddered and she felt the left rear tire sink into a deep rut. "Rats." She opened her door and glanced around. "We pretty much have to keep moving forward. There's no spot to turn around."

Ava deposited Mimi in Carmela's lap. "Not to worry, I got this." She stepped out of the car and into the mud, then flexed her arms in a weight lifter's pose. "I'll push us out of here. This is where my Pilates finally pays off."

"Okay, now," Carmela called out once Ava had positioned herself at the rear bumper. "I'm going to rock the car. Push real hard on the forward bounces, okay?"

"Got it," Ava called back.

Carmela put her car in first gear and rocked. Gave a little spurt of gas, then let the car settle back. Then another spurt. With Ava pushing and Carmela rocking they managed to gain about ten inches of forward progress.

"This isn't working very well," Carmela yelled above the grinding of the engine.

"Tell me about it," Ava called back. "I can't get much traction with these stupid boots!"

Carmela jumped out to survey the situation. "Probably because you're not wearing boots. Those are just skinny straps of leather with a miniature brass buckle attached."

"They're cage boots. They give the *illusion* of boots but technically they're not really boots," Ava said.

"How about you get in and drive. I'll push."

"Your car's a stick shift?"

"You know it is. Just put it in gear and then . . ."

Ava crossed her arms and shook her head. "I can't drive a stick shift. Not very well, anyway. My cousin Emerson tried to teach me once on his brother's Camaro that had a welded chain for a steering wheel, but we ended up in . . ."

"Ava?"

"Huh?"

"I'll put it in first *for* you," Carmela said. "Then you just give it a shot of gas while I push. Got it?"

"Natch," Ava said as they traded places.

Standing behind the car, Carmela widened her stance and grabbed hold of the bumper.

"Okay, Ava, give it a touch of gas," Carmela called out as she pushed with as much force as she could muster.

There was a high-pitched whirring sound, and the car's tires began to spin wildly.

Huge clumps of mud flew everywhere. A torrent of juicy brown slime spattered Carmela's clothes, her face, and her hair.

Stunned, Carmela just stood there as she watched her car fishtail forward onto drier ground. Swearing to herself, wiping mud from her eyes, she stormed up to the driver's side and yanked the door open. "Ava, what were you *thinking*!"

Ava gaped at her. "*Cher,* what happened to your face? Your clothes?" She blinked. "Oh no, did I do that?"

"Yes, you did!"

"The wheels started spinning a mile a minute and we shot forward," Ava cried. "But that's a good thing, right? I mean, we're not stuck anymore."

"Ava, look at me!"

Ava bit her lip as she dug in her purse and pulled out a miniature pack of tissues. "Tissue?" She looked and sounded extremely contrite.

Carmela wiped her face and hands. Then she reached in the back seat and pulled out Mimi's blanket. Wiping herself with the dog blanket helped dislodge the larger hunks of mud that were stuck to her.

"We could exchange clothes," Ava offered. "This was all my fault, so I'm prepared to take responsibility."

Carmela shook her head, still wiping. "Thanks. I'll be okay."

"I guess I'd better not drive anymore, huh?"

"Honey, you just said a mouthful."

Carmela took the wheel and drove until they reached a signpost that was leaning halfway into a ditch.

"This must be Royalton," Carmela said.

"Sounds better than it looks," Ava said.

Carmela turned onto an even narrower road and bumped along slowly.

"This makes me nervous," Ava said. "Mimi's worried, too."

"That makes three of us," Carmela said.

They crawled along in the dark until they came to an old-fashioned one-and-a-half-story wooden house. It was set back from the road in a shroud of weeds and trees.

"Is this it?" Ava whispered.

"I don't know." Carmela coasted to a stop. The house was half falling down, and there was a junky fishing boat parked in the yard.

"This reminds me of that scary movie *The Last House on the Left.*"

"At least somebody's at home."

"Yeah, I see a faint glow through the drapes," Ava said. "Maybe a lantern? Or actual electricity?" She let loose a shiver and said, "Now what?"

But Carmela wasn't exactly sure what to do, either. Was this even the right address? And who lived here, for heaven's sake? Her eyes searched the old place, looking for a mailbox with a name, or numbers over the front door. But there was nothing. Then her eyes landed on a vehicle that was parked behind a grove of trees.

"Maybe we took a wrong turn," Ava suggested.

Carmela stared at the blue SUV that was the mirror image of the one that'd chased them last night. And her heart skipped a beat.

"No," Carmela said. "This is it. We've come to the right place."

CHAPTER 30

"You see that?" Carmela asked.

Ava peered around anxiously. "See what? Who's out there? Please don't tell me there's an escaped maniac with a hook for a hand."

"Calm down and take a look at the SUV that's parked over there."

"What? Where?" Ava craned her neck and glanced around. "Oh yeah, back in the bushes. What about it?"

"Recognize it?"

"You're scaring me, Carmela."

"You should be scared. Because I'm pretty sure that's the same SUV that chased after us last night."

Carmela's words were like an electric shock to Ava.

"Then we have to get out of here!" she cried. "This is dangerous! Just like that trip wire thing Babcock warned us about."

"Not so fast. Right now, we're the hunter,"

Carmela said. "Closing in on our prey."

"Don't you mean *pray*? Like in asking baby Jesus to please help us? Because this is not only scary, it's super hazardous to our health!"

"I need to get out and take a look," Carmela said.

"You don't *need* to, you *want* to," Ava said. "And that's such a bad idea, I can't tell you how bad an idea that is."

"I need to find out *who's* in there."

Ava swallowed hard. "We know it's not T.J. There's no way he could have driven any faster than you did."

"Agreed. And Babcock already eliminated Richard Drake."

"Could it be Roy Sultan or Colonel Otis?" Ava asked.

"Too old."

"Then who?"

Carmela stared at the SUV and then at the camp shack. "You wait here, Ava. I'll be back in a couple of minutes." Carmela's nerves strummed wildly, but she was excited at the prospect of finally getting one step closer to ferreting out Devon's killer.

Ava grabbed Carmela's hand. "Don't go," she pleaded. "I hate the idea of you stumbling around out there all covered with mud. Looking like one of those wild mud men from Borneo."

"Take care of Mimi," Carmela said as she pulled free. "I'll be back in two shakes."

Carmela crept slowly across the yard, letting her eyes become accustomed to the dark, trying desperately not to trip on a fallen branch or a root. She ducked under an old clothesline, still heading for the shack. She'd spotted a window, and it seemed like a good place to start. Maybe if it was unlatched, she could even crawl inside and take a quick look around.

Carmela's fingers had just touched the rough wood of the windowsill, when she felt a tap on her shoulder. With her heart nearly beating out of her chest, she spun around wildly to find . . .

"Ava! You scared me to death!"

"I had to get out and follow you," Ava said. "Sitting in the car all by my lonesome, I thought . . . well, if we're going to die, it's better that we die together." She gazed past Carmela's shoulder. "Did you look inside? What did you see in there?"

"Nothing yet."

They both stepped up to the window, stood on tiptoes, and pressed their noses to the glass.

"Dark in there," Ava said. "But I can see

shapes. Furniture, though, not actual people."

Carmela stared in, too. "Looks like a really messy office."

"Do you think drug dealers work from an office? That they have, like, files and invoices and stuff like regular people?"

"There's only one way to find out." Carmela seized the edge of the window frame and slowly pushed the window up. A creak sounded and they both held their breath. But no one came rushing to investigate.

"Give me a boost," Carmela said. "So I can crawl inside."

Ava backed away. "No way, it could be a trap. We're out here in the middle of nowhere. Even if Babcock circulates a million missing person posters, no one will ever find our poor mangled bodies."

Carmela held up an index finger. "One quick look. You stay out here and be my lookout. Now come on, hurry up and give me a boost."

Grudgingly, Ava laced her hands together and hoisted Carmela through the window.

As Carmela landed quietly, her first impression was of dust and mildew. Awful. Made it difficult to draw a breath. Stifling a sneeze, she crept over to an old-fashioned rolltop desk with a scatter of papers on top.

She reached out and stirred the papers around, looking for something — anything — that might give her a clue as to who lived here. Her fingers touched an old leather-bound address book.

This could be something.

Picking it up, Carmela thumbed through the pages but didn't recognize any of the names or addresses.

A noise in the next room made Carmela jump. Her throat went Gobi Desert dry, and the tiny hairs on the back of her neck prickled and rose up.

Fear. This is what fear feels like.

She tried to swallow her feelings and dig down deep for some courage. She was here, maybe even inside the killer's house. She had to come away with something!

When nothing happened, when nobody came flying into the room to attack her, Carmela rifled through the papers again but couldn't find anything that seemed related to drugs or even to Dulcimer Antiques.

Did I make a bad call on this? Please, no.

She glanced around the dreary room and, off to one side, noticed an ancient Remington typewriter sitting on a timeworn metal stand.

Typewriter?

Something clicked in Carmela's brain.

403

Hadn't Babcock told her that all the anonymous notes sent to the NOPD had been typed? Yes, he had.

Carmela searched around the typewriter stand, looking for scraps of paper filled with jottings or cryptic notes. There wasn't a thing. She stood there, feeling as if she'd somehow let Babcock down, let Devon Dowling down, too. She frowned and shook her head, disheartened, ready to concede.

That's when her eyes landed squarely on the typewriter ribbon.

Without hesitation, Carmela reached out and ripped the two spools out of the typewriter. As she started to unwind them, she stepped closer to the door where a thin crack of light shone through. Squinting, she tried to read the words that were imprinted and overprinted on the old cloth ribbon. As she eased the ribbon through her trembling fingers, bit by bit, she was shocked to discover a number of key words.

Colonel Otis. Knife collection. Richard Drake.

Carmela stared at the typewriter ribbon that was smudging her fingers. Suddenly, she had no doubt that the anonymous notes left on Babcock's and Gallant's car windshields had been typed on this machine!

The sound of a ringing phone in the next

room startled Carmela and caused her to drop the ribbon on the wooden floor. *THUNK!* She froze, praying that whoever was in there hadn't heard the noise.

Five, ten, twenty seconds dragged by, but no one came to check. Carmela bent down, scooped up the ribbon, and tucked it in her jacket pocket. She felt shaky and knew she should get the hell out of there. Beat feet back to civilization. And Babcock. But her curiosity was still amped to a fever pitch.

Carmela tiptoed closer to the door and put her ear against the crack.

A low, hoarse voice was spewing anger. "No, you freaking idiot! Your delivery boy screwed up royally. Yes, it was the wrong address. I had to send a guy in to grab it, but he decided to get creative and made a mess of things. I had to clean things up myself!"

The voice grew louder and more venomous, and Carmela had no doubt that the speaker, whoever he was, was surely Devon's killer. As her mind fought to process this notion, she suddenly froze with fear as she heard footsteps heading in her direction. Whoever was spewing anger on the phone was also about to open the door and step into this room!

Biting back her panic, Carmela rushed for

the open window and dived out headfirst just as the door opened . . .

CLICK!

. . . and she landed in Ava's waiting arms.

As they both tumbled to the ground, Carmela slapped a hand across Ava's mouth to stifle her screams.

They huddled together, quiet as a pair of mice, as someone moved about in the grubby office. Finally, Carmela removed her hand from Ava's mouth and shook her head. *Don't talk,* she mouthed.

"What?" Ava whispered. "What's going on?"

Carmela touched an index finger to her lips. *Hush.*

"But I want to see."

Carmela nodded. She got it. She wanted to know what was happening, too.

Stealthily, carefully, they both stood up and peered cautiously in the window.

And there, stomping around the room like a caged animal, was Peter Jarreau!

Ava's lips silently formed the words *holy crap.*

Carmela nodded as Jarreau's obnoxious aftershave drifted out at them. Then she quickly pulled Ava to a safe distance away from the window where they could talk in low voices.

Ava was rocked to the core by their discovery. "That's the officious little jerkwad who works for NOPD, right?"

"Peter Jarreau," Carmela said, her lip curling. She was thunderstruck at the realization that Jarreau was the dope dealer they'd been looking for. Worse, he was also a traitor to the police department. He could have put Edgar, Bobby Gallant, and the whole force in terrible danger. "He's around all the time. Right under Edgar's nose. Close to all the inside information."

"So he's a dope dealer? He's the one who was supposed to take delivery of the cocaine?"

"Worse than that, he's probably Devon Dowling's killer," Carmela said in a low voice. "And the one who probably sliced Sonny Boy's throat to keep him from talking."

Ava's brows puckered. "Who woulda thunk it? Peter Jarreau."

Carmela pulled her mouth into a twisted grin and dropped her voice to a harsh whisper. "Gotcha."

CHAPTER 31

But if Carmela thought she'd cornered Peter Jarreau like a rat in a trap, she was sorely mistaken. Jarreau continued to jabber away, cursing up a storm, as he rummaged through a drawer.

"Listen to that guy swear," Ava said. "What a potty mouth. And I thought I was bad."

"Maybe he's stoned out of his gourd."

"You know what they say," Ava said.

"What's that?"

"Don't get high on your own supply."

"Let's see what he's going to do next." Carmela's nerves were tingling from excitement and outrage as they crept back to the window.

Jarreau was standing there as if in a trance. Then, suddenly, his phone rang.

"What!" he yelled, then listened for a moment. "You're kidding. *Now?* Awright, yeah, whatever."

They watched as Jarreau clicked off his phone, then rummaged through a second drawer.

"Too many foul-ups," he muttered to himself.

Finally, Jarreau pulled out a black snub-nosed pistol, studied it for a moment, then stuffed it in his jacket pocket. He gave a final look around and left the room.

Holding hands, Carmela and Ava rushed for their car. But before they could jump in, Jarreau came storming out of the camp house.

"Oh jeez," Ava whispered. They collapsed behind a magnolia tree and held their breath. Would he spot them in the shadows?

But Jarreau didn't glance left, he didn't look right, he just jumped in his SUV and took off like a scalded jackrabbit.

"We have to follow him!" Carmela yelped. She was up and running, reaching out to yank her car door open.

Ava, following closely on her heels, jumped in and grabbed for her seat belt. "Where do you think he's going? To meet his dealer? Do a sneaky deal somewhere?"

"I don't know, but I doubt he's up to anything good." Carmela glanced over her right shoulder. "Hang on again, Mimi!"

She cranked her engine and fishtailed

down the road after Jarreau.

Carmela had been following Jarreau for a good five minutes, driving without her headlights on, when he suddenly juked right.

"Wait, we didn't come that way," Ava said.

"He's taking a different road out of here," Carmela said as she followed him.

"I didn't know there was one."

They trailed Jarreau along a twisty-turny dirt road and over a couple of rickety bridges. They bumped to a sudden halt when they reached a stop sign and their tires hit blacktop.

"Which way did he go?" Carmela wondered.

"Left, I'm positive he turned left," Ava said. "He's gotta be heading toward U.S. 90."

"Going to New Orleans?"

"Maybe. Probably."

"That's not good," Carmela said.

They made the turn onto the wider road and, as they drove along, slowly began to pick up traffic. Thank goodness, Carmela could finally put her headlights on.

"We're definitely headed for U.S. 90," Carmela said.

"Be sure to keep a car or two in between

us," Ava said. "It's a chase technique I picked up watching *Private Eyes.*"

"Watching what?"

"TV show with that dreamy Jason Priestley. He used to play hockey and . . ."

Carmela slowed down to allow a banged-up maroon truck to pull onto the road in front of her.

"There. Happy now?" Carmela asked.

"Mostly I'm just scared. And hungry."

"Grab your cell phone and see if you can scare up Babcock. I gotta let him know what's going on."

"Won't he be mad?" Ava asked as she pulled out her phone and dialed.

Carmela sighed. "Probably."

"He's not answering. It just goes to voice mail."

"Okay, we'll try again in a few minutes."

They bumped along, the maroon truck puttering away in front of them, Jarreau's SUV a distant speck on the road ahead.

"Maybe I should try to get around this truck," Carmela said, just as the truck's brake lights flared. "Oh, wait, he's turning."

The truck turned into a lane marked *AGGIE'S FARM.* But now the road in front of them looked surprisingly empty.

"Where'd he go?" Carmela asked. She was breathless and her nerves were on edge.

411

"Ava, I thought you were keeping an eye on him."

"I was. But it's like he disappeared into thin air." She peered ahead into the gloom. "Wait, that might be him, that little dot on the horizon."

Carmela saw a distant flicker of light, like a firefly, on the road ahead.

"He's really moving," Carmela said as she hit the gas.

They accelerated like a bat out of hell, picking up speed. The trees and bayous flew past their window like crazed images from some kind of herky-jerky, old-time movie. As the speedometer continued to climb upward, Carmela flipped on her brights.

And Ava suddenly screamed!

"Watch out, there's a log in the road!" Ava lifted her legs and planted her feet against the dashboard, bracing for the oncoming collision. Her hands flew up to cover her eyes.

Carmela saw the obstruction on the road and slammed on her brakes at the very last moment. Her tires squealed in protest as she slewed across the road and spun around in a dizzying half circle. Mimi started barking and didn't stop until they came to a jouncing halt on the road's gravel berm.

"Whew." Ava uncovered her eyes, reached

back to grab Mimi, and cuddled the frightened dog in her lap. "That was some kind
of crazy, huh? Some truck must have
dropped . . ."

"That was no log," Carmela said.

"Then what was it?" Ava pushed open the
door and stepped out, Mimi still in her
arms.

"I wouldn't do that if I were you."

Ava stopped and spun around. "Huh?"

"Just bring the dog back."

Ava deposited Mimi back in the car, as
Carmela crawled out to join her.

"You see that?" Carmela said. She pointed
to an enormous brown and green animal
whose body practically filled the road. It sat
just inches from her car's front bumper.

"What on earth is that awful thing?" Ava
asked. "It looks like it crawled out of *Juras-
sic Park.*"

"It's a turtle."

"Don't be ridiculous, that's a gator. It has
an alligator head and tail."

"Yeah, but look at that humpy-bumpy
bony shell. It's an alligator snapping turtle.
I saw one once at Shamus's camp house."

"He looks more like a turtle that swallowed an alligator," Ava said. "Honk at it,
get it to slither off the road."

The turtle blinked as if listening to their

conversation.

"Or maybe we could just give him the old heave-ho," Ava said.

"That guy probably weighs two hundred pounds. With jaws that can snap your wrist in half. If he ever got hold of Mimi, he'd consider her a tasty appetizer."

Ava stared at the turtle. "Well, he's an ugly mother, I'll say that."

The turtle let out a loud hiss.

"Uh-oh, I think I offended him."

"Maybe I can hurry him along," Carmela said. She opened her trunk and pulled out a tire iron. She walked to the rear of the turtle and clanged the tire iron hard against the blacktop. The sharp, metallic sound rang out. *CLANG. CLANG. CLANG.*

The turtle whipped around and opened its mouth.

Carmela hastily retreated.

"Plan B?" Ava said.

But the turtle had had enough. Slowly, creeping along and taking its own sweet time, the alligator turtle waddled off the road and disappeared down the embankment into a murky pond.

When they finally got going again, there was no sign of Peter Jarreau, and Carmela was feeling desperate and out of sorts.

"Jarreau is miles ahead of us now, so we definitely need to get hold of Babcock."

"I'll try him again," Ava said. She punched in his number, then held the phone out so Carmela could hear it going to voice mail again.

"Where is he?" Carmela wondered.

"Busy doing cop stuff, I guess."

When they finally hit U.S. 90, Carmela pulled into the far left lane and accelerated to seventy miles per hour.

"We'll make good time now, *cher*," Ava said. "And we probably won't have to contend with any more insanely huge turtles."

But Carmela was still fretting. "Maybe . . . call Bobby Gallant."

Ava nodded. "I can do that."

She punched in the number Carmela gave her, and two rings later, Gallant picked up.

"Bobby, you sweet thang," Ava purred.

"Who is this?" Gallant asked.

Carmela snapped her fingers and gestured for Ava to hand over the phone. Ava obliged.

"Bobby?" Carmela said.

"Carmela?"

"Yes, it's me." Carmela was thrilled that Bobby had picked up. Now she could say her piece. "Something really wild just happened and I need you to help us deal with it. It's a really . . . huge problem."

"Sorry, Carmela, no can do. I'm rushing out the door right now. On my way to the big press conference."

Carmela realized that's where Babcock must be as well. *Oh no!*

"Dear Lord, the press conference is happening now? With the mayor?"

"In twenty, maybe thirty minutes, yeah. It was delayed so everything's in a total panic, so I gotta go. Sorry."

"Listen, you have to tell . . ."

But Bobby had already hung up and Carmela was talking to dead air.

"He hung up," Carmela said, handing the phone back to Ava. She felt both hollow and defeated.

Ava was incredulous. "How rude."

"We have to get to New Orleans and tell Babcock about Jarreau. We have to somehow interrupt that press conference."

Ava gave Carmela a strange look. "But isn't Jarreau their media liaison? Won't he be *part* of that press conference?"

Panic rose inside Carmela.

"You're right!"

Of course, that's exactly where Jarreau was headed. And with a loaded *pistol* at that.

All Carmela could do was whisper a prayer and focus on the road ahead.

And worry about the danger that lay ahead, too.

CHAPTER 32

Faster, faster, faster was Carmela's mantra as she spun off U.S. 90 and roared down Poydras Street. From there it was a matter of twenty minutes before she turned onto Loyola, cruised past the Superdome, and reached the edge of the French Quarter.

And slammed to a dead stop.

Directly ahead of her, the street was closed. Black-and-white wooden barriers had been set up. And just in case you didn't get the full message, two police cruisers were parked in front of them, nose to nose.

"What's going on?" Ava asked. "Do you think it's a second line march? Or maybe a jazz funeral?"

"I don't know." Carmela backed up her car, skirted around another block, and came up against another barrier. This one had a uniformed police officer shaking his finger at drivers, warning them the road was definitely closed.

418

"Now what?" Ava asked.

"I don't know. Looks like the whole French Quarter is blocked off. There must be another Jazz Fest parade. We're going to have to find a place to park and then get out and walk."

Ava grimaced. "In these shoes? I couldn't even push a car wearing them, let alone walk a half dozen blocks. I swear, this is the last time I buy Louboutin knockoffs!"

"You want to wait here?" Carmela eased her car into a super tight space that she figured would have to do.

"Not really, I might miss all the fun."

"Okay, then, put Mimi in her tote bag and let's start hiking."

They managed to walk two crowded blocks when they suddenly encountered the parade. A high school marching band, with students in snappy navy and gold uniforms, was playing a syncopated rendition of "When the Saints Go Marching In."

"How are your feet holding up?" Carmela asked.

"They're not," Ava said, as the band halted directly in front of them and continued to high-step in place.

"We need to get across this street somehow," Carmela said, eyeing a line of snare drummers.

"Better we should squeeze through the clarinet section," Ava said. "They seem to be the least lethal when it comes to musical instruments."

Dashing, dodging, and subjecting themselves to more than a few angry comments, Carmela and Ava scurried their way through the band.

"This is like playing the old video game *Frogger*," Ava called out.

A second later, the band members executed a snappy turn and resumed their marching, trapping Carmela and Ava in the middle of the street as the band members streamed by them.

When the band had finally passed by, the women turned to run and were immediately engulfed by the Beastmaster Puppets!

Now they had to fight their way through a sea of oversized puppets and dozens of ninja-clad puppeteers who were manipulating the puppets. A ginormous, twenty-five-foot-tall bat puppet seemed intent on bearing down on them.

Ava turned to Carmela with a look of panic on her face. "It's like we're being swept along in a tsunami of weirdness!"

Carmela grabbed Ava's arm and pulled her close. "Just stand still, stay in place, and they'll swoop right by us."

Didn't work that way.

Five seconds later, they were confronted by a masked man wearing a tuxedo and sporting a top hat and cane.

"Not you two again!" he cried. "Are you trying to drive me insane or just completely ruin Jazz Fest!"

"Drake?" Carmela quavered. "Richard Drake?"

"Yes, it's me," Drake thundered as he pulled up his mask. "I'm a member of this organization. What's your excuse?"

"We blundered in," Carmela said. "We didn't mean to, it's just . . ."

"It's my shoes," Ava chimed in. "I think I'm getting a blister."

"Actually, we're trying to get to the mayor's office," Carmela stammered. Maybe it was better to tell the truth?

Drake stared at Carmela, then at Ava. "You think the mayor gives a damn about your blister?"

"Listen," Carmela said, putting a hand on his arm. "We know you're upset at us. But you have to believe us, we never pointed the police in your direction. But the thing is, we just . . . well, we stumbled upon something . . . and we're desperate to get to City Hall."

"We know who killed Devon Dowling!"

Ava blurted out.

Drake stared at her. "What are you talking about?"

"We found the person we think is responsible for Devon's and Sonny Boy Holmes's deaths," Carmela said. "I know . . ." She drew a shaky breath. "I know this all sounds ridiculous and quite implausible, but we have to get in touch with the police. Like . . . immediately."

"Before the mayor's press conference happens," Ava added. "And the real killer goes scot-free."

Drake gazed at them for a hard moment. "You're not making this up?"

Carmela and Ava shook their heads.

"You have to talk to the police. At City Hall." Drake was still digesting their words.

"But all the streets are blocked," Carmela said.

"I can help," Drake said. "Our parade route goes right past City Hall."

"Oh, wow," Ava said.

Drake waggled a finger, and they stepped to the side of the street where a gray Subaru was parked. "You're lucky you caught me at the start of the parade." He opened the car and pulled out two costumes. "Hurry up, put these on."

"The man comes prepared," Ava said, impressed.

"Thank you," Carmela breathed to Drake.

Within minutes they were suited up, Carmela in a furry bat costume with gauze wings attached to her back, Ava in a flying monkey costume complete with curly tail.

"Now get in line," Drake instructed. "And try not to cause too much of a scene."

They marched along, the crowd cheering and waving at the puppets. Walking at the back of the pack, Carmela and Ava waved back. Mimi had popped her head out of her tote bag and stared in awe at the crowds.

"This is cool, huh?" Ava asked. "Reminds me of when I was in the Miss Teen Sparkle beauty pageant. Of course, that was much fancier and we rode on the back of a shiny convertible."

As the marching band and Beastmaster contingent continued down Basin Street, Carmela and Ava executed a fast left-hand turn. They skirted past a police barrier and made a beeline for the plaza just outside City Hall.

"Hey!" a uniformed officer called after them. He made a pro forma attempt to chase them but petered out after fifteen feet.

"Keep going!" Carmela cried as they ran toward the plaza ahead.

"I see TV cameras," Ava huffed as she ran

alongside Carmela.

"Good. The more press, the better."

They were in the thick of reporters, TV vans, and camera crews now, and one reporter yelled out, "Hey, Batgirl," as Carmela flew by.

"What am I, chopped liver?" Ava asked as she tried to keep up.

Carmela looked about frantically. Where was the mayor? Where was Babcock? Better yet, where was that murdering skunk Peter Jarreau?

Suddenly, she spotted a wooden podium just up ahead. There was a barrage of bright lights set up around it, camera lenses were aimed at the podium, and microphones were clipped to its front edge.

Okay, Carmela thought, *now we're getting somewhere.*

But were they really? Because dressed as they were, in goofball costumes, they looked awfully ridiculous.

Her fear soon came home to roost when a policeman reached out, pinched her shoulder, and yelled, "Stop, right there!"

Carmela's forward progress ground to a halt as she gazed into a face that told her he was dead serious.

"I need to talk to Detective Babcock," Carmela said. "It's an emergency."

"Let me guess, you double-parked your Batmobile?" the officer said.

Ava tried to intercede. "This woman is Detective Babcock's fiancée," she said. "And it's really important she talk to him. A matter of life and death."

The officer stared at Carmela, as if trying to make up his mind.

Carmela gave him a look of intense concern. "It has to do with the mayor's press conference." Her bat wings bobbed as she spoke.

"It's going to have to wait," the officer said.

"It can't wait," Carmela said. "I have information about a homicide that's under investigation."

"Two homicides," Ava said. She held up two fingers, trying to be helpful. Then she reached into her tote bag and pulled out Mimi. "You see this cute little dog? Her owner — her most favorite person in the whole world — was murdered in cold blood."

At having Mimi shoved in his face, the officer released Carmela's shoulder so he could raise his arm and push Ava and Mimi away.

That was all Carmela needed.

Like a sprinter bolting from the starting

425

block, Carmela dashed toward the podium. "Detective Babcock!" she cried out. "I have to talk to Detective Babcock." She couldn't see him anywhere, but maybe he would hear her?

Bright lights swung her way as cameramen suddenly turned and focused on her. Carmela was aware they were probably rolling tape but didn't much care. She kept running, her breath coming in shallow bursts, the whoosh of blood in her ears.

And then, seconds later, the mayor appeared, smiling, waving, looking dapper and polished in his two-thousand-dollar suit. And at his side . . . Babcock.

"Edgar!" Carmela screamed. Even though her heart was hammering inside her chest, and she was almost out of breath, she managed to make her voice carry above the babble of the crowd. And then suddenly, thankfully, Babcock's head swiveled, and he saw her running toward him.

"Carmela?" The blood drained from Babcock's face, and he looked positively baffled as he ran to intercept her. "What are you doing here? You shouldn't *be* here."

"Sonny Boy was a thief, not a killer," Carmela managed to stammer out. "You're accusing the wrong man!"

CHAPTER 33

"Carmela, what are you saying?" Babcock shouted. He looked angry, but there was urgency in his voice, too.

"I tried to call you. Ava and I figured it out!" Carmela cried.

"Figured what out?"

"Devon's killer," Carmela said. She was so out of breath she was nearly choking as she danced around on the balls of her feet, trying to make Babcock understand, trying to make him listen. "And Sonny Boy's killer, too."

"Carmela . . ." Now his voice carried a warning tone.

There was an enormous commotion off to their left. People applauding and reporters and cameramen trying to edge closer as the mayor stepped to the podium.

"Now is not the time," Babcock told her. "I'll listen to you, but not until this is over."

"That's what I'm trying to tell you. Jarreau is the one. Peter Jarreau is the killer!"

"What?" Babcock said this so quietly, Carmela was afraid he hadn't heard her.

"I said . . ." Carmela gazed past Babcock's shoulder and practically gasped. There was Peter Jarreau, bearing down upon them. He wore a determined, steely-eyed look on his face and carried a stack of press releases — probably text of the mayor's speech — that he'd hand out to the media afterward.

Jarreau walked directly up to Babcock, glanced at Carmela, and said, "Get rid of her. She's a distraction."

"I know what you did," Carmela said from between clenched teeth.

Jarreau had turned away, but now he hesitated and looked back at Carmela. "I could have you arrested for interfering in police business."

"Now just a minute," Babcock said. He seemed torn between the two of them.

"Stop wasting time," Jarreau said. "Get her out of here. We have a lot on the line tonight."

"You killed Devon Dowling," Carmela spat at him. "You stabbed Sonny Boy Holmes. And you're a drug dealer. I have a brick of cocaine that proves it!"

Jarreau's face turned bright red as he shook his head. "You're completely crazy, you know that? I always knew you were trouble, and now you're making lunatic accusations that you can't possibly prove."

"Oh no?" Ava screamed as she rushed up to him. "Tell that to Mimi. She was a witness!"

At hearing her name called, Mimi popped her head out of the tote bag. She looked around, saw Peter Jarreau, and suddenly went crazy. Barking and snapping at him, she fought her way out of the tote bag, then launched herself directly at Jarreau.

"Aggh!" Jarreau cried as Mimi landed squarely on his chest. She scrabbled to gain purchase with her hind feet and sunk her teeth into the side of his neck. Jarreau's papers fluttered everywhere as he staggered backward. His right arm flailed in the air for a moment, and then he whipped the pistol out of his pocket and aimed wildly.

BOOM!

Time seemed to stand still as people screamed, ducked, and tried to scramble out of the way.

Luckily, Jarreau's shot went wild and struck the statue of a minor Louisiana dignitary that stood at the edge of the plaza. The man's head blew off as if it had been hit by mortar fire, then landed on the patio and rolled away.

There was no second shot. Babcock had already wrestled Peter Jarreau to the ground, and three uniformed officers had jumped into the fray to help handcuff him.

Standing at the podium, the mayor looked terrified for a split second, then a grin creased his face and his dignity was once again intact.

"What?" he said in a joking tone. "Have the redcoats come back? Should we alert Andrew Jackson and Jean Lafitte?"

The crowd erupted in laughter.

The mayor held up his hand. "One moment please while I confer with a couple of my guys."

Babcock and Bobby Gallant hurried to the mayor's side and spoke into his ear. The mayor registered surprise, shock, and then agreement, as he listened. This wasn't his first rodeo. He was a political pro.

Finally, the mayor gripped the podium with both hands and addressed the crowd.

"I actually have two important announcements to make tonight."

There was a buzz of excitement, then the mayor continued.

"My first announcement is that the man who murdered two of our citizens, Mr. Dowling and Mr. Holmes, has been apprehended by members of our outstanding

New Orleans Police Department. I will release all pertinent details once they conclude their investigation."

"Hey, don't we get any credit?" Ava asked as she and Carmela stood and watched.

The mayor straightened up and looked a little less serious.

"My second announcement is that Detective Edgar Babcock has been promoted to deputy chief!"

Babcock gazed in surprise at the mayor, then his eyes sought out Carmela as she stood nearby. He quietly mouthed, *You okay with this?*

I'm so proud, Carmela mouthed back.

"Me too!" Ava shouted.

CHAPTER 34

Carmela waited anxiously as reporters jostled around the mayor and Babcock, asking questions, jotting notes, grabbing sound bites.

Finally, Babcock walked over to where Carmela and Ava were standing.

"Excuse me," he said as he took Carmela by the hand and led her a few steps away, out of the hubbub of the crowd. Then he wrapped his arms around her.

"You did it," he said. "I don't know how — I probably don't want to know how, but you did it."

"And you're not mad?" Carmela gazed up at him.

"Of course I am. But I'll get over it, like I always do. My main concern has always been your safety." His mouth crinkled in a wry grin. "You do tend to hang it all out there."

"I'm good," Carmela said. "You know I'm good."

Babcock shook his head. "No, you're very, very bad. You never listen and you take ridiculous chances."

"But I . . ."

"And, excuse me, ma'am, but what's with this costume? And the wings?"

"I'm supposed to be a bat. Don't you like it?"

"I wouldn't say it's my idea of a sweet, romantic outfit." Babcock touched his nose to hers. "Truth be told, I'd much prefer you in a wedding dress."

"This is all I had in a pinch," Carmela said. "Besides, don't you know it's bad luck for the groom to see the dress before the wedding?"

Babcock grew very still. "Is there a dress?" he growled. "Is there a wedding? Can we finally set a date?"

Carmela rose up on tiptoe and whispered in his ear.

Babcock whispered something back that made Carmela smile, and then his lips closed on hers.

SCRAPBOOK, STAMPING, AND CRAFT TIPS FROM LAURA CHILDS

Dip Dye a Scarf

Turn a plain white scarf into an of-the-moment dip-dyed scarf. Prepare a dyebath in your favorite color, then completely wet your scarf. Dip one end of the scarf into the dye until you get the color saturation and "dipped" effect that you want. Then dip the middle of the scarf in the dye to create a fun accent area. Simply let your scarf dry, and it's ready to wear!

Autumn Burlap Flowers

If you've ever made paper flowers, then you can easily make these sturdy blooms. Just cut your burlap into petals, pinch one end, and tack or use hot glue. You can make large blooms to ring a candle or even create an autumn wreath.

Snow-Covered Wine Bottles

Select 3 wine bottles of varying sizes and spray with white primer. Allow to dry. Now spray bottles with adhesive and, while still tacky, roll each bottle in Epsom salt, making sure to coat the entire bottle. When your new vase is dry, tuck in silver floral stems from the craft store. Clustering votive candles or ornaments around the base of your arrangement makes it even more festive.

Little Felt Critters

Make small ghosts, cats, and pumpkins using felt and fringe yarn. Using a cookie cutter for a pattern, trace 2 images on felt and cut out. Place the felt pieces together and sew the edges using a blanket stitch, feeding in a piece of fringe yarn with the thread as you go along. Before finishing your critter, pull the fringe out from under the thread so you get a nice shaggy border. Stuff critter with fiberfill and finish stitching.

Decoupaged Bears and Dogs

Buy a couple of brown papier-mâché bears or dogs (or cats) from the craft store. Now gather up scraps of all your fun papers and tear them into random pieces. (Note: The thinner the paper, the easier it is to work with.) Brush glue onto your papier-mâché animal, then begin to stick on bits of paper. Be sure to keep brushing on glue as you overlap the various bits of paper. If you hit a tricky spot (legs or head) cut a few slits in the paper so it will lie flat and not buckle up.

Driftwood Art
Add a beachy look to your wall with this driftwood art project. Start with a flat piece of wood and a bunch of driftwood pieces that you've collected. Arrange the driftwood pieces in a fun design (fish, sailboat, crab, etc.) and glue to your board. Now paint the whole thing using white or cream-colored paint. Frame and hang on your wall. (Note: If you use a small piece of paneling, you can replicate a tongue and groove look. Or if you use old barnwood for your background, you may want to leave it natural.)

FAVORITE NEW ORLEANS RECIPES

CARAMEL BREAD PUDDING

1 cup brown sugar
5 slices buttered bread, cubed
2 eggs
2 cups milk
1/2 tsp. salt
1/2 tsp. vanilla

Place brown sugar and bread cubes in top of double boiler. In a separate bowl, beat eggs lightly, then add in milk, salt, and vanilla. Stir again and pour over bread in top of double boiler. Cover and cook on medium heat for 1 hour or until bread pudding becomes firm. Run knife around edge and turn pudding upside down onto a serving dish. Serve with a dash of cream or whipped cream. Yields 4 to 6 servings.

PARTY HEARTY SHRIMP DIP

1 3/4 oz. pkg. cream cheese, softened
1/3 cup chili sauce
1 tsp. fresh lemon juice
1/2 tsp. fresh dill, minced
1/4 tsp. garlic powder (optional)
1 can shrimp (4 to 6 oz.), small shrimp or
  diced

Mix all ingredients together, adding shrimp last. Chill approximately 2 hours and serve with crackers or chips. Yields approximately 2 cups of dip.

BOURBON HOT DOGS

3/4 cup bourbon
1/2 cup ketchup
1/2 cup brown sugar
1 lb. hot dogs, sliced diagonally

Mix bourbon, ketchup, and sugar in medium pan. Add hot dogs and simmer for 45 minutes. Serve hot with slaw and beans. Yields 6 servings.

CARMELA'S APPLE DUMP CAKE

2 cans apple pie filling (21 oz. each)
2 tsp. cinnamon, divided
1 box yellow cake mix
2 sticks butter
1/2 cup chopped pecans or walnuts

440

Preheat oven to 350 degrees. Spread apple filling in bottom of 9-by-13-inch baking pan. Sprinkle on 1 tsp. cinnamon. Pour dry cake mix evenly over apple filling. Cut butter in small squares and dot on top of cake mix. Sprinkle with nuts and an additional 1 tsp. of cinnamon. Bake for approximately 45 to 50 minutes. Cut into squares and serve with whipped cream. Yields 8 servings.

PECAN JAZZ TARTS

2 sticks butter, softened
5 Tbsp. powdered sugar
2 cups flour
1 tsp. vanilla
1 1/2 cups chopped pecans
additional powdered sugar to roll cookies
  in

Preheat oven to 350 degrees. Mix together butter, powdered sugar, flour, vanilla, and chopped pecans. Roll out in small oblong balls and place on lightly greased cookie sheet. Bake for 20 minutes until golden brown. Roll still-warm tarts in additional powdered sugar. Yields 15 to 20 cookies.

AVA'S SLOP-IT-ON HOT DOG SAUCE
1 can chili (15 oz., no beans)
1 can tomato paste (6 oz.)
1/4 cup chopped onion
1/4 cup chopped green pepper
1/2 tsp. chili powder (or to taste)
1 tsp. prepared mustard

Mix all ingredients together in saucepan. Bring to boil and simmer for 15 minutes. Serve as topping for cooked hot dogs. Yields 1 1/2 cups sauce.

EASY APPLE BUTTER
5 apples, cored and chopped
1/4 tsp. salt
2 Tbsp. lemon juice
1 1/2 tsp. ground cinnamon
1/4 tsp. ground cloves
1/4 cup pure maple syrup

Stir all ingredients together in a medium-sized pot. Cover and cook on low heat, stirring occasionally, for 2 hours. Remove pot from stove and let cool. Put apple mixture in a blender or food processor and blend/process until it's smooth and buttery. If you'd like it to be thicker, cook apple butter an additional 30 minutes to 1 hour. Serve apple butter warm. Stays fresh when refrigerated for about 1 week. Yields 1 to 2 cups, depending on size of apples.

TANDY'S BUTTERMILK JUMBLES
1/2 cup butter
1 cup sugar
1 egg
1/2 tsp. vanilla
1/2 tsp. cinnamon
1/2 tsp. salt
1/2 tsp. baking soda
1/2 cup buttermilk
2 1/4 cups flour

Preheat oven to 350 degrees. Using an electric mixer, cream together butter and sugar. Add in egg, then vanilla, cinnamon, and salt. In separate bowl, mix baking soda into buttermilk. On medium speed, add both buttermilk mixture and flour to mixture, alternating ingredients until fully mixed. Drop using a teaspoon onto greased baking sheet. Bake for approximately 18 to 20 minutes. Yields about 40 cookies. (Note: You can also add your favorite nuts or dried fruit.)

CROCK-POT PORK CHOPS
4 bone-in pork chops
2 cans (14 oz. each) diced tomatoes
1/4 cup brown sugar

1 green pepper
1 red pepper
salt and pepper to taste

Brown pork chops in skillet then place in Crock-Pot. Add diced tomatoes and brown sugar. Cut up peppers and add them to Crock-Pot. Add salt and pepper. Cook on high for 1 hour, then turn Crock-Pot to low and cook for an additional 3 hours. Enjoy! Yields 4 pork chops with about 2 cups of sauce.

WATERMELON DESSERT BOMB
2 cups lime sherbet
2 cups lemon sherbet
1 quart raspberry sherbet
1/4 cup mini chocolate chips

Chill a medium-sized bowl for 30 minutes in freezer. Then pack lime sherbet into bowl, covering only sides and bottom. Return to freezer to firm. Pack lemon sherbet into bowl the same way. Return to freezer to firm. Fill cavity completely with raspberry sherbet mixed with chocolate chips. Freeze until very firm. To serve, invert bowl on a serving plate and wrap a warm wet towel around bowl to loosen dessert. Slice dessert into wedges that will now resemble a watermelon and serve. Yields 6 to 8 slices.

ABOUT THE AUTHOR

Laura Childs is a pseudonym used by Gerry Schmitt. Before becoming a full-time author, she was a Clio Award-winning advertising writer and CEO of her own marketing film called Mission Critical Marketing. She writes the Tea Shop Mystery series, the Cackleberry Club Mysteries and the Scrapbook Mystery series.

The employees of Thorndike Press hope you have enjoyed this Large Print book. All our Thorndike, Wheeler, and Kennebec Large Print titles are designed for easy reading, and all our books are made to last. Other Thorndike Press Large Print books are available at your library, through selected bookstores, or directly from us.

For information about titles, please call:
(800) 223-1244

or visit our website at:
gale.com/thorndike

To share your comments, please write:
Publisher
Thorndike Press
10 Water St., Suite 310
Waterville, ME 04901